THE RENEGADES
RAFE

GENELL DELLIN

D012515?

AVON BOOKS
An Imprint of HarperCollinsPublishers

This is a work of fiction. Names, characters, places, and incidents are products of the author's imagination or are used fictitiously and are not to be construed as real. Any resemblance to actual events, locales, organizations, or persons, living or dead, is entirely coincidental.

AVON BOOKS
An Imprint of HarperCollins*Publishers*
10 East 53rd Street
New York, New York 10022-5299

Copyright © 2001 by Genell Smith Dellin
ISBN: 0-380-81849-3
www.avonromance.com

First Avon Books paperback printing: June 2001

Avon Trademark Reg. U.S. Pat. Off. and in Other Countries, Marca Registrada, Hecho en U.S.A.
HarperCollins ® is a trademark of HarperCollins Publishers Inc.

Printed in the U.S.A.

10 9 8 7 6 5 4 3 2 1

Prologue

New Orleans, Louisiana
April 25, 1862

The whole world was on fire, and so was every drop of blood in her veins. Rafe's hands had always done that to her—and so had his eyes, his voice, just the scent of his skin, even. But this time it was his words that set her ablaze with wild longing.

He said them again.

"Run away with me, Maddie. Now."

Then he added, "Before the Yankees get ashore and set up their roadblocks."

He grinned that devilish, crooked grin, the one that always made her heart turn over, and said, "We can be in Texas before the Yankees know we're gone."

Oh, dear Lord, how she wanted to go with him! His hot, whiskey-colored eyes held her with a gaze even more powerful than the strong hands gripping her shoulders.

She tore her gaze away to try to think.

Smoke from the Yankee fleet was visible now. She didn't have much time. She didn't have any time. The city was burning.

The pressure in his fingers grew.

"I love you, Maddie. Come with me."

She looked up at him again, made herself fight the entreaty in his eyes and the desperate need in her heart. Both, together, were almost too much to resist.

"How can I, Rafe? Daddy's not well, you know that, and he doesn't have another soul in this world but me."

"He has good friends all over this city. He's lived here all his life. He'll get by. We'll write to him and come see him when we can."

"Write to him! How can that take the place of his only daughter in his house and at his business?"

He stiffened.

"That's it, isn't it? Your precious newspaper means more to you than—"

Angrily, she pulled away from his hands, but she felt hurt when he didn't stop her. She turned her back on him and stared at the awful chaos along the levee, at the men driving axes into barrels of whiskey and pouring it over the cotton while others touched the torches to it; at the crowds farther downriver, shaking their fists to the Yankee ships; at the flaming sheds, docks, wharves, and ships and the long blaze of burning cotton that lined the opposite bank of the Mississippi.

"Everything has gone to destruction, Rafe," she said. "Can't you see that? How in the world could I just run off and leave Daddy now?"

"How can we part when we may not ever see each other again? Life is short, Maddie. Haven't you learned that from this war?"

She whirled to glare at him.

"Rafe, how unreasonable can you be? You're giving me no time at all to decide whether to leave my old, sick daddy all alone, with his employees gone to the war and a scandal on his hands!"

"We'll get married in Texas."

"I'm sure that would comfort him a lot."

Her sarcasm irritated him; he made a visible effort to hold onto his patience.

Then suddenly, worry filled his eyes.

"Madeleine, you'd be living under Yankee occupation. Print the wrong thing in the newspaper and you could wind up in jail!"

"Even the Yankees wouldn't jail a woman."

"You don't know that. With your quick tongue, no telling what you might say."

She saw the shadow of his teasing grin. His eyes were somber, though. He was worried sick about her.

And she about him. He wouldn't be in battles unless the Yankees invaded Texas, but being a secret agent would take him into plenty of danger.

"With your quick temper, no telling what you might get into," she said, and her voice broke completely.

He reached to comfort her, but she stiffened and walked off a little way, her fist jammed against her mouth to keep it from telling him she'd run away with him. She couldn't leave her father like this, she just couldn't.

But, dear God, she couldn't let Rafe go. Never could she do that.

Inside, she was shaking all over. Farther down the levee, the crowd growled and yelled, the air filled with the sweet odor of burning tobacco, and another ax crashed into another barrel of whiskey to fire the cotton. A hundred people were working at destruction as if their very souls depended on disappointing the Yankees.

She couldn't escape and leave her father here while her beloved city was falling into a shambles. Why, that grief alone might bring on his angina. If she left, too, it might cause his death.

And she couldn't let the *Times* go silent as long as she had breath in her body.

Her heart screamed that she had to go with

Rafe, but her bones went cold with the knowledge that she couldn't.

The flatboat that had been towed out into the middle of the river burst into a sheet of living flame.

Rafe's arms went around her and pulled her to him for one sweet second of warm safety with her weak, trembling backbone resting against the big, hard, muscular power of his body. Then, gently and surely, he turned her around in his embrace.

His face was terrible—he already knew what she would say.

"Oh, Rafe," she cried, "I can't. My darling, I can't go with you now."

She flung her arms around his neck, threw herself against him, seeking shelter from her words.

"Rafe, I love you . . ." she tried to say, but he crushed her lips to his and took her to another place.

A place that held only the hot, insistent pressure, the sweet, pulsing joy of his mouth on hers, and the hope that maybe it wasn't true after all—for after a kiss such as this, how could they ever be parted?

She gave to his tongue, to his lips, she poured her soul into telling him without words that she loved him. He had to believe it because that would be her only comfort.

It lasted forever and a lifetime too long for her

ever to live while parted from him. But it was over and done way too soon.

He broke it off and held her away from him.

"I'll wait for you, Rafe," she cried. "You know that, don't you?"

"I'll slip through the Yankee lines and come see you," he said, his voice low and hard and dangerously determined. "Count on it."

He spun on his bootheel and left her, disappearing into the smoke and haze in an instant. She didn't know how long she stared at that spot through the tears she'd been holding in check. At least she'd managed to do that. It always broke his heart when she cried, and she could never have sent him away brokenhearted.

As if he weren't already, and she with him.

She picked up her skirts and ran blindly toward the *Times* office, which sat at the bottom of the levee. Sobs racked her whole body and tears soaked her shirtwaist even before the sudden, hard downpour of rain began.

Chapter 1

Mexico
1874

The house was deserted.

He'd known it from the instant he rode into the yard, but Rafe couldn't stop himself from calling out again anyway.

"Juanito! Señora Ruiz!"

No answer. No face at the window, no opening of the door. Only the wind, banging a shutter against the cracked adobe.

They were gone. Sand had blown and piled against the doorsill, which his son's grandmother never would have permitted. Rafe tightened his hand on the reins, yet he couldn't turn the horse away.

A fear like none he'd ever known knifed his heart.

Someone must know. Los Pinos was a tiny village—*everyone* would know what had happened to the old woman who had always lived in this house and to her grandson who had been born in it.

He wheeled around and took off at a high lope toward the square, which was bustling as usual with border-town business. He scanned it for children, in front of the merchants' stalls or playing around the well. None was big enough to be his son.

As he neared, the sound of his horse made the two women drawing water turn to watch him come. He recognized them by sight but he didn't know their names.

"Señoras! Donde está la Señora Ruiz?"

He shouted the question before he was even close enough to hear the answer. He didn't need to. Each woman crossed herself the moment he spoke the name.

Dead. The fear slashed him again. What about his son?

"Y el niño?"

One of the matrons turned and pointed toward the river where the children often played. Rafe tipped his hat in thanks, and when he dropped his hand he saw that it was shaking.

Thank God. Thank God.

He swerved, headed in the direction the woman had pointed. People stuck their heads out of the cantina to see what the hurry was as he pounded past and several stepped away from the stalls to watch him.

Rafe barely noticed the adults, however, because children began to pop up over the riverbank, drawn by the rapid hoofbeats ringing against the hard earth.

He scanned each small face as he rode toward them, the sudden, sharp fear growing as he drew nearer and nearer and Juanito did not appear.

What if the woman hadn't understood him correctly? What if she'd been wrong? What if something had happened to Juan Rafael, too?

Juanito loved horses more than anything else in the world—every time Rafe came to see him he paid more attention to whatever mount he was riding than to him. A dozen other children had heard Beau and come to see what horse was loping toward them, so where was Juan?

What if something had *just* happened to him, was happening at this very minute, when all the others were looking the other way? A tree root holding him, trapped, underwater . . . a blow to the head when he dived in . . .

The river, always, lay so shallow . . .

Two boys ran up over the bank, water streaming from their nearly naked bodies, and Rafe's gaze flew to them—but they were too tall, too lanky. No. Could that be Juanito on the right?

He stared in wonder as they stopped and looked at him shyly, like the others. Yes! It was Juanito.

His perfect oval face, so like Angelina's—except for the whiskey-colored eyes only a bit darker than Rafe's own—had thinned a little, his high cheekbones showed up more. And he was so tall! How could any child have grown this much in only six months?

"Whoa."

To his shock, Rafe's voice broke on the word. He sat back in the saddle for the stop, and relief tried to pull his shoulders into a weak slump. But he held them straight. His emotions weren't going to rule him, no matter how surprisingly deep they ran.

He was almost close enough to reach out and touch his son. His son who, thank God, was alive and well. They weren't in the habit of embracing or touching very much; usually Rafe only tousled his hair in saying hello or good-bye. Was he too old now to have his hair tousled?

The boy was fine, he looked healthy. He was too thin, though—all over, not just in his face.

"Hola, mi hijo," Rafe said.

Juan gave him the ghost of a shy smile in answer and met his gaze for an instant before he ducked his head in embarrassment. But not for long.

Despite the fact that all the others were staring at him, he spoke.

"Tu caballo se llama Beau, no?"

"Sí."

He remembered the black from three years ago! Juan Rafael had been only six the last time he saw this horse.

That stunned Rafe, then saddened him. The last time he'd ridden Beau to Los Pinos was the time he'd brought a pony to Juanito. The grandmother had sold the animal by the time Rafe had crossed the river going north again. Months later, when he'd returned, the child still had been heartbroken.

Anger, pity, and sorrow flooded him. And something else, too: guilt. He was the father of this boy and he should've made sure the child had a horse. That was the least he could've done.

At that moment, he knew he could never leave the boy again.

"You must come with me now," he said, thinking only of finding the Spanish words to convey the message, not of the unending complications of what it meant. "Let's get your things."

He gestured for Juan Rafael to mount behind him, slipped his toe from the stirrup, and held down his hand. The boy moved forward, slowly, then he stopped and looked back at his friend.

"La casa de Diego es mi casa," he said.

Rafe nodded and motioned for Diego to come, too. Both boys, in turn, took his hand, stretched up to step into the stirrup, then leapt on behind the saddle. The other children watched enviously and ran alongside as Rafe started Beau off at a trot.

Diego had been Juan Rafael's best friend since babyhood. The Martinez family would have been the logical first place to look for Juanito. Why had that fact totally left him when he'd found the house empty?

Because fear had taken over. Just the memory of the panic he'd felt then made his pulse quicken again. Where was his famous gambler's cool head? He had to get a grip on himself.

Quickly he turned to glance at the boys.

Juanito sat behind him, wet and grimy, barely holding onto the cantle. He rode with his seat, with his balance: back straight and shoulders squared, as he'd ridden the pony for those few days he'd had him. Juan Rafael was a natural horseman.

Pride surged through Rafe as the child leaned down to pat Beau. Then he pointed to a tiny house at the edge of the village where several smaller children played in the dooryard.

Diego's weary-looking mother stepped out and watched them ride into her yard, Rafe slowing the horse, trying not to raise too much dust. He gave the boys a hand, then swung out of the saddle.

La Señora Martinez greeted him softly, not by name, which he wouldn't expect her to remember, but with recognition in her eyes. After all,

Rafe had visited the village at least twice a year since Juanito's second year of life.

He thanked her for taking care of his son, then asked for her husband, who she indicated was not home. He spoke with her then, telling her that he was taking Juan Rafael to Texas. Both boys stood still as statues to listen.

Sudden tears filled her dark eyes.

"*Sí, señor,*" she said, and turned away so he wouldn't see.

Awkwardly, he waited in the yard with her as Diego and Juanito went silently into the house. The mother pulled herself together and called the other children to come and say good-bye to Juanito. Her voice trembled as she told them Juan's father was taking him to Texas and they ran to her side, shyly glancing at Rafe with large, wondering eyes.

He felt like a kidnapper.

Thankful for something to do, he reached into his pocket and took out the money for Juan's support that he'd meant to give to Señora Ruiz, then found a coin for each child. At first Señora Martinez tried to wave the money away, but Rafe insisted and she accepted it gratefully. The children were quietly thrilled.

He felt like a kidnapper who was also paying the ransom.

Diego and Juan Rafael came outside again, each now wearing a shirt, each with a small bundle in hand. The *señora*'s eyes widened and she gave a gasp of surprise, her hand on her heart.

"*Y Diego?*" Juanito said shyly, gesturing from his friend to Beau before he forced his gaze to meet Rafe's.

Rafe understood. They didn't quite have the nerve to say it, but they wanted to stay together. Two pairs of wide, hopeful eyes fixed on him said that they wanted it very, very much.

Dear God. This made him feel even worse than Señora Martinez' tears.

He glanced at Diego's mother's face and knew he could never do it. She had seven or eight children, she was desperately poor, but she didn't want to lose even the one who hadn't been born to her.

He remembered the fear he'd felt for Juan at the river and a great pity for this tired, worn woman came over him. She had all these many children to make her feel those terrors, over and over again. How could she bear such a burden?

Abruptly he turned toward Beau. He couldn't linger here to take on other people's troubles; he needed to be on the road.

"Your mother needs you here," he said to Diego in Spanish.

As he spoke, he made himself look into those huge, dark, pleading eyes again, but only briefly. And one quick glance at Juanito's sad face was enough.

"We must go now, Juan Rafael," he said, more abruptly than he had intended. "Tell your friend good-bye."

He went straight to Beau so as not to see the boys as they said farewell. He checked his cinch, tightened it, and mounted. He moved his saddle bags from behind his saddle to in front of it. Then he gathered his reins to the same length and crossed them in his fingers, smoothed Beau's mane, and patted his neck.

Quickly, he looked at the tightly huddled group, Señora Martinez held onto Diego and kissed Juan Rafael on the head.

"Juan Rafael," Rafe said gruffly. "*Vámanos.*"

The other children opened a path and his son came to his stirrup. He didn't look at Rafe as he pulled him up onto the horse.

"Tie on your bundle," Rafe said.

Somehow, his voice didn't seem to work right, but he cleared his throat and called out a last "*Gracias*" to Diego's mother, tipping his hat as he smooched to Beau to move out. Swiftly they left the little house and then the village behind in the dust.

But that lift of the heart he always felt when leaving one place behind and starting toward the fresh adventure of a new one didn't stir in him. He couldn't even feel his heart *beat*.

He could feel nothing but the small, silent presence on the saddle skirts behind him. Was Juanito hating him for refusing to bring Diego?

"I'm sorry," he said, half-turning in the saddle to make sure Juanito heard, "but Diego needs to stay with his family."

He thought maybe the boy gave a slight nod to show he'd heard, but he couldn't be sure. Most certainly, he never said a word in answer. He seemed to be staring off into the far distance.

"*La señora* would be very sad."

No reply.

Maybe Juanito was just afraid that he would cry if he spoke. Boys had their pride; that's what made them into men. He would give his son some time to himself and put his own mind where it needed to be: on the journey. He—they—had five or six days to go.

To his suite at the Menger, filled every night with smoke and poker players. That was no home for a boy.

The thought froze Rafe. Life was repeating itself.

Instantly, *he* was the boy of nine years, horseback behind his father, leaving the Choctaw village and his mother's grave on the wild banks of Lake Pontchartrain, being carried toward the closed walls of the mansion in New Orleans which he had never seen. His heart had been so torn—with grief for his mother weighing it down and guilty joy at being with his father trying to lift it up—that he'd thought his body could not remain whole.

But *his* father had had a home to offer him.

* * *

Six days later when they rode into Goliad, one of the "good" gambling towns with a high-stakes card game always in progress, Rafe's heart lifted. Work would be a relief, a welcome distraction from trying to be a father. So far Juanito had talked to him only about horses, and very little about even them.

In Goliad, he could leave the boy with Dora, the livery stable owner's wife. She loved sticking her nose into everyone else's business and she loved children.

Dora happened to be the one who met them at the barn.

"Who's this?" she demanded gruffly, hands on her hips. "Who is this handsome lad riding with the likes of a no-count rambler like you, Rafe Aigner?"

As they dismounted in the center aisle, she ruffled Juanito's hair. To Rafe's surprise, his shy son gave her a huge grin and stood still beside her while he told her his name.

"Get out of here, Rafe," she said briskly. "Me and Juanito's having supper together tonight. Anybody knows a child's got no call to be at a gambling game."

Four hours later, well into the game, well into winning it, Dora's last words still rang in Rafe's ears. He picked up the new cards dealt him and arranged them in a fan in his hand, but her voice drowned out the other players' calls. Dora was right. What would he do with Juanito when they got to San Antonio?

"I'll pass," said the rancher sitting to his right.

"Raise a hundred."

That was the next man, owner of the mercantile here in town, Thomas McNaught.

Rafe looked at his cards, thought about what had already been played, speculated about what the others were holding.

"I'm putting up my newspaper," snapped the man who'd introduced himself as Sutton Calhoun. He tossed an IOU onto the pile in the middle of the table that already held markers for his saddle and his horse. Calhoun was starting to sweat.

"Hm, never played for a newspaper, I don't believe," Rafe said, in the careless way he used to lull his opponents into thinking he wasn't paying attention. "Don't know what I'd do with it."

"Don't worry, you won't win it," Calhoun muttered, his hands shaking as he rearranged his cards.

They'd shake worse than that if he could see what Rafe held.

Rafe kept his face impassive, but inwardly he smiled. At least he'd have a horse for Juanito to ride out of here tomorrow. Maybe having his own horse would loosen his tongue.

At Rafe's turn, he threw his cards on the table, face-up.

He flicked his glance over all the others'

hands, and saw Calhoun, the last man to play, lay down exactly what he'd thought he had. Rafe reached for the pot.

A high-pitched scream, more animal sound than human, tore the air. Calhoun was coming up clawing for his gun, scraping his chair back with a desperate screech, his accusing eyes fixed on Rafe as sweat poured off him.

"You're a cheat, Aigner! A lowdown card-sharping cheat, with an ace up each sleeve and a heart black as night."

For the longest moment, Rafe's hands froze on the winnings while his mind clung to the image of Juanito's face. He'd caught no hint that Calhoun might react like this. If he hadn't been thinking about his boy instead of his business . . .

If he died, what would happen to Juan Rafael?

Chapter 2

Calhoun pointed his gun at Rafe, his hands shaking, his chin set with determination to hold the muzzle steady.

Rafe reached for his own handgun, uncharacteristically slow and awkward. Before he could clear leather, another gun blasted. Rafe waited for the stinging burn of a bullet that never came.

It was Sutton Calhoun who fell, sweeping a bottle and a glass from the table with one hand as he dropped to the floor.

"That's all, men," someone shouted. "Trouble's over."

Sheriff Wade Brown stepped away from the bar where he'd been watching the play for an hour or more and holstered his gun.

"He's a goner," Thomas McNaught said.

He and the rancher were kneeling beside Calhoun's body, searching for a pulse. The rancher shook his head.

Rafe looked at Calhoun, then at the quick-thinking sheriff who had fired so accurately.

"Much obliged, Wade," he said. "You saved my bacon."

"Any time," Wade Brown said.

While some volunteers carried Calhoun's body to the undertaker's, the hotel manager found a canvas money bag for Rafe and helped him gather up his winnings. The other players went to the bar for drinks but Rafe had no desire to join them.

Calhoun was dead, two-bit bad loser that he was.

And *he* was going to be dead if he couldn't keep any better lookout than he had done just now. This attempt to be a father was going to get him killed, or at the very least, ruin his career. Either way, it would destroy his son's life. Every single decision he had ever made about Juan Rafael had been wrong.

As he walked to the livery, he added another to the list: leaving the boy with Dora. Rafe stood in the livery stable aisle holding the reins of Calhoun's big-headed mustang mare, and stared down at his son. Juanito was sound asleep in the hay Beau had strewn around the stall after he'd eaten his fill. The big Thoroughbred stallion stood over the child, dozing. And keeping watch. He lifted his head and muttered to Rafe, low in his throat.

Then he noticed the mare.

"Sorry, old man," Rafe said softly. "I know she's not much to look at, but we won't have to be seen with her for very long. We'll trade her as soon as we get to San Antonio."

Beau rumbled that that had better be true.

The side door to the stable opened and Dora came in.

"I'm sorry," she said, going straight to the stall to see about Juanito. "Me and Virgil tried everything but we can't get him out of here and into the house."

"Aren't you and Virgil quite a bit bigger and stronger than he is?" Rafe said, trying to keep his tone light.

"Yep," she said, "but I couldn't bring myself to part them. He clung to your horse and looked so pitiful and begged to stay with him—I reckon that's what he was sayin' in Spanish—that I didn't have the heart to take him away."

"I'm going to have to start *making* him do some things. Did you try after he went to sleep?"

"Woke the instant Virge picked him up, and cried out so sharp and sad he had every horse in this barn calling back to him."

"Has he had anything to eat?"

"I brought his supper and he ate it in there."

"That's ridiculous! If you hadn't done that, maybe you could've starved him out."

Dora snorted her disgust.

"He drank a gallon of milk and ate a whole skilletful of cornbread and a bowl of beans. You're the one who's been starving him."

"You're the one who's supposed to know all about children," Rafe said sharply. "And here you've let my son sleep in a stall. Well, I've had a hard night and I'm ready for bed, so we'll be going to the hotel."

"You'll be taking that new nag you've got a hold of there to your room, too?"

The woman was as impossible as the boy.

"Find me another stall, will you, Dora?"

Rafe unsaddled the mare and carried the fancy saddle that had belonged to the luckless Sutton Calhoun to the tack room while Dora found an empty stall. Then he went in with Beau and Juanito, petted the horse, and picked up the boy.

Instantly, Juan woke and stiffened alarmingly as Rafe carried him past Beau toward the aisle. He reached for the horse and made such a piteous sound, as if he were afraid to cry, that Rafe stopped.

"Not even a stick of horehound candy nor a orange straight out of the Valley would do the trick," Dora called. "He's carryin' a load of distress. Let him be for tonight. I'll watch him."

"I'll watch him myself, damn it, I'm his father," Rafe said.

He returned Juan Rafael to the hollow spot in the hay.

"See you don't wake him up no more," she said, as she latched the door of the ugly mustang's stall.

Rafe let her have the last word as she left.

She stopped in the doorway, though, and turned back.

"He's a sweet boy, Rafe Aigner, and don't you be teaching him none of your gamblin' ways."

"Dora, when did you take up preaching?"

She snorted her disgust.

"You ain't never heard preaching, if you think this is it." After a moment, she added a last thought. "Juanito says you're his pa. You're a lucky man, Rafe."

A quick knot formed in his throat.

"I know," he said softly. "I know I am, Dora."

Once he knew she was gone, Rafe removed his coat and vest and folded them carefully over his saddles, then picked up a saddle blanket to lie on to protect his dress shirt. His bags were at the hotel, where he'd bathed and shaved and dressed for work, but he'd get them in the morning.

Suddenly he felt as tired and weak as a kitten. He pulled off his boots, picked up a second saddle blanket, and padded to Beau's stall. He added hay to the bed and arranged it as best he could without waking Juan. Then he blew out the lamp in the hallway and crawled in beside him.

Well, so much for dignity and comfort. So much for the reputation that had served him so well, the show he lived by: the perfect and expensive guns and boots, the snowy shirts and silk cravats and waistcoats that proclaimed him to be such a successful gambler that his rivals might as well give up.

Rafe's eyes widened as he stared into the dark. One of the Aces, one of the top-notch gamblers like himself, had been heard to say that he'd rather follow his son to his grave than to have his son follow him into a life of gambling.

Now *he* had a son, whom Dora was forbidding to follow him into this gambling life. Would he?

He shifted in the hay, tried to get the blanket under his head. The more urgent question was whether the boy would ever talk to his father, much less follow in his profession.

A piece of hay stuck his cheek and he moved the blanket again. This was not only aggravating, it could be damaging, too. If word of his sleeping in a haystack travelled all the way back to San Antonio to Big Jim Thompson, the rumor would be all over town by tomorrow noon that Rafe Aigner was broke and vulnerable.

Juanito would not be sleeping in a stable in San Antonio. There, he would make him behave as he should.

At that moment, Juanito gave a great sigh in his sleep and scooted his small, warm body up right next to Rafe's. Startled, Rafe stiffened. In his unconsciousness, the child insisted on fitting himself into the curve of his father's big body, spoon fashion, as tightly as he could.

A smile erased the frown from Rafe's face. A smile he didn't even know he had in him.

He folded his arms around his son and held him close, then finally slept.

Madeleine Calhoun glanced at her reflection in the mirror of Mrs. Bolander's Millinery Shop one last time. Then, slowly, she removed the flower-trimmed, wide-brimmed hat, the utterly *charming* hat with the blue ribbons that matched her eyes, and reluctantly handed it back.

"I'm sorry, Mrs. Bolander," she said. "I would love to take it home with me, but I'm afraid it's a little too dear."

Even more reluctantly, when Mrs. Bolander had gone to return the luscious creation to its display stand, Madeleine made herself meet the gaze of her friend, Sophie Langston.

"Your eyes looked as deep blue as bluebonnets beneath that brim," Sophie said in her Southern drawl. "That hat was made for you. It makes me sad for you not to have it. Please, Maddie, let me—"

"I couldn't possibly permit you to do such a thing."

"Well, then, barring my being allowed to make you a small present in appreciation for the many generous ways you have given help to me over these past years . . ."

"Help us all, Sophie," Madeleine said, bursting out laughing, "you're making a *speech*. Do you want me to publish it in the *Star?*"

"Yes. If you won't listen to it, perhaps you'll read it when you do the edit."

"I could buy the hat myself if I wanted."

"I know that. But I also know that you won't. You need to be good to yourself, Maddie."

"I am good to myself! Why, I—"

"Hush," Sophie said. "I can't bear to hear those old fantasies again. The luxuries you allow yourself, like food and water, are simply too much to believe."

"I'm saving my money to buy a new spring-form pan," she said firmly.

Although I may have to buy the food to go in it if Sutton keeps on gambling as he's been doing.

She might as well have said it out loud.

"You need to make Sutton give you more of what he wins . . . *when* he wins," Sophie murmured under her breath.

They put on their hats and picked up their reticules.

"It's the very latest style," Sophie whispered temptingly, "too deep a crown to be a 'flat,' too daring, with the brim turned up by that bunch of flowers, to be called a bonnet . . ."

"Get away from me, Devil," Maddie whispered back.

"Good day, Mrs. Bolander," they said in unison.

They waved to her and her other customers, all of whom they knew, then the two best friends opened the door and stepped out onto Travis Street.

"Do *not* tell me that you must go back to work now," Sophie said. "We haven't had a shopping day for ages and ages." She pouted. "And this *is* a shopping day whether you buy anything or not."

Madeleine turned to the north, anyway, toward the newspaper offices of the *Star*.

A wagon sat at the edge of the street right in front of it and she startled.

"Is that a coffin in that wagon? Sophie?"

"It appears so to me. It's a long, narrow box shaped like a body, after all. Wearing a strip of black cloth."

"Can't they tell we're a newspaper? How could they mistake us for the undertaker?"

"Maybe they're here to request an obituary."

"It's hardly the custom for me to observe the body of the deceased."

The driver climbed down over the wheel and started for the door of the *Star* while his companion remained on the seat. Madeleine walked faster.

For some reason, her heart was in her mouth.

"Sutton's been gone for nearly a month without a word," she said.

"Madeleine," Sophie said dryly, "I don't think you have that kind of luck."

"Sophie!"

"I don't care," Sophie said, tossing her head, "any husband who gambles *your* money all over Texas, yet makes you feel you can't even buy a new hat, deserves to die."

"Sophie!"

The irrepressible Sophie merely shrugged.

"I'm your friend," she said. "Sutton isn't. Remember that."

She quickened her pace to keep up with Madeleine's.

Madeleine reached the door of the *Star* just as the wagon driver opened it to return to the street.

Her printer, Charlie, called out to her from the press in the corner of the room.

"Mrs. Calhoun, this man's here to see you."

"Mrs. Sutton Calhoun?" the man said.

Madeleine managed to nod before blurting her questions.

"What is this? Why are you looking for me?"

Respectfully, the man took off his cap.

"My name's Ronald Ferguson, ma'am. I'm sorry to tell you I'm hauling your husband home. He's done been killed."

Madeleine froze where she stood.

Ronald Ferguson held his cap at his side and waited for her to speak. She couldn't.

"Let's go inside, shall we?" Sophie said.

She took charge of both Madeleine and Ronald Ferguson and led them through the office and into a small parlor at the back. Madeleine felt as if she'd stepped outside of her body, watching Sophie help her into a chair.

"What happened to Sutton?"

Madeleine knew she was the one who'd asked the question but the voice wasn't hers. Emotions coursed through the self she was watching— sorrow, wonder, relief, disbelief—but her other self, the watcher, felt numb.

No more Sutton coming in and out of her life, grasping for every penny she made with the *Star*; his every greedy word, his very presence reminding her that marrying him had been the biggest mistake of her life. How could she ever have believed that he loved her?

She wouldn't have, if she hadn't thought she loved him. She wouldn't have if she hadn't been so unsettled by the war and the Yankee occupation, if the whole society of her beloved New Orleans hadn't been in a shambles and Papa dead, leaving her utterly lonely for the first time in her life.

She wouldn't have if Rafe hadn't been killed in the war.

But she should've known what love was. Because of Rafe—and because the news of his death had nearly killed her, too. How could she *ever* have believed Sutton Calhoun loved her or that she loved him?

"Mr. Sutton was shot in a dispute over some winnings at poker, ma'am."

"Where?"

"Goliad. At the Lone Star Hotel."

Stunned and a little excited, she could not think of a single question more. Sutton was gone and she was, at last, in charge of her life.

"Sheriff Brown killed him, ma'am. He had to. Mr. Calhoun was drawed down on another player he was calling out for a cheater."

Madeleine stood up. "Take Mr. Calhoun's body to Traywick's Undertaking Parlor," she said. "On Crockett. How much do I owe you?"

She paid, then accepted the traveling bag of Sutton's clothes to which had been added his gun and wallet, along with the other contents of his pockets.

"What about his horse and saddle?"

"Sheriff said he lost them in the game."

"Very well. Thank you, Mr. Ferguson."

When he was gone, she turned to Sophie.

"I'm a wicked person, Sophie. I feel so . . . relieved—and deep down, sort of free—much more than I feel sad."

"You're human, Madeleine. You're a good person. Which Sutton was not."

Sophie took both her hands and Madeleine held on as if a high wind were trying to lift her off her feet.

"I *am* sad, though," she said. "I'm sad he never loved me; I'm sad we lost our child. I'm sad we never tried to have another."

"Even if he didn't love you?"

"Even so. A child would be a comfort to me now."

"You have friends to comfort you."

"I know. But I've always wanted a child, and now I know for sure I'll never have one. I'll never marry again."

"You don't know that."

"I won't, Soph. I loved Sutton at the beginning—at least, I truly believed that I did—and I truly believed he loved me. What would keep me from making that same mistake again?"

Absently, she unpinned and untied her bonnet and took it off. Sophie put it away.

"The sheriff shot him," Madeleine said suddenly. "Maybe he was the one who was cheating and accusing someone else as a distraction. Do you suppose?"

Sophie gave her a long, knowing look that somehow settled her a little bit inside.

"That sounds like Sutton to me. Since he often accused *you* of losing all y'all's money."

"Yes, he did," Madeleine said. "If I think about that I can get mad and not mourn him at all."

"Here, Maddie," Sophie said, "sit and put your feet up. Let me make you some tea and we'll talk."

"You always know what to do in a crisis, Sophie."

"Tea," Sophie said. "Or whiskey. It depends."

She turned from the stove and smiled. "But whatever the drink, it's really the talk that helps."

As they sipped their tea, Sophie sat on the footstool and listened with all her attention while Madeleine sorted through her tangled feelings out loud.

"Don't feel guilty at all," Sophie said, as they finished their second pot of tea. "You did the best you could. Don't feel guilty about any of your feelings, 'cause Sutton's the one who created them."

People started arriving to pay their respects, because word had spread from the undertaker's parlor and from Charlie. Big Jim Thompson brought a potted azalea and spent half an hour answering the door to all the friends Madeleine had made through the *Star*, her charity work for children, and her efforts to bring culture to San Antonio. He informed them all that he, with his new theater on the second floor of his gambling palace, the Golden King, was one of Madeleine's strongest supporters in her cultural efforts.

Once Big Jim was gone to prepare for his game of the evening, Sophie took over receiving the food and the flowers and protected Madeleine from too much conversation. Finally, it was late, the spring evening faded into night, and they were left alone again.

"Duncan's out of town," Sophie said, bustling

around to set the room to rights, "but even if he weren't, I'd stay here tonight. I want you to try to sleep, but if you can't, we'll talk."

Madeleine's eyes filled with tears.

"I could never have a better friend than you, Sophie."

"Maybe not, but you have a lot *more* friends than me."

"I know," Madeleine said, with gratitude. "I'll never leave San Antonio. I'm so glad this is where Sutton left me."

On the day after the funeral, Madeleine whole-heartedly accepted Sophie's advice. She wasn't going to feel guilty about anything, not even the fact that her heart felt light with freedom and her spirit strong with eagerness for her work.

She was not even going to feel guilty about loving her work more than she'd ever loved Sutton, even during their courtship. *If* she'd ever loved him. Surely she had, just not in the same way or with the same intensity that she'd loved Rafe.

At any rate, it didn't matter any more. After all the grief she'd been through, she wasn't going to get deeply enough involved with *any* man to need to know whether she could trust her feelings or not.

All morning and most of the afternoon, she

worked on the accounts and the advertisements which brought in the bulk of the *Star*'s income. Apologizing for her need to appear in public so soon after being widowed, but explaining with the bald truth that she must make a living, she visited several establishments and actually sold more space than usual because people felt sympathy for her plight.

But she resolved not to feel guilty about that, either. Sutton had used her for years, had squandered her inheritance and made her a slave by taking her profits. She might as well use him to her advantage now.

Back at the small, rickety building that held her home and the *Star*, she talked to Charlie, met the new printer's devil he'd hired, and then told them both good-bye for the day. Then she stacked all the condolence notes on her desk and Sutton's obituary into a box which she carried into the living quarters and put away.

After that, she relaxed at her desk in the front office to go through the mail. Five letters to the editor raved with anti-Mexican sentiments because of the increasing frequency of cattle-stealing, murdering raids by *bandidos* all up and down the Nueces and the Rio Grande. All of them blamed every theft on Cheno Cortinas, the famous Mexican rebel pushed into Mexico years ago by Texas Rangers.

Probably rightly so. Cortinas was ruthless, he

had a huge number of men at his disposal, and he held a great grudge against all Texans. Madeleine chose three of the letters to publish.

Then she took paper from the drawer and her pen and inkwell from the cubbyholes in her roll-top desk. What she needed now was an editorial that would set people talking and cause them to buy newspapers.

After a few minutes' thought, she began to write about her friend Big Jim Thompson. She named him a powerful and respected pillar of the community, owner of the largest, most elaborate gambling establishment in Texas, and supporter of culture in the city of San Antonio.

The latest of his generous gifts is a lavish theater on the second floor of his new gambling palace—a theater which will bring us the very best plays from the East. This is only one of the ways in which Big Jim Thompson shares his wealth with the citizens of San Antonio . . .

The words came swiftly and smoothly, they flowed out of the tip of her pen and filled her with the inexpressible satisfaction that her work sometimes brought her. She included a detailed description of the new theater, and a list of the plays and the dates they would be presented there, then finished the piece with a strong encouragement for San Antonio society to attend and support every performance. Then she threw down her pen and stood up to stretch her legs and her hand.

She smiled to herself as she walked to the window. That would set the cultural mavens who strongly disapproved of gambling but wanted to lead the city in enlightenment and refinement, like Mrs. Frank Begley, into a swivet.

It might even bring those disparate elements of the town together eventually, by making them realize what they held in common. That would be a wonderful satisfaction to her.

Suddenly, she realized what she was looking at outside.

A big-headed, scruffy mustang mare the color of wheat straw bearing a hundred-dollar saddle trimmed with silver. Tied at her hitching rail.

She blinked and looked again as a cold hand clutched her stomach. Sutton's horse and saddle.

Her mind flew to her precious freedom, half-expecting to see him coming to take it away again. Her breath caught in her throat.

No. Sutton was dead.

She turned toward the door as it swung open. A man and a boy stepped inside.

Her heart stopped.

The man was Rafe.

Chapter 3

*R*afe! Rafe was *alive!*

A great, spirit-piercing joy burst into her veins.

"Madeleine?"

The incredulity in his voice didn't change its true nature. It was low and rich and dark as his skin; it was Rafe's voice, all right. And the years had made him even more handsome, not less.

She ached to say his name out loud—to him—and hear him answer, in the flesh, in reality, just as she had done a million times in her dreams. But she could not speak.

"Maddie. What are you doing here?"

His voice had turned so sharp it cut her tongue loose.

"I live here. I own the *Star*."

He stared at her, his face hard and impassive. He looked almost as if he hated her. What was wrong?

"Why didn't you wait for me?"

Shocked, she struck back in defense. "You were dead, if you recall."

"That was a lie for the Yankees, but you knew lots of the casualty reports were wrong."

Maddie couldn't believe what she was hearing. How could he be so unforgiving? He thought she had betrayed him!

His amber gaze held hers in an uncompromising stare.

"I could hardly go looking for your body, Rafe!"

"Did you notice that it was never shipped home?"

"From *Mexico*? That's what I managed to find out—you were shot somewhere across the border. You were still a special agent, still trying to keep the Port of Brownsville open. I never expected your body to be recovered from Mexico."

"Did you expect me to sneak back into the city to see you?"

"Not after you were *dead!*"

He was relentless.

"I promised you that I'd get past the Yankees and see you—it was the last thing I said when we parted. Did you have no faith in me?"

"Not after you were *dead!*"

"But you had faith in your newspaper, didn't you? In the blessed *New Orleans Times.*"

Her anger began to build.

"I refuse even to answer that. I didn't choose the *Times* over you. That wasn't the choice."

He dismissed that with a slashing gesture of his hand.

"And then later you had faith in Sutton Calhoun. I'm assuming you are his widow, right?"

"I never knew you could be so mean, Rafe."

"I'm only stating facts."

"The fact is that I believed you were *dead.* More than one list said so. The officials I inquired of said so. Dear God, Rafe, why didn't you get word to me that it wasn't true?"

"I came back to do that, and found you'd married."

"Oh? Not until over a year of mourning had passed. A year that nearly killed me. Another black year on the heels of the one spent mourning my father."

"I couldn't get there sooner. There was a war, Madeleine, if you'll recall."

"A war that has been over for nearly ten years. How come you never found me and told me you were alive?"

"How come you never sat on your veranda and watched the roads, never haunted the harbor or the train stations, like thousands of women did when the war was over? You knew men in Northern prisons had been reported dead."

Maddie was stunned. He would never forgive her what was not her fault. She'd just found him alive, only to have the horror of losing him again.

Sorrow became a weight on her heart. If only she had known he was alive years ago. Before Sutton. Before she lost her ability to tell love from charm, and interest from greed. Before she lost that sense of joy that used to live within her all the time.

His whiskey-colored eyes burned a hole through her.

"You were *dead*," she said, searching those eyes for a shred of understanding. "Your name was on the list at the post office, at the telegraph office, at the church, in all the papers. I had to print it in the *Times!*"

She struck herself on the chest with a shaking hand as if to show him what a blow that news had been to her heart.

He didn't care. He had no pity, no remorse.

He wasn't Rafe anymore. He had been wild and dangerous as a young man, but he'd been warm and fun-loving, too. These ten nightmare years had taken that away.

"Well, now you can print in the *Star* that this newspaper has a new owner: Rafe Aigner, who was alive enough to win it in a poker game."

Maddie felt her eyes go wide. She stared into his agate eyes as her pulse nearly stopped.

But, thank God, she kept her voice level.

"Of course," she managed to say. "I should've known when I saw the horse and saddle."

"Those, too," he acknowledged, with the barest of nods.

Her very heart and bones froze. If not, she would've screamed, cried, flown at Rafe, and flogged him. She would have driven him out into the street again.

But all she had were words.

"You don't need a newspaper, Rafe. You wouldn't know what to do with one."

His face grew even harder.

"But you do, don't you, Madeleine? You need a newspaper in the worst way. You always have."

His voice and his eyes were terrible now, so cutting she'd have bled if she hadn't been frozen.

"My work means a great deal to me—if that's what you're saying."

"Yes," he drawled viciously. "It always has meant the world to you. More than honor, more than love."

She stared at him.

"Are you still saying that when I didn't run away to Texas with you—*without* benefit of clergy, I might add—it was because I wanted the *Times* more than you?"

He only stared at her, his eyes cold as sunshine on snow.

"Rafe, my father was ill, his business was foundering with all the help gone to war, *and the Yankees were invading New Orleans!* I was seventeen years old and you gave me five minutes to decide the rest of my *life!*"

He slashed her with the end of the look, as if inflicting one last punishment, then turned away.

"I came to inspect my new business," he said brusquely.

There was a cold spot in the middle of the room, like people said they felt when there was a ghost, and she was standing in the middle of it. She was the ghost. Madeleine Calhoun, Editor, was invisible now.

The *Star* was no longer hers. Her moment of freedom and power had been fleeting as a bird's flight.

Sutton had taken everything away from her, after all. He had kept on and kept on until he'd managed to squander the entire fortune for which her father had worked so long and hard.

No, she had done it to herself by being so stupid as to marry such a man.

Suddenly Rafe turned back to her.

"Was Sutton Calhoun the man you married while you were supposed to be waiting for me?"

"*Yes!* How many times do you think I've been married?"

"Even once is hard for me to imagine," he said, in a sarcastic drawl.

He looked right through her again.

"I told you we'd marry in Texas," he said. "There was no time in New Orleans, with the harbor on fire and the Yankees coming up the river."

"My point exactly," she said coldly. "If there wasn't time to find a clergyman, there wasn't time to make a decision, either."

"Long ago, I'd have said you married beneath you with Sutton. But since you broke your pledge to me the way you did, now I say maybe you didn't."

Her lips went stiff with anger and unshed tears.

"Leave it," she said. "I won't hear insults from you when you're the one who lied to me!"

The enormity of his lie, the memory of the black depths that had claimed her when she'd first seen his name on that list, made her dizzy. He must have had this streak of cruelty all along and she didn't know it.

"Rafe, did you never care for me at all? Did you not know that I might grieve myself to death?"

She thought she saw a flicker of regret or shame flash in his eyes, but it was quickly gone.

Then he raised one black eyebrow and fixed her with a hard, cynical glance.

"You shook off your grief, didn't you, Maddie? You found solace in Sutton's arms."

Madeleine stood very still.

All the love had gone out of him. Or maybe he had never loved her. How could he have and still be so hellishly brutal?

Did he not feel the slightest breath of happiness at seeing her again after ten long years?

Maybe all of their happiness, that brief, most treasured joy of her life—the memories of the idyllic rides along the shores of Lake Pontchartrain, the marvelous balls and soirees and long talks together—had been nothing but the fantasy of a foolish girl.

The Rafe she had loved *was* dead, after all.

She turned away and walked to her desk, surprised her legs would hold her until she got to that refuge. But it wasn't hers anymore.

Desperately, she glanced around the place she'd come to love during these past three years. Thank God Charlie was gone, and his helper, so she could break the news to them more gently in the morning.

A hot rebellion burst into fire in the pit of her stomach.

Damn it! She ought not to have to tell them the *Star* was no longer hers. Rafe might not keep them on—he might not even keep the *Star*, for he didn't know one thing about running a newspaper and he didn't need this one. From the clothes he was wearing, he had plenty of money.

Her mind raced to try to find a way out, something to offer Rafe in exchange, but she had nothing left. He had won every single thing of value that Sutton had owned.

She looked up. Rafe was gone, back into her private quarters, which he also now owned.

A chill took her. She couldn't just pack up her meager belongings and go live with Sophie, or something! She *would* not!

He strode back into the office from the short hallway that led to her rooms.

"Where's the boy?"

From the instant she'd seen Rafe, she'd forgotten about the child who'd come in with him.

"Where'd he go—the boy who was with me?" he barked.

"I don't know. He isn't my responsibility!"

He turned back to the living quarters and she followed.

"Maybe he's in my bedroom. There's a stray cat who sits on that windowsill in the sun."

"I already looked in there."

"Then maybe he went into the back yard. There's an outside door in the kitchen."

"I saw it. You're sure he isn't in the office?"

"Yes."

She went out into the big back yard right on his heels, suddenly caught up in the urgency emanating from him.

"What's wrong? Does he have seizures or something? Who is that little boy, Rafe?"

He strode on.

"My son."

She stopped short.

His son! And she had hardly glanced at the child because she'd been so shocked to see Rafe.

"Do you think he ran away?"

"He'd better not have!" he said fiercely.

He stopped in the middle of the wide yard and raked the place with his gaze. It came to rest on her small stable with its attached pen, empty now. Charlie, who sometimes delivered papers in the gig, always took care of putting Dolly up when he left work.

"You have horses?" Rafe snapped.

"Dolly. An old mare who came with the *Star* when we bought it."

He started toward the stable door and Madeleine saw that it stood half-open.

"Charlie would've closed the bottom half," she said quickly, "I'll bet your son is in there."

Why was she trying to comfort him? He didn't deserve it.

He opened the door and stepped inside, into the dimness striped by the late-afternoon sun. She got there just as Rafe came to an abrupt stop at the door of Dolly's stall. He stared down into it intently.

Madeleine ran to look.

Dolly was lying down on her side, her eyes open and her head up. Curled against her old sway back was the boy, sound asleep.

Rafe made the strangest sound, like a whimper of relief, deep in his throat. His hard face softened.

Madeleine's heart went out to him. Maybe he did have some love left in him.

"I should've known," he said.

"You did know," she said, wondering again why she bothered to reassure him. "You asked if I had a horse."

A low-slanting sunbeam fell across the child's perfect face. His long lashes lay tightly against his brown cheek, his chest rose and fell in the deep-sleep rhythm.

Rafe stood still, completely silent. She glanced up at him.

Suddenly he looked so *lost*.

"He's all right. He's just a tired little boy," she said softly, gazing at the gorgeous child again.

Comparing his face to Rafe's, she thought she could see a slight resemblance. He must look most like his mother, though, and she must be a stunningly beautiful woman.

Rafe reached for the latch to the stall door, then stopped with his hand on it.

"I hate to wake him," he said, and his face softened even more.

"Don't."

He pulled an ornate silver-backed watch from the pocket of his waistcoat.

"I'll have players at the door of my suite at the Menger in an hour. I have to get things ready."

Madeleine looked at the little boy again.

Leave him. I'll take care of him.

She bit her tongue before she said it aloud. She couldn't let herself get attached to this child. He was Rafe's, and Rafe was going to hate her forever.

But she had trouble taking her eyes from the sight before her. The boy's hair was ruffled against the mare's back, sticking up in a cowlick that gave him a mischievous air in spite of his angelic, sleeping face.

"What's his name?"

"Juan Rafael. Juanito."

"He looks like he'd be a lot of fun," she said.

"Not much," Rafe said bitterly. "He likes horses better than people."

"Well, that doesn't mean he isn't fun. Just that he has good sense."

"Not if it means sleeping in stables instead of beds."

"He won't sleep in a bed?"

"He hasn't since I've had him."

"How long is that?"

"About a week," he snapped, as if he were sick of questions.

A dozen more were swarming on her tongue.

Why such a short time?

Why won't he sleep in a bed?

And the most pressing one of all.

Where is his mother?

"Damn!" he muttered, and pulled the latch, started to swing open the door. "This is a hell of a deal. I've got to make a living."

Go on. Leave him with me.

Once more, she managed not to say it.

"If word of this ever gets around, Big Jim'll make hash out of my reputation."

She turned to stare at him.

"Big Jim Thompson? He's a friend of mine. He's not in the habit of hashing other people's reputations."

He stopped and glared at her.

"Most other people aren't professional gamblers in his same class, bringing competition into his town."

"I'm sure there're pigeons enough in San Antonio for you both to pluck," she said tartly.

Pigeons like Sutton.

"Tell Big Jim that, if you're such good friends." He glared harder, as if that friendship were a personal insult to him.

"Big Jim's an important citizen in San Antonio. What makes you think he'd bother to spread rumors about you?"

"He wants this town all to himself. He's the king of the Golden King, most elaborate gambling hall in the West."

"He's not that petty," she said. "He'd never gossip about your child—"

"Madeleine," he said wearily, "even ten years later, you're still an innocent belle. It's no longer your job to try to keep everybody happy so we'll all have a good time at the dance."

A terrible anger flared in her heart.

"Rafe Aigner, I haven't been a belle since the day you left New Orleans," she said. "That's the day I became a woman and a businesswoman. I *know* what a job is!"

He glanced at his son, then at her.

"You didn't marry Sutton to have someone to run the *Times* for you?"

Her fury flamed higher.

"Sutton couldn't even run the *Star*, which is half the size of the *Times*."

But Sutton could take them both away from her, and he had done just that. Now Rafe had the *Star*, and he couldn't run it, either.

While she, the only one who'd done any work, was left with nothing. No work, no home, no means of livelihood.

Rafe swept his eyes from hers scornfully, as if she were lying, and went to his son, bending to wake him.

The idea hit her, then, like a lightning bolt.

"Rafe, listen!"

He looked up at her.

"You're a gambler. You won the *Star* in a poker game."

"I told you that."

"You're not afraid to take me on, are you? Innocent belle that I am?"

He waited.

She gathered her courage. "Gamble with me. Let me try to win back what's rightfully mine."

"You'd be a lamb to the slaughter. Talk about ruining my reputation! Then Big Jim would be telling the town I take advantage of helpless women."

His eyes bored into hers.

"Madeleine, you can't play poker."

"I can learn! We can set a date that'll give me time to learn. Big Jim can teach me."

His face turned into a storm cloud.

"My skill and experience can't be matched," he said.

"How arrogant can you possibly be, Rafe Aigner?"

"Even coming from your powerful friend, Big Jim," he said, his tone dripping with sarcasm, "a *hundred* lessons wouldn't make a dent in the advantage I have over you."

"That's *my* lookout," she said.

"And my reputation is mine."

He pierced her with his sharp eyes.

"What would you put up against the *Star* in this great poker game of yours, Maddie? Would you borrow a stake from Big Jim? If so, how would you pay him back if all you won was the *Star*?"

Her heart sank through the floor. Of course. She'd have to have something to *gamble*, for goodness' sake.

"*My* skills," she said quickly. "Then no one can say you took advantage of me, and your precious reputation will be safe."

"What skills?"

"My business skills. My writing skills. Let's not have a poker game at all. I'll publish the *Star* for you for a year. If I make a profit, I get the newspaper and the building back. During that year, you get the income."

He glanced at the boy again.

"I need a nanny more than I need a newspaper."

Her pulse quickened. He was taking her seriously. Maybe she would talk him into this, she would make a profit, and then her troubles would be over.

"I can help you with Juanito."

"Only for tonight," he snapped. "Until I can get someone else. Watch him tonight and I'll consider this wild idea of yours."

"No!" she cried.

She looked, but Juan Rafael didn't wake.

"You'll do more than consider it," she went on, in a lower tone but one made hard as steel by her need. "You'll tell me yes or no right now."

She looked into his eyes as hotly as he'd looked at her.

"That paper was *mine!*" she said, fighting back tears of fury. "Sutton had no right to gamble away my inheritance, but that's exactly what he did. The *Star* was in Sutton's name only because he was my husband. That's abominably unfair, and you know it!"

Rafe's cynical eyes looked a hole through her.

"All right," he said harshly. "I'll raise you. If you're such a businesswoman and publisher, get after it. Take three years. It'll give you a better chance to turn a profit. Run the *Star*, live in your rooms, and I'll give you a small salary for food."

Hope—pure, raw hope—took her breath away.

"Make a profit one year of the three, and the *Star* is yours, lock, stock, and barrel."

"All right. Three years."

"One more stipulation. You have to at least break even all the time, because I won't put one cent into this newspaper. None."

"Done," she said, and held out her hand for him to shake like a man's.

It wasn't until she sat in the stall with Juanito and Dolly, her back to the wall, her eyes on the brilliant sunset, that she realized what else she had done.

She had tied herself to Rafe for three more years.

Chapter 4

~∽∾~

Rafe looked up from the cards in his hand and signalled the waiter who'd brought up the coffee to refill the cups all around. Night was turning into early morning now, and the players had all had plenty of whiskey—no sense having another scene like the one when Sutton Calhoun had been killed.

He tried to keep away from that thought because it led to Madeleine. His nerves felt frayed already, from dealing with Juanito and leaving him asleep in another horse's stall, so he certainly didn't need to think about Maddie.

Damn! What were the odds she'd even be in the same town, much less be the owner of the newspaper he'd won? They must be astronomical.

Madeleine Cottrell. God help him. The most fascinating, most treacherous woman in the world, and their paths had crossed yet again. Twice in one lifetime was too much for any man.

And she was a friend of Big Jim Thompson, into the bargain! Well, that fit. Big Jim was pretty damn treacherous, too.

He watched the waiter while the players pondered the new hands they'd been dealt and re-arranged their fans of cards. He ought to hire a valet, but he hated to run the risk of getting a ringer sent in by Big Jim to spy on his every move and every game. So when he'd found that this young man had an interest in gambling, he always asked for him and found him very helpful.

Maybe *he* was a friend of Big Jim, too.

The cynical thought made him smile to himself.

He felt a little better as the game resumed. Big Jim would soon do something to try to nudge him on his way—he was famous for running other gamblers out of his territory—so Rafe had that to look forward to. A good challenge always livened him up.

"Your call, Mr. Aigner," someone said.

Abruptly, he banished his wandering thoughts. Thinking about Juanito had nearly gotten him killed in Goliad, and thinking about Madeleine and Big Jim could do the same.

"Raise you five hundred."

What had he been doing, letting his mind

wander like that, anyway? Didn't he even care about money anymore? This was a high stakes game.

The erstwhile jovial rancher with the brand new John B. Stetson hat frowned fiercely at his cards. Rafe's research had shown that the man, Dirkson, had well-nigh unlimited resources— several ranches and other business interests.

"Raise," Dirkson said.

He laid his cards face down on the table and reached for his pocket.

Rafe unobtrusively cradled the butt of his holstered gun in his palm.

The man pulled out a piece of paper and began scribbling on it.

"A note for fifty head of cattle on my North Forty place," he said. "Steers and young bulls."

He threw it onto the heap in the middle of the table.

Rafe won the hand.

"I don't know where I'll put these cattle," he drawled. "Reckon the manager will mind if I run them up the front stairs to get them in here?"

The drummers on each side of him—who had each won enough during the evening to stay in a fairly good mood—were the only two who laughed. Things were serious now; this was a high-stakes game and it was nearing its end.

"Fold," Blackie Matson said. "You've cleaned me out, Rafe."

Blackie wasn't cleaned out, but he wasn't risk-

ing any more money that night. He was the most
disciplined small-time professional gambler Rafe
had ever seen.

"Fold," another man echoed.

Suddenly Rafe wished everyone else would
fold, too, and they'd all get up from the table and
get out of his rooms. He felt a supreme, jaded
weariness overtake him. He needed quiet, time
to think. He needed to be alone.

Maybe he could raise the stakes even higher
and drive them out. He took ten hundred dollar
gold pieces and stacked them in the center of the
table.

The drummers both stayed in.

And Dirkson the rancher wouldn't quit.

"Deed to the ranch," he said, taking a stiff paper from the inside pocket of the coat hanging
on the back of his chair. "I'm glad we're upping
the ante, boys, for I'm aimin' to get lucky at last."

Rafe forced himself to concentrate as he dealt
the cards.

They all took at least two new cards, and then,
it seemed, they all laid them down fast, like
dominoes falling.

Rafe won the pot.

"Now you have someplace to put your cattle," one of the drummers said, and the evening
ended on a fairly level note.

Dirkson was disappointed, a little sick about
his losses, but not angry. He was a good loser,
unlike Sutton Calhoun.

"I'll have my men drive your cattle into the hill pasture," he said, "and get the rest off there as soon as I can."

"No hurry," Rafe said.

After they were all gone, Rafe walked back through the messy parlor, ripping off his shirt and tie while he unfolded the deed with one hand and read it. He threw it onto the bed and himself across it, propped up one knee, and set his bootheel into the damask coverlet. Then he reached for a cheroot on the bedside stand and lit it.

Staring at the ceiling, he began to survey his situation. He had a son, he owned a newspaper and a ranch ten miles out of town stocked with fifty head of cattle. He was no rancher, but it appeared that if he got some mama cows to go with the young bulls, he'd be in business.

For a gambler like himself, who never stayed put more than a month or two, it was a hell of a note. Add Madeleine into the mix and it was nothing but trouble.

It'd been stupid to agree to her little proposal, but it was truly unfair that Sutton had lost the last of her inheritance. Of course, she'd brought it on herself by marrying the bastard.

Rafe Aigner was known for his fairness, though, and he never wanted it said that he took advantage of a woman. She owed him, too, for doing him so wrong. It'd serve her right to work for him three years for room and board, and three years would give her plenty of chance to decide where she'd go and what she'd do.

And he didn't have to worry about ever loving her again, so handling her wouldn't be that big a deal.

Rafe grinned his most wicked grin. His seeming to settle in here was going to chap Big Jim's hide. He might just stay around for a while and watch the big man suffer.

Madeleine opened her eyes to a pale dawn. The sun wasn't up yet; the air smelled like hay and horse and roses. There was a snuffling sound coming from the corner. But this wasn't her room.

For an instant, she didn't recognize her surroundings, then she knew. The stable.

She hadn't intended to fall asleep here.

She leaned forward to look at Juanito, the hay prickling her skin through her thin wrapper and nightgown. The child looked fine, snoozing with his hands beneath his cheek on the pillow she'd brought out for him. He had rolled over onto the blanket, too, she noted. Good. He needed that rest.

Getting to her feet, she touched his hair, but very lightly, so he wouldn't wake. She'd better get to the house and get the stove heating for the breakfast she'd promised him at midnight.

Dolly was standing drowsily over Juanito, her

head hanging, and Maddie gave her a couple of pats.

"You're a good, good girl," she whispered, and then ran toward the house.

After she got the fire started and the coffee on, she tried to stretch out the stiffness of sleeping sitting up. Then, yawning drowsily, she wandered into her bedroom and threw herself across the bed to wait for the coffee to heat.

Her dream came back in bits and pieces, and she tried to hold onto them, put them back together again, but they slipped away. She remembered the dream, though.

Her baby had been alive in her, kicking, still safe inside her huge belly.

Which truly had been a dream, for she had lost her child after only four months. That baby had never filled her or made her huge, and she'd never had another chance, because Sutton wouldn't make love to her after that. It was like he thought she was bad luck for him, or something.

Restless at the old, old pain starting to creep into her again, she got up and set her feet on the floor. Coffee ready or not, she couldn't stay in here another minute.

She couldn't stay away from Juanito.

It was her little voice of truth, but she ignored it. Juanito was the one child in all the world that she must *not* get attached to. Maybe she shouldn't have promised him breakfast, but surely Rafe wouldn't be here before noon, considering the life he led.

Rafe. Dear God. Rafe.

How could she have slept the night after the resurrected Rafe walked through her door? Not to mention the news of her financial ruin!

She'd always been one who had to have her sleep, though, and sleep had saved her sanity more than once in these last long ten years. Running through the kitchen, opening the back door with one hand, carelessly tightening the belt on the wrapper with the other, she went out into the flower-scented yard.

The sun had come up while she'd been in the house; pink light streamed across the trees and bushes, and the stable's open door. It probably hadn't waked Juanito, though, down behind the wall of the stall.

Halfway to the stable, a slight movement in the shadows of the big live oak by the alley stopped her in mid-step. A man dressed in black leaned back against the trunk, one knee bent, the sole of his boot resting against the tree.

Her heart leapt into her throat.

Rafe.

She couldn't see his face, but every line of his body proclaimed it.

The snowy white of his shirt gleamed in the dark like a light.

His relentless gaze was taking her in. Slowly. Every inch of her.

She could feel it on her skin everywhere it touched.

"Maddie."

The low, rich sound of her name, said the way only Rafe could say it, brought memories rushing through her.

"Rafe."

Now that she thought about it, had she heard a trace of anger in his voice?

The sharp crack of a striking lucifer and then its fire dancing at the end of his cheroot held her mesmerized. It flared and she glimpsed the glint in his eyes and then the shape of his mouth as he blew out the flame.

Yes, he was angry. To think that she could know him this well, this stranger. And only because she used to love him.

The breeze picked up a strand of her hair and brushed it against her neck. Finally he spoke.

"Come here."

It was an order. He'd always been arrogant.

She stood where she was.

"I'm going to see Juan Rafael," she said.

"He's still asleep. How come all the doors are wide open?"

The sun burst over the treetops. For an instant, the breaking light blinded her, but she could still see the hard line of his jaw.

"I thought he might be afraid to be locked in again."

That stopped him for one beat.

"Damn! What did y'all do, sit up and talk half the night?"

"He was awake when I checked on him at midnight, but he went back to sleep after I opened all the doors. Juanito's not used to closed places."

She walked toward him.

"And Juanito's not used to you."

"He'll get used to me," he growled. "And he'll damn well get used to doing what I tell him. I *told* him to get in the bed and go to sleep."

"In a room alone, in a strange place."

"I was in the next room, for God's sake! With a connecting door. He had no business in the room where we were playing."

"Rafe," she said dryly, "isn't ordering someone to go to sleep a lot like leading a horse to water?"

She thought she saw the ghost of his old sideways grin.

"He's horse crazy," he said.

"As you used to be."

He shrugged that away and fixed her with his hard glare.

"Forget it," he said harshly. "I'll take care of him."

Her anger flared to match his.

"I don't know what right you think you have to be angry," she said coolly, "when *you're* the one intruding on *my* life and robbing *me.*"

"Of what? According to the deal you talked me into last night, you still have your newspaper and the hovel your husband so generously provided."

She stepped closer to get the light out of her eyes.

"But neither is really mine anymore, is it, Rafe? Now my whole life hangs by a thread that you could cut at any minute of any day."

He only smoked his cheroot and stared at her through narrowed lids.

"You could sell the *Star* or gamble it away and I couldn't do a thing about it."

When he spoke, his voice was a cold knife.

"Are you saying I'll go back on my word?"

"No. I'm saying I'll let you out of it if you want out."

"Why?"

"Because I don't know if I can bear the suspense for three years, since you're already out here the very next day fuming mad that you ever agreed to it."

"Maybe you'll turn a profit the first year and that'll put an end to it."

"I'll sure do my damnedest."

"Well, well, Madeleine Cottrell," he drawled, and took a drag on his smoke. "When did you take up bad language and shameless behavior?"

"When I needed them. I only use them at appropriate times."

"I'm flattered."

"Why? Because talking to you somehow brought profanity to my tongue?"

"I'm thinking more along the lines of your nakedly shameless behavior."

His gaze moved over her slowly, lingered, and then came to rest on the low vee neck of the wrap. Her skin burned.

She pulled the flimsy wrap tighter around her, and retied the belt with fumbling fingers. Then she resented the fact that she had let him make her do it.

"Don't flatter yourself too much, Rafe," she said, walking toward him again to prove that he didn't intimidate her in the least. "I didn't even know you were here, remember?"

He kept his eyes on hers.

"What a surprise," she said wryly, "at this hour of the morning to find you idly lurking my backyard."

"Don't forget it's my backyard now."

She stopped right in front of him and tilted her head so she could look him squarely in the eye.

"Not for three years, it isn't."

He threw away the cheroot, grabbed her by the shoulders, and kissed her, hard.

Kissed her senseless in an instant.

She was gone, in a heartbeat, into the wild heat of his mouth that once had been her sun. A sun as new as this day, yet old and familiar and filled with a power she couldn't fathom.

He ended the kiss as quickly as he'd started it.

However, he kept his hands on her as if he owned her. She stepped back but he didn't let her go.

Her lips were still on fire and bruised, begging for more, more of his taste, in spite of the fury pounding her brain. The raw desire racing through her made her even more furious.

"You have a *nerve*, Rafe Aigner. What do you think you're doing?"

"What any sane man would do in this situation."

She glared at him.

"This isn't a situation."

"Oh, yes, Maddie, it is. Just the sight of you obviously right out of bed, your charms hardly covered by that scrap of silk, is enough to create a situation in any man."

Accusation and anger, cold and controlled, rang in his every word.

"You sound as if I deliberately set out to seduce you, Rafe."

She was trying for just as cool a tone as his—with her blood running so hot, her pulse couldn't slow from his kiss.

"You denied me your body and then sold yourself to another man."

"Sold myself! For what? What did I get from Sutton?"

He only stared at her.

"Did you love him?"

Madeleine looked him straight in the eye.

"Yes."

Not a muscle in him moved.

"He shared your bed."

It was not a question. Rafe thought he knew everything, when he knew nothing about what had happened to make her who she was now.

She should walk away and refuse to say another word, but she wanted to hurt him.

"Yes, of course. Sutton *was* my husband, after all."

There. Maybe he'd suffer the way she was suffering right now. He'd had no right to grab her and kiss her and start all this incredible turmoil raging in her body after he'd become so different, so hard and cold that their love could never live again.

"Then why didn't you have children?"

The question, so baldly put, shocked her.

"What are you trying to do with this inquisition, Rafe? Say that since I have no children, Sutton didn't share my bed, therefore that proves I never loved him?"

He raised one black brow and stared into her eyes.

"You're the only one who knows."

"Thank you for admitting that much," she said scornfully. "If you're trying to make me feel guilty for marrying Sutton, you can quit right now."

She wrenched free of his grasp and stepped back.

"You're the one who ought to carry the burden of guilt. If you'd loved me half as much as you said you did, you would've come to see me, married or not, when you sneaked back into New Orleans."

"To see you with another man?"

He was incredulous.

"To set my mind at ease! To stop my grieving!"

"I don't see it that way."

"Obviously not," she said, in a snippy tone. "And that's because your pride is all that matters to you. You don't ever consider other people's feelings."

"You're wrong."

"I am not. The way you treat your son is perfect proof of that. He probably would have slept if you hadn't locked him in that room."

That cracked his facade of coolness.

"What'd you want me to do?" he shouted. "Let him run the streets in the middle of the night to get back to his horse? Bring the horse into my hotel suite? Drop out of the game so I could watch him every minute? How am I supposed to make a living? Hire a nanny? What nanny is willing to sleep in a stall?"

He fixed her with a mighty glare.

"Look here, Madeleine, you don't know the half of it. I slept in the livery at Goliad, but I'm not about to make myself a laughingstock by doing that every night."

"You're borrowing trouble," she said sharply. "When Juanito begins to feel closer to you, he'll get weaned away from the horses."

"You're dreaming," he said scornfully. "If I hadn't been horseback, he'd never have come one mile with me. Horses're all he cares about. He's not going to get close to me."

She sensed a wistfulness in him in spite of his tone. He was holding a barely perceptible hope that she would contradict him.

A trace of treacherous pity crept into her heart.

"You can't expect him to let you get close until he knows you'll stay with him," she said. "He's afraid you'll be together only a day or two, as on one of your usual visits, and then he'll be alone here in this strange place."

He flashed her a piercing glance.

"How do you know all that?"

"I'm guessing. But I'm going by a few things he said when I came to see about him in the night. When we talked about the locked doors."

He stared at her. "He woke, sat up, and blurted out his deepest feelings to you, a perfect stranger?"

"No. He was already awake, grooming my mare in the middle of the night and telling her his troubles. He'd checked to see if Tortilla was still in front of the shop. I told him you took her to the livery. We got to talking."

"About the mare? He only talks to me about horses."

"About everything. It was just some remark he made."

"You speak Spanish?"

She frowned at him.

"No, we both used Comanche, since that seemed easier. Of course I speak Spanish. I've been in Texas five years."

He shook his head as if to say he should've known. "Like you needed to speak Cajun for the *Times*."

"It's the only way to get a lot of stories," she said.

"All right. What else did he tell you?"

She shrugged.

"If you'd stop quizzing people and just listen, Rafe, you'd be surprised what they might tell you."

His sharp gaze left hers, shifted to something behind her.

She turned.

Juanito, his hair sticking up in all directions, was coming out of the stable, sleepily rubbing his eyes. He was leading her mare, who looked about as tousled as he did. Poor thing, her peaceful routine had certainly been turned upside down.

Just the sight of them made Madeleine smile.

"What the *hell?*" Rafe muttered.

He fixed his piercing glare on Juanito.

"That isn't your horse, is it, Juan Rafael?" he said sternly.

"No, *Papá*," the child said, barely loud enough to be heard above the slow clopping of hooves, "she is my friend."

The way he said "*Papá*" was so sweet, Madeleine marveled that Rafe could keep frowning at him. He walked to Madeleine and stopped, the mare snuffling at his shoulder.

"Go and put her back where you found her. She belongs to the *señorita* . . . the *señora*. You know that."

Juanito's huge amber-colored eyes, so much like Rafe's, went straight to Madeleine's face.

"*Mi Lena*, may I take her to see my mare? I will bring her back."

"What are you *talking* about?" Rafe said. "That's the dumbest thing I ever heard . . ."

He did have the grace to hush when Madeleine looked at him.

"Your *papá* says no," she said, thinking fast, "but it would be nice if your horse and mine could meet sometime."

Her reward was a beautiful smile from Juanito which transformed his usually sober face.

"You and I," he said, with a gesture that flowed through the air between them, "*amigos.*"

"Yes," she said, aching to reach out and take him into her arms, "we are friends. It would be nice if our horses could be, also."

His quick, brief nod said that was what he'd had in mind.

She could feel Rafe's eyes on her.

"You must do what your *papá* tells you," she said, "but perhaps he would let you bring your horse to visit mine sometime soon."

She turned and met Rafe's incredulous stare.

"What do you think?" she said.

"I suppose so," he said abruptly.

"There," she said, turning to Juanito, "bring your horse here anytime you like."

"*Gracias, Papá,*" he said. "Perhaps we will bring Beau, too?"

He looked so innocently hopeful that even grouchy Rafe couldn't deny him that.

"Yes," he said shortly, "sometime we will."

"Are you on foot right now, Rafe?" she said.

"Yes. After a long night at the table, I needed to stretch my legs."

His gaze drifted from Juan Rafael to the mare and suddenly she knew the real reason he was walking instead of riding. Her heart went out to him, although she tried to hold it back.

He might not even realize it, but he'd been hoping for a few minutes with his child when he wasn't distracted by one of his equine true loves.

"We must go, Juanito," he said gruffly. "Papa must sleep."

A sudden, lonesome feeling came over her.

"He could stay and help me here," she said quickly. "I told him I'd cook his breakfast, since we thought you'd sleep until noon."

"No," he snapped, even more quickly.

Then she saw that the Southern manners ingrained in him by his father, that most gracious gentleman, Lucien Aigner, wouldn't let him rest. The wheels turned almost visibly in his head as he realized he must set an example for *his* son.

"Thank you, Miss Madeleine," he said, "that was thoughtful of you but we must go."

Then, more sharply, he added, "You have work to do and a profit to make."

He turned to Juanito.

"Put the mare back into her stall," he said.

Juanito immediately turned to go do as he was told, reaching up with one hand to stroke the mare's nose as they walked.

Rafe turned to her again.

"Don't encourage him in this silliness," he said, his tone harder than ever.

"He's going with you, isn't he? Without my mare? I doubt you'll even have to lock him in your room."

He only looked at her.

"Madeleine, stay out of this," he said finally. "I have to learn to deal with him myself."

"Yes," she said dryly, "you do."

"And what is this *'mi Lena'* business? That's what he calls you?"

"Last night we went from Miss Madeleine to Señorita Magdalena and, somehow, when I mentioned that you and I had known each other long ago, we wound up with *'mi Lena'* and *'mi Papá'*."

He gave her a long look she couldn't read.

Was he jealous? Would he keep Juanito away from her because the boy had a term of affection for her?

"Don't ever say *I'm* the one who kept him from sleeping," he said.

That gave her hope after they'd vanished through her back gate and into the alley behind her place. Rafe must be thinking they'd at least be talking about Juanito again.

How could she have become so attached to the child in one brief encounter?

Surely Rafe would let her have more time with him!

The old Rafe never had been petty or jealous—except of her other suitors—but she must remember that he had become someone else altogether. Her breath caught in her chest as it had when he started that fierce, angry kiss.

He tasted like the old Rafe, only more dangerous. She could never forget that this rough stranger was not the man she had loved.

Chapter 5

Rafe sat across the breakfast table from his son and watched him swirl a bite of pancake into the pool of syrup. At least Juanito was eating, even if he wouldn't cooperate about anything else. Yesterday, he had only picked at his food.

Breakfast at Madeleine's would've been a treat—for the food. She'd always loved to cook and evidently that was the one thing about her that hadn't changed. She'd never been so direct or so tart-tongued, or so . . .

He fought back the memory of how sweet she'd tasted.

And she'd never been one to pay a lot of attention to little kids, not that he remembered.

76

How come *she* had had no problem getting along with Juanito?

Rafe tore his mind away from Maddie and put it firmly onto the boy. He needed to get him some more good clothes. His son's appearance reflected on him, and appearances were ninety percent of the game for a gambler—especially one in the top echelon of the game.

He sighed. Clothes, food, nannies, places to sleep, *persuasions* to sleep: it seemed there was always something else to think about when a man was responsible for a child. He felt inadequate and half the time he was; Maddie's remarks about locking him in the hotel room made sense. But what if that wouldn't have worked, either? How could he have known what to do?

Maybe any woman would've instinctively known. Why hadn't he simply left the child with that whole big family who loved him?

Because something even deeper than the instincts he constantly honed and lived by had told him not to leave his son again.

Rafe sipped at his coffee and looked at the top of Juanito's dark head, bent over his plate. Juan Rafael might be eating but, as usual, he certainly wasn't talking—at least, not to him. If Madeleine had been there, words would likely be flowing from his mouth.

Mi Lena. He still couldn't believe that the boy felt so familiar with her after one, just *one*, short visit—and at midnight, no less. What the hell was *he* doing so wrong?

"I talked to Señor Hobbs at the livery," he said. "He'll let you help him with the horses today if you'd rather be there than at the hotel."

The sound of the word "hotel" brought a wary look from Juan Rafael.

"Don't cut your eyes at me like that," Rafe said, regret tugging at him. "I wouldn't have locked you in if you hadn't kept trying to go back to the horses."

The little imp had left the room *three times*—*after* the game had started. He'd had no choice but to lock him in, no matter what Madeleine said.

Madeleine.

He never should have kissed her. No matter what his intention, no matter that he'd meant to convey anger instead of love, he never should have touched her.

He never even should have looked at her in the dawn light. That image of her creamy breasts glowing in the vee of the peach-colored silk haunted him still. Her mass of black hair all mussed from the warm pillow, and her blue, blue eyes still glazed with sleep—until she saw him—that picture would not leave him, either.

Rafe closed his eyes but that only made the memory more real, so he opened them again and tried to concentrate on his son. His son, whom he'd brought to a foreign country to help out at the livery stable and sleep in other people's horse stalls.

Juanito picked up his glass of milk and drank half in one gulp. He'd never had much except an occasional cup of goat's milk in his life, and he was learning to like cow's milk. At least his body would be stronger for Rafe's having brought him to Texas.

"I won a ranch out west of town," he told the boy. "This afternoon we'll go out and see if it has any place to keep cows that give milk."

Juanito's eyes widened and fixed on his.

"Does it have *muchos caballos*—hor-ses—on the *rancho*?"

"I don't know. If so, they won't be ours."

"We could buy some!"

Rafe laughed. At least Juanito was still talking to him about horses.

"We might," he said.

Dirkson had better get on out there and gather up any of the horses on the place, or Juanito would have them all in his personal herd and be making a bed to sleep beside them when the sun went down.

"Who will go there?"

"You and me."

"And Beau and Tortilla?"

"Yes," Rafe said, trying to hide the irritation the question sent through him. "It's too far to walk."

The child certainly didn't mind making it plain that he cared more about Beau and Tortilla's company than his own father's.

"We will come back to San Antonio?"

"In a few days."

"You and me and Beau and Tortilla?"

Rafe leaned forward and looked into the child's big eyes, so like his own. He would never have recognized the underlying fear in that question if not for what Madeleine had said.

Pity squeezed his heart. It was a terrible thing to be a child and helpless to decide your own fate.

For a year, at least, after his own father took him to New Orleans, he'd wondered how long it would be before he returned him to the Choctaw village. Sometimes he had longed for it to be soon; at other times he never wanted to leave his father.

"Yes," he said. "You and me. We live together now."

But *his* father had had a home and community to take him to, a community that included the very best families and the belle of New Orleans, Madeleine Cottrell. *He* had no place at all in society here to offer Juan Rafael.

He shouldn't have left him the first time he ever saw him, when Juanito was a chubby, bright-eyed two-year-old sitting on his grandmother's lap. But how could he have taken him from the only mother he'd ever known?

Juanito ate another bite of pancake and looked at Rafe solemnly.

"Beau and Tortilla live with us?"

Rafe sighed. He would never be able to trade off the raggedy mustang now, embarrassing as she was.

"Yes."

"We live *aquí*, in San Antonio? Or at *el rancho?*"

"Wherever. We'll be together for a long time. Until you grow up, Juan Rafael, and become a man."

Looking shocked, Juanito considered that, searching Rafe's face as if expecting to find the truth there instead of in the words.

"It's true," Rafe said.

"Y mi Lena?"

For a second Rafe didn't understand. Then he did.

Was the child *that* attached to her already?

"I suppose she'll be here in San Antonio. At least for three years—*tres años.*"

He shrugged.

"Maybe. I don't know."

Juanito was through with him. He stared off into the middle distance and Rafe raised his hand to signal the waiter.

Sleep would help. If he could get a good day's sleep, he could figure out what to do with the boy. If he did stay in San Antonio, he needed to put him in school.

Vague visions of a teacher chasing after Juan

at the stables, trying to bring him back to his desk in the classroom, made him smile wryly. Any school trying to deal with Juan Rafael would probably double his tuition charges on the second day.

Rafe woke in the early afternoon from a thin, restless sleep in the too-hot room. For a few minutes, he tried to fall back into his crazy dreams where Madeleine and New Orleans and his father and Juanito and the Choctaw village where he grew up were all mixed up together. He couldn't, though, he kept tossing fitfully and tangling his feet in the sweaty sheets. Finally, he gave up and got up.

He needed to get out of town, get out into the countryside, and forget the past. He had a son to raise in the present.

Quickly, he dressed in an old, soft blue cotton shirt and some Levi Strauss jeans, then threw a few things for overnight into his saddle bags, for himself and for Juan. The next game he had scheduled was two days away, so he might as well take this time to spend with the child. On the ranch—where the horses surely would be in a pen near the house for the night—surely he could persuade Juanito to sleep inside in a bed.

Then it struck him that he didn't even know whether there *was* a house on the ranch. Or any horse pens. No matter; they could camp outside, the way they'd done on the way back from Los Pinos—the four of them, him, Juanito, Beau, and Tortilla.

By the time he had all the gear together, he was carrying two bedrolls and two sets of saddle bags. Crossing the hotel lobby unnoticed beneath his burden, he felt a sudden lift of freedom. Surely when he and Juanito were alone again, when the boy truly believed that he wasn't going to leave him, they could begin to be *amigos*—like Juanito and Maddie.

He thought about it while he strode across the crowded street, the bags slung over his shoulder. His short rest had not been deep or good, but he felt more hopeful, somehow, than he had before. Juanito had seemed reassured when he told him that they would live together until he was grown.

But when he arrived at the livery, Juanito wasn't eagerly awaiting his father's arrival. He wasn't even there.

"He saddled both your horses," Hobbs told him. "And rode out of here riding the buckskin and leading the black."

"When?"

"Not twenty minutes ago. When I asked where he was headed, he said La Señora's. Seemed to think you knew who that'd be."

"I do," Rafe said tightly.

"You leaving town?"

Hobbs eyed the saddle bags suspiciously, as if thinking Rafe might be trying to run out on an obligation.

"I'll be back in a couple of days," Rafe snapped. "Don't worry about it, Hobbs—I'm paid through the end of this month, if you'll recall."

He ignored the man's blustering apology, whirled on his heel, and strode away. No sense fooling himself about Juanito's attachment to *him*; it was Madeleine he wanted.

Well, what man wouldn't want her?

His lips curved in a bitter smile.

Juan Rafael was growing up in a hurry.

By the time Rafe reached Travis Street and turned south to go toward the offices of the *Star*, he had met two men who were regulars at his poker games, the proprietor of the tobacco shop where he bought his cheroots, the young waiter who liked to serve his poker games, and the tailor who had measured him for a dozen more of his custom-made shirts—all of whom inquired as to why he was on foot carrying his saddle bags. Every man jack of them had some supposedly funny remark to make about it.

Rafe took it all in good humor, accepting that the sight he presented today *was* in sharp contrast to his usual portrait of a stylish man superbly mounted. However, it did irritate him a bit that Big Jim Thompson just happened to be sitting a huge gray gelding—one that looked to be of fine Thoroughbred breeding—on Travis Street not far from the *Star*, holding forth to what appeared to be a couple of pillars of the town.

Rafe thanked God that he wasn't riding Tortilla.

Big Jim's audience roared with laughter at something he'd just said. Thoroughly pleased with himself, he removed one foot from the stirrup, hooked his leg loosely around the horn, and slumped in the saddle in the most leisurely fashion while he turned away to wave to all the fine citizens in the streets of San Antonio who were lucky enough to get to see him.

Then he turned back and spotted Rafe coming down the street.

"What's the matter, Aigner?" he called, loudly enough to attract attention. "Did your horse get away from you? Turn around! Let me see if he tossed you off on your backside and dusted your pants."

Not only did the little group he'd been talking to turn and look, but so did several people in the street and a couple walking just ahead of Rafe. Thompson clearly thought he was hilarious, he was grinning wide enough to split his fat face.

Rafe ached to ignore him and his loud mouth, but he wouldn't give him the satisfaction of knowing he'd irritated him.

"He dusted me, all right, but I'll get hold of

him again in a minute," he called back. "I've got him hemmed up somewhere over on the south bank of the San Antonio River."

That brought a jovial guffaw from Big Jim and a laugh from everyone else.

"Glad to hear it," he boomed. "Glad to hear it. I was getting scared that maybe the famous Rafe Aigner had lost that big, beautiful black equine in a poker game."

Now, *that*, according to the loudness of Big Jim's laughter, was the very funniest thing he had ever conceived. His friends thought so, too, and they watched Rafe closely to see if *that*, perhaps, got his goat.

Not one of the three turned toward the sudden sound of galloping hooves that came from the street behind them; not one of them saw that the young man on the fast bay horse was not going down the street, but was headed straight for Big Jim. The kid's hat was pushed back on his head, he was coming on at a lightning pace—bareback, strangely—and his eyes held a killer gleam. He wore a six-gun.

Rafe let his saddle bags fall, reaching for the gun at his hip. But as Big Jim's eyes widened in shock at Rafe's behavior, Rafe saw that the kid wasn't going to draw at all.

He intended to collide with the gray.

Rafe shoved his handgun back into the holster, dashed to the edge of the sidewalk, and grabbed the bridle of Jim's horse. There was no time to circle the gray out into the street and no room to bring him up onto the sidewalk, so he had to make him back up.

In spite of screams and shouts now coming from every direction, he smooched calmly to the gelding and clutched the reins beneath his chin to push him backward. He got no interference from Big Jim, who was still trying to regain his balance from the first lurch backward. Seconds after the gray moved, Rafe felt the rushing wind of the boy on the bay at his back, and then the sharp, flaming sting of a spur rowel slashing through his skin from shoulder to shoulder.

When Rafe let up pressure on the gray, the gelding stopped short and Big Jim came tumbling off like a big, chubby doll. Rafe got there in time to break his fall, then he looked up to see that the young man on the bay had not gone crashing up onto the sidewalk, as he'd thought he would surely have to do, but had managed to stay right at the edge of it. He was galloping down the street in a cloud of dust.

It had all happened so fast that it was nearly incomprehensible, but dozens of people had seen the whole thing and they gathered around in a chattering, shouting mob as Big Jim struggled to his feet, vainly brushing at the dust on his clothes. A great cheer went up.

"Ride 'im, Big Jim!" somebody yelled. "Git back on and show 'im who's boss!"

The loud general laughter turned Jim's face bright red.

"He didn't even rear up on you, man! Nor try to buck, neither! How come you couldn't stay on top?"

"Yeah, whose backside is it that got dusted now?" someone else called.

"You saved him—and us—from a bad wreck, there, Mr. Aigner," said one of Jim's important looking pals who had recovered enough to step down off the sidewalk. "Much obliged. Tom Rivers is my name."

He walked out into the street to shake Rafe's hand.

"I'm another one in your debt," said the other, coming up behind him. "Henry Oliver. Privileged to meet you."

"Glad to be of service," Rafe said, shaking Oliver's hand, too.

"If that kid had collided with Jim, why, he'd have knocked you two with him all the way through the window into the barber shop," another man said. "Likely to have killed you both."

"And coulda broke up a few bones in the barber shop, too," a bystander added.

"And outside," said another. "All that flying glass."

"I know," Rivers said. "We were beyond lucky

to have Mr. Aigner right there in the right place at the right time."

Other men, people Rafe didn't know, came up to slap him on the back and talk to him.

"Yeah, you're mighty salty, Aigner," one of them said. "That took a lot of guts. You coulda been killed in a heartbeat."

This was beginning to embarrass him.

"I just happened to be there," he said. "Anybody else would've done the same."

He turned to look for a way out of the crowd and his eyes met Big Jim's. They were filled with resentment. Hatred.

Shock stopped Rafe in his tracks and he stared. The look vanished. Surely he'd been mistaken.

"I reckon I should thank you, too," Jim said loudly, and held out his hand to shake.

But he didn't move toward Rafe.

"Git on over there and shake the man's hand, Thompson," someone yelled. "He saved your life, and again after the bay horse passed. You came tumbling off of there like Humpty Dumpty."

That brought another round of loud laughter. Big Jim didn't join in.

"He's put back together again, though," somebody else yelled. "Thanks to Aigner."

Big Jim did come over to Rafe and shake his hand, but that made his face flush even brighter.

"Thanks," he said loudly. "You can move fast, Aigner. I'll have to give you that."

Rafe nodded.

"Don't mention it, Thompson. Glad to help."

"Maybe you ought to've thought twice about it, though," Big Jim said, trying to sound jovial. "Now that I'm a laughingstock for falling off my horse, I'll have to beat you at poker to get back my rep."

"Well, then, I'll have to confess to the truth, I guess," Rafe drawled. "I was mainly trying to save that good-looking gray. He's too good a horse to let get hurt."

That brought the loudest round of laughter of all, and Rafe turned away.

It *would* be embarrassing to have to be rescued in front of the whole town. Especially by someone you'd just been hurrahing.

At that instant, he saw the smiling faces of Juanito and Madeleine coming toward him through the crowd. He met Juanito's eyes and his heart stood still. They were full of hero worship and they were fixed on his face.

He went to meet them and squatted down to be at eye-level with his son. All he wanted to do was to take him into his arms, but that would embarrass a nine-year-old with the whole town looking on.

"Papa, you saved a terrible *accidente*," he said. "You are *muy rápido*."

"Did you see it?"

Juan Rafael could only nod.

"We both did," Madeleine said. "You were *magnificently rápido*."

The look in her eyes went all through him. She, too, thought he was a hero.

"Oh, my goodness, you're hurt!"

It was a woman's voice from somewhere behind him.

Madeleine's face paled.

"What? Let me see."

He straightened up and turned around.

Juanito cried out. So did Maddie.

"Oh, Rafe, you're bleeding!"

"Mr. Aigner," said the other woman, her voice closer now, "you need someone to clean and bandage that wound. My shop is just down the street . . ."

Madeleine was beside him now, taking his arm as if he had to have help to walk.

"Thank you so much, Mrs. Bolander," she called. "But I'm taking Mr. Aigner into my place right this minute to take care of him."

"We will take care of my papa," Juanito called to her firmly.

Rafe stared down at him in amazement as the boy went to his other side and reached up with both hands to support his left arm.

The strangest feeling came over him as they made their way into the front door of the *Star*. Rafe couldn't put a name to it, but he liked it.

"Does it hurt, Papa?"

"Like fire," Rafe said.

"Do not worry," his son told him. "I will wash it with cool, cool water."

Unexpected tears stung behind Rafe's eyes. Suddenly he felt as if he *did* need them to hold him up.

He must be getting old if one little dust-up like that one could shatter his nerves.

"We heard all the laughing outside and then the galloping horse," Madeleine said, "and we got out onto the sidewalk just in time to see you drop your bags and go for your gun."

"I thought at first the kid intended to shoot Big Jim," Rafe said. "Then I couldn't believe he was trying to run him over."

"He was *estúpido*, that man," Juanito said as they made their way, three across, down the little hallway.

He ought to tell them that he could make it on his own. He really should. But it was too late now; they were into Maddie's parlor.

"Why do you say that, son? Maybe he was just mean. *Bajo*."

Juanito shook his head.

"No. *Estúpido*. His horse, the bay, he was *pequeño*, the gray horse *grande*."

Rafe smiled down at Juanito.

"Sometimes it's the *pequeño* ones you have to watch," he said. "*Pequeño* can also be *muy fuerte*. Very strong."

Juanito thought about that.

"*Sí*," he finally said.

Rafe tousled his hair.

"You don't miss much, do you, son? You didn't see that horse for more than an instant."

"I am *rápido*, too," Juanito said. "Me and *mi papá. Rápidos.*"

And he made the same flowing gesture in the air between them that he had made that morning when he proclaimed he and Maddie were *amigos.*

Rafe bent down and pulled his son into his embrace, his heart beating faster than it ever had in his life. His wound hurt like hell but he barely felt that for an instant.

Because Juanito put both his skinny arms around his papa's waist and gave him a big hug.

Then, when Rafe let him go, he shyly went to help Madeleine turn a chair around at the kitchen table.

"Straddle it," she said to Rafe, and went to a tin cabinet in the corner to get her supplies.

He did as she told him and Juanito stood at his elbow like a small shadow.

"I remember when you fainted at the sight of blood," Rafe said, teasingly. "Are you sure you can do this, Maddie, or should I send for Mrs. Bolander?"

"Very funny," she said dryly. "You should be on the playhouse stage, Rafe."

"I *am* funny," he said, teasingly. "I made the whole town laugh."

"Except for poor Big Jim. He was a tad embarrassed."

That hit him wrong, somehow.

"If I hadn't jumped when I did, you'd be saying 'poor Big Jim,' for sure," he said sharply.

Juanito gave a gasp of surprise and turned toward the door.

"You drop our bags! I get them."

"I'll help you in a minute, son," Rafe said. "They're heavy. No one will bother them."

"No. I go. I am *pequeño* and *muy fuerte.*"

He grinned shyly as Rafe and Maddie laughed, then darted out to do his errand.

Rafe took up the argument again as Maddie came back to the table and began to set out her cloths and medicines.

"I don't know why you feel sorry for Big Jim," he said stubbornly, although he'd had the same emotion—but briefly—himself. "He could be splattered all over the barber shop."

She grinned. "I know, but compared to you, he did look sort of foolish," she said. "I couldn't help but feel just a little bit sorry for him."

That was so irritating.

But she *had* said, "Compared to you."

"You just have too soft a heart, Madeleine." He willed himself not to flinch as she started peeling away his shirt from where it was drying to his skin.

"Do you want me to take it off?" he said.

She got a funny little hitch in her breath, right beside his ear.

"No."

He couldn't resist.

"Are you sure?"

"Rafe Aigner, you are totally at my mercy, if you will but realize it," she said tartly. "I am in a position to hurt you really bad."

"Just trying to help," he drawled, and set his teeth against the pain.

"Holler if you want to," she said.

Now how had she known? She couldn't see his jaw.

"You can even cuss if necessary."

Small footsteps ran across the front office, coming toward them.

"No, I have to set a good example," he muttered.

"He truly is *muy rápido*," she murmured.

"They are in there, the bags," Juanito said. "Someone put them there for us."

He sounded very disappointed.

"Because they admire what your *papá* did," Madeleine said, and touched something to his back that hurt fiercely. "He is a hero today."

"*Sí*," Juanito said, and came to stand beside Rafe again.

He was shifting back and forth from one foot to another.

"I help you, *mi Lena*," he said.

"You know what I need you to do most?" she said.

"What?"

"Would you go put the horses up for me?"

"Not our two," Rafe said quickly. "We're headed out to the ranch, since I don't have a game for a couple of days."

"Juanito told me. Where is it?"

"About ten miles west of town. I'm not sure exactly where but I can find it."

"This bleeding needs to be stopped for a while before you ride. You'd better wait until morning."

Juanito started for the door.

"If I have to do that, I'll take the horses back to the livery myself."

Juanito turned back.

"Stay here, Papa," he said, "so I sleep beside you and help you not to bleed."

Then he was out the door.

Rafe sat stunned, his back numb.

"Did he say what I thought he said?"

"Yes," Madeleine said. "He'll sleep inside if you stay here. But I don't believe he will at the hotel."

He turned around and their eyes met.

"That puts me in a hell of a fix."

"I might say that, myself," she said wryly.

"I can't see that we have any choice, though."

"Neither can I."

She picked up the iodine and started with that, but somehow he didn't feel any pain.

That was because something that felt almost like happiness was creeping over him. Where had this come from, this unexpected, extremely pleasant warmth that was growing between him and Madeleine?

Chapter 6

$\sim\!\!\text{O}\!\!\text{O}\!\!\sim$

Maddie's fingertips touched him like brushes of a feather, like cool drops of rain that still held heat in their centers. A lot of heat. Even through the fabric of his shirt, they left their imprints.

A wet cloth held against the most stubborn spot didn't entirely take the heat away.

He thought of that angry kiss in her garden at dawn.

"Rafe," she said, and again he heard that little catch in her voice, "you are going to have to take this shirt off, after all."

He turned to look over his shoulder.

"Are you sure it's safe? You won't try to take advantage of me, will you?"

She cut him a look from her blue, blue eyes.

"I won't, but Mrs. Bolander might. You want to change your mind now so you won't have to walk down the street half-naked?"

He started to unbutton his shirt, but he kept his gaze locked with hers.

"You've got it all wrong, Maddie," he drawled. "You're the one who ran off poor Mrs. Bolander. I never had a chance to take her up on her invitation."

Her eyes narrowed until her long, black lashes almost touched her cheeks and that mischievous grin that he remembered touched the corners of her mouth. She took hold of the collar of his shirt and started peeling it away from his shoulders.

"All right, then, if that's the way you feel, I'll just rip this all the way off now because it'd give all the ladies at the millinery shop a thrill to see you without your shirt."

She bent over to look him fiercely in the eye.

"I didn't mean it, I take it back, I'm *glad* you forced me to come home with you, Maddie."

"*Forced* you?"

"Just don't hurt me, please."

"I'm making no promises," she said.

Her touch felt like a caress as her palms slid over his shoulders and down his arms. It brought a sharp thrill, although she, doubtless had not meant it that way.

She *had* kissed him back, though, there beneath the live oak tree. There was no way to deny that.

Her scent was the same as always. He breathed it in as she bent over him to ease the sleeves down his arms. He had bought it for her, once, in a shop over on St. Charles, but he could no longer recall its name.

His lips parted to ask her, but he caught himself in time.

"Rafe, this one spot goes pretty deep," she said, as she pulled the shirt completely away and dropped it on the floor. "It's going to take me a minute."

"I'm in no hurry," he said.

That was one of the truest statements he'd ever made. His mind was leaving him completely and his body was taking over. Every touch of Madeleine's hands, every gesture she made that stirred the scented air around them, every tantalizing rustle of her skirts, made him more aware of her.

It brought back the taste of her to his lips.

How could he sleep here tonight, under the same roof with her, and not kiss her again? And again?

Rafe did sleep, though, much to his own surprise. After the cold roast beef supper Maddie gave them and the evening of well-wishers dropping by, including some of Madeleine's friends who wanted all the details of the recent excitement, and an outwardly cordial visit from Big Jim, who'd brought him a new shirt as a very public thank-you gesture, he'd stretched out on the day bed in her kitchen/parlor to rest—with Juanito by his side to watch for bleeding—and passed out completely, his last coherent thought being that he must undo this tangle of their lives with Maddie's as soon as possible.

So now, the next day, with half the morning gone already, how could he explain the fact that the three of them not only had just shared a large batch of her feather-light pancakes like a family, but were now out in her backyard, tacking up their horses and heading for the same destination?

Juanito was how he could explain it. The boy had slept inside last night, he had shown constant concern for Rafe, he had talked to Rafe and listened to him. Juanito wanted Maddie to go see the new ranch with them, and Rafe hadn't been able to refuse him.

Neither had she. She had tried, but rather weakly, he thought, and that was because she clearly adored the boy—her eyes warmed every time she looked at him.

Right now, however, her eyes were on Beau as Rafe brushed him down to ready him for the saddle. Every move he made hurt the cut across his back, but he tried not to show any stiffness. Maddie might insist on doctoring it again, and he didn't have the strength to bear the sweet torture of her touch and her scent again.

Madeleine walked past them, leading her old

mare. Juanito was saddling Tortilla not far away.

"Rafe," she said, "your father knew what he was doing when he bred this Beau Monde line of horses. This is the most gentlemanly stallion I've ever seen."

In spite of himself, he smiled.

Not only because she'd said the word "stallion" right out loud, which no proper lady would ever do, but because her words brought him back to the days when she visited the Aigner plantation, River Oaks.

"Here he is with these two mares and he's a picture of decorum," she went on.

"He knows how to behave," Rafe said, stroking Beau's glossy black neck. "We've been around lots of women, haven't we, boy?"

"*Sí, Papá,*" Juanito piped up a little breathlessly, since he was standing on tiptoe, heaving on the latigo to tighten the cinch. "But *mi Lena* is the most beautiful, no?"

Rafe's gaze met Maddie's.

"*Papá?*"

He was insisting on an answer.

"Yes, son, she is."

She's the most treacherous, too.

A strange weakness settled through his muscles and his mind as he tried to hold that thought against the wild, sweet memories that came flooding back. In all these years, he'd never known another woman who could even hold a light to Madeleine Cottrell.

"Who is Beau's dam? Do I know her?" she called.

He made his feet move, started walking toward her.

"Best I recall, she was that Rainmaker mare with the four white stockings my father brought from Virginia."

She turned back to Dolly, who was melting beneath every stroke of her gloved hand. "That mare always had a sweet disposition. I'm not surprised she passed it on to him."

"Well, now," he said, pretending to take offense, "are you saying that the old man, Beau Monde, had a *sour* disposition?"

"I am. And I'd say it right now to his gorgeous face if he were still with us."

For one fleeting second everything felt as if they were young again, back in Louisiana, the whole world blissfully lost to them while they reveled in the wealth of horseflesh in his father's stables. Madeleine loved a good horse as much as he did.

He ran a quick eye over her mare, which was slightly sway-backed but not as shabby-looking as Tortilla. Obviously not royally bred, however. Sutton certainly hadn't indulged his wife's tastes when it came to horses.

Or houses. The no-good son-of-a-bitch. He'd deserved to die for making her live in this poverty-stricken condition.

Rafe wanted nothing more in that instant

than to walk up to Dolly, lay his hand over Madeleine's, turn it over, strip off that glove, one long, slender finger at a time, and press his lips into her soft palm to comfort her.

No, to be honest, so he could taste her again. So he could hear her quick intake of breath, that gasp of desire that made his blood run hot.

The thought made him furious with himself.

She had betrayed him in the worst way, had broken his heart. Hadn't he had enough misery from Madeleine Cottrell to last him a lifetime?

He threw the saddle bags over Beau's rump, tied on his bedroll, and turned to Juanito who was doing the same.

"Ready?"

"*Sí, Papá.*"

The one thing Madeleine had refused Juanito, thank God, was to camp with them on the ranch.

"You're sure you can find your way back alone this evening, Madeleine?"

She backed her mare into the shafts.

"Merciful heavens! I go all over this country alone all the time investigating stories. Of course I can find my way back."

She began buckling the harness.

"As a matter of fact, I need to go on out to the Blakeley Ranch, five miles farther on, when I leave your place. I'm writing an article about a cattle broker Mr. Blakeley has had dealings with."

Good. Maybe that was the real reason she was going along.

"I have lots to do," she said. "I must also write the story about the attack on Big Jim yesterday."

That stirred his irritation again, for some reason.

"Aren't you afraid you'll *embarrass* your good friend?" he said sardonically.

"I'll be tactful."

"Who was that kid who tried to ram him, anyway? I heard Big Jim say something about that last night."

When he was talking to you for an hour or more.

"Some poor boy who'd lost everything, including his saddle, to Big Jim in a game. He'd never gambled before."

Sudden pity swept through Rafe. He hated that.

"Well, if he'd any sense to begin with, he wouldn't have bet his saddle," he said sharply. "Any six-year-old could've told him that."

He and Juanito went to help with the harnessing, which only took a minute or two with all three of them working together.

"You should just ride her, *mi Lena.*"

"Dolly doesn't ride, Juanito. She only drives."

Sutton Calhoun should've been hanged instead of shot. Madeleine was a superb horsewoman and he hadn't even provided a horse for her to ride.

Gallantly, they helped her into her gig and she picked up the lines.

"Thank you, gentlemen," she said.

And she smiled at each of them, studying them calmly with those eyes so blue that a man could fall into them and be lost forever. It took a minute, but Rafe made himself speak.

"We need to get on," he said gruffly. "Mount up, son."

"Wasn't it Turner Dirkson who lost the ranch?" she said, as they turned to their horses.

"Yes."

She gave a brisk nod.

"Then I can show you where it is. Y'all can be my outriders and I'll be your guide."

"We are outriders, *Papá*," Juanito said proudly, as they mounted and began to move out.

But this is the last time.

"How'd you know it was Dirkson's ranch, Maddie? Did I say that?"

Then it hit him that she also knew where it was.

"He mentioned that it wasn't the ranch where he lives. How'd you know *which* ranch he lost?"

"Big Jim was telling me all about it last night," she said, rearranging the lines in her hands. "You must've been talking to somebody else at the time."

"The trusty gamblers' grapevine," Rafe growled. "Most reliable source of information in the West."

"That's what Jim always says."

He tried not to ask the next question but it popped off his tongue anyway.

"What'd Jim say about my owning the *Star?*"

"He said he heard it as a rumor before you ever got back to town but he didn't tell me for fear it wasn't true."

"Thoughtful of him," Rafe said sharply. "Peach of a guy, that Big Jim."

"Now, now, Rafe," she said, laughing a little with that old lilt in her voice, "remember he gave you the shirt on your back."

That made him laugh, too, although he tried his best not to.

The ranch wasn't half bad, and there *was* a house, although it had been deserted for a while.

"Good, solid old farmhouse," Rafe said.

He and Madeleine were walking through the house while Juanito explored outside.

"Yes. I love this style, with the Texas limestone walls and the wide gallery all around the outside."

"Not a bad night's work," he said. "Even has pens and outbuildings, too."

There was a homey feel to the place, nestled as it was in a valley between rolling hills. It had big live oak and cottonwood trees scattered through the pastures and several in the yard. This was a lot to win from a man on the turn of a card.

"So Dirkson didn't live here," Rafe said, although he'd already known that.

He and Madeleine left the dust-covered parlor and nearly empty kitchen for the pleasantly shady back porch.

"No, Dirkson owns a much bigger and better house than this one," she said, turning to lean against a porch post while she looked at the house again. "He bought this place to run more cattle on."

Somehow, that made Rafe feel better about winning it.

That thought froze him where he stood. Pitying his opponents, even for the loss of a home, would be a treacherous path to take. Next thing he knew, he'd be lending them money to bet against him and giving back things they'd lost.

He'd actually been worrying about it, or he wouldn't have sought reassurance from Madeleine. Realizing that worried him even more.

And he'd felt pity for that kid who'd lost his saddle to Big Jim, too! Even though the young idiot could've killed half a dozen people with his shenanigans.

He had to get a grip on his emotions.

If he'd had them in hand earlier today, he'd have left Madeleine there instead of giving in to what Juanito wanted. Then he wouldn't be hanging around her now, angling for her reassurance that it was all right that he owned this ranch—a property that he had won fair and square.

He was acting as if that spur cut had let his brains leak out.

"So," he said abruptly, "Dirkson can afford to lose once in a while."

He had to change the subject.

"Maddie, do you know everything about everybody for miles around?"

"I try," she said lightly, shading her eyes with her hand as she looked around for Juanito. "Besides the fact that it's a newspaperwoman's business to poke her nose into everybody's affairs, I've really come to feel a part of the community these past couple of years."

That remark took him back to the last time he'd felt that way.

"As much as you did in New Orleans?"

She thought about that.

"Yes, in a different way," she said. "Now it's a place I've created for myself, instead of being born into it."

"That's what Juanito is used to. Being born into a place where he knows everybody. I can hardly remember how it feels."

He felt her quick glance come to rest on his face.

"It's a comfort, Rafe," she said. "It's an encouragement in a person's life to have friends who care."

Softly, she added, "You surely remember what

it was like in the village for those first years with your Choctaw people and then at home in New Orleans."

He did remember growing up in New Orleans. He also remembered falling in love there. Memories assailed him from every direction, sweet ones and then the bitter ones.

"Oh, yes, Maddie, I remember," he said bitterly. "I had friends who cared and those who didn't."

He turned in time to see the hurt spring to life in her eyes.

"If you're going to take that tack, then let's not talk about the past," she said. "Forget I mentioned New Orleans."

"I will," he snapped.

"*Mi Lena! Papá!*"

They turned to see Juanito coming out of the barn.

"There are no other horses here," he said. "Now I go to look for the cows who have milk."

Maddie laughed.

"All right," she said. "Good luck to you."

"*Gracias!*"

Juan opened the gate, marched purposefully out of the yard, and started up into the hillside pasture behind the barn.

"Close the gate," Rafe called to him. "On any ranch or farm, close any gate that you find closed when you get to it."

Juanito obeyed.

"I see. The cows are up there, in the trees," he called back to them as he started out a second time.

Rafe glimpsed a calf in among the trees, then another.

"Dirkson hasn't moved his other cattle yet," he mused out loud. "What he put up in the game was fifty head of steers and young bulls, not mama cows and calves."

He looked at Maddie, who hadn't taken her eyes from Juanito.

"As I'm sure your grapevine informed you."

To his vexation, she ignored that.

"Juanito's really comfortable here," she said with a fond chuckle, still watching the boy. "Look, he's gone a long way from our horses and he's not even looking back."

"That's a wonder, all right," Rafe said, unaccountably irritated by that observation and the fact Juanito had also gone away from the horses at Madeleine's house. "Next thing I know, he might even be living under the same roof with me."

Abruptly, he leapt from the porch to the ground without using the steps. It was enough to wear a man down, never having any time to himself. He had to get away from her and Juan, too, for a little while.

No wonder his nerves were raw. He was accustomed to a solitary life.

He walked the fence, away from them both,

striding faster and faster, searching for a sign of the steers that belonged to him. It would be necessary to brand them again, he supposed. He'd have to hire some hands.

Putting both hands on the top of the fence, he threw himself over it and started out into the middle of the big open pasture.

He didn't need to be hiring any hands; this place needed to go on the auction block. Settlers were pouring into the area as they moved west, and San Antonio was booming,

That was one thing that made it such a good gaming town. He *was* a gambler, not a rancher, and he must remember that.

And he ought to sell the damnable newspaper, too. That was one possession that would prove to be more trouble than it was worth if he kept it—his gut told him so.

He walked faster, pulling out his handkerchief to wipe the sweat from his face. He'd find those steers and see what he could do about selling them when he got back to town.

But there seemed to be no cattle at all in this pasture. Could it be that Dirkson had meant to say fifty cows? Or could he have the steers on another range, far from the house?

Rafe recalled from the deed that the ranch consisted of half a section of land. Those steers could be grazing a long way away, and with his back still stinging, he didn't care for the thought of a long hike in the sun.

He turned back to get Beau and saw the small figure of Juanito, halfway up the hillside pasture, stalking a peacefully grazing cow. She was ignoring him.

As far as Rafe could see, she had no calf to protect, so she'd probably continue to ignore him until he came a good deal closer, and then she'd run away. He'd been in Texas enough to know that the longhorns were half wild, not gentle, like the cows on his father's plantation had been. Juanito could actually have learned to milk one of those cows, but this one he would never be able to touch.

If he kept this place, he'd have to buy some real milch cows.

"Juanito!"

The breeze carried Madeleine's voice to him, a high, fearful screech.

Juanito turned quickly toward the sound.

Rafe started to run at the urgency in her voice. He turned to look for her, too, and saw her running toward Juanito faster than he could have believed possible. She held her skirts up with both hands, then let one hand go to point up the hill while she streaked toward the boy.

Rafe looked where she'd pointed, searching for what was wrong as he raced toward his son. His heart stopped in his chest.

A young bull had come out of the trees farther up the hill, butting a log ahead of him, trying out his own power, playfully testing his strength. He was headed straight for Juan Rafael, who was standing stock still, paralyzed by the danger.

As Rafe watched in horror, the log hit a rock, the bull lunged after it, and both came lurching down the hillside faster and faster every second. The animal shook his horns and pretended to hook at the ground in frustration, but he didn't give up following his lost prize, which was gathering speed with an inevitable force.

Juanito watched it all, mesmerized.

Rafe jumped the fence as his heart fell into a hundred pieces. He was too far away to have a hope of reaching his son in time to save him.

"Juanito!" Madeleine screamed.

"Get out of the way!"

The boy stood still.

Madeleine threw herself at him, headlong, and the two of them went flying in a tangle of dark skirts and arms and legs. The log hit the spot where they had been one short second earlier.

Rafe couldn't see where they landed for the curve of the hill. The bull was again worrying the log, which had hit a big rock that stopped it, but what if the bull went after them before he could get to them? What if they had broken bones and couldn't get out of its way?

He ran up toward where they must be, and found them—flat on their backs, with Madeleine half on top of Juanito in a little gully among the rocks and mesquite brush. Neither was moving.

Juanito's eyes were closed, Madeleine's open. She stared at the sky, not moving. As Rafe slid down the side of the shallow depression, though, she turned her head.

"Where . . ." she croaked.

Laboring for breath, she struggled to sit up.

"Where have you *been*," she rasped, gasping air as she reached for Juanito. "You're his *father!*"

Her eyes flashed fiery accusations at him. Juanito lay deathly still.

Fear had him in a fit already.

"I damn sure am!" he roared. "So get away and let me see about him! He may have broken a bone."

"Now's a fine time to think of it," she snapped, going onto her knees. She made as if to gather Juanito into her arms.

Rafe took her by the shoulders and sat her down to one side.

"Listen to me, damn it! Do as I say!"

He lifted Juanito's eyelids, peered into his eyes, and felt for the pulse in his neck.

"He's alive."

"No thanks to you."

Hot fury surged through him. He refused to answer.

He felt Juanito's arms and legs for broken bones. Relief began to weaken his own limbs as he found none.

"Nothing broken," he muttered. "At least, no arms or legs."

"How would *you* know?"

"See for yourself," he snapped. "But don't move his neck or back yet."

"I could not believe you just walked off and left us without a word—"

"What the *hell* are you ranting about, Maddie?"

"About you. And your beautiful child you can't even be bothered to watch."

A whole new anger surged into Rafe.

Along with the beginnings of a whole new guilt.

Juanito turned his head and moaned. He opened his eyes but he looked right through Rafe without really seeing him.

On her knees again, Maddie tried to get past Rafe to gather Juanito into her arms.

"Come on, honey," she said, "you need to be out of the sun with a cold compress on your head."

"You can't carry him," Rafe snapped. "He's half as big as you are. Let me have him."

To his surprise, she moved back and let him pick Juan up. As he took the first step, he realized the reason. She was having trouble getting to her feet.

"Here," Rafe said gruffly, reaching down one hand. "You're half dazed. That's why you've been talking out of your head."

"I have not! I knew exactly every word I was saying."

But she let him pull her up to stand beside him.

As they started up the slope, she staggered.

"Hold onto my arm," he said. "I should be carrying you, too."

"So now you're all protective and caring. Too bad that notion couldn't have come over you earlier. It might've kept Juanito from getting hurt."

"Madeleine," he said, with exaggerated patience, "you need to lie down for a while. I'll get you into the shade and put a cold compress on *your* head, too."

He wanted to shout her down, to roar at her until she lapsed into silence. Good God, didn't she realize what a fiery hell of regret he was living in?

He tightened his grip on his son, tried to cradle him more comfortably. *God in Heaven, make him be all right.*

"I will *not* lie down," she said, through gritted teeth. "Somebody has to see about this child, and you obviously are not the one to do it. You couldn't take care of a cat, much less a child, Rafe Aigner."

Chapter 7

Her saying it out loud made it seem profoundly true. He'd been telling himself that since the moment he rode out of Los Pinos with Juanito behind his saddle.

"It's a good thing I came along today," she said, gasping to steady her breath. "I can't believe you weren't even *watching* him!"

"He's a big boy," Rafe growled, "not a baby."

But Juanito seemed so small in his arms, small and helpless and silent and hurt.

Madeleine stumbled and, reluctantly, finally took hold of his arm as the slope down steepened. Her hand was trembling and so was her voice.

Nothing about Rafe was trembling. He was frozen rock solid out from the bone. Except for his guilt. Why had he ever thought Juanito would be better off with him?

"Juanito's not *that* big a boy! And he's never been around cattle before, and . . . !"

She took in another long, trembly breath.

"For someone who just got the breath knocked out of her body, you sure have a lot of wind," Rafe said.

Madeleine flashed him a look.

"You could pay enough attention to tell him to close the *gate*, for pity's sake, but not enough to find out what animals might be lurking in the pasture he goes into! You were more worried about your cattle than about your son!"

"That's not true, and you know it!"

"I cannot believe . . ."

"You're starting to repeat yourself, Maddie," he snapped. "How about holding your tongue until you regain your composure?"

She tried to reach across Rafe to touch Juanito's pale face. Her whole body was shaking and she flashed Rafe such a beseeching look it made him feel human again.

Suddenly blame wasn't even in the picture. All that mattered was saving Juanito.

Terror was giving wings to his feet. They were through the gate, into the horsepen, out into the back yard of the house.

"I think some cold water will bring him around," he said, praying that would prove to be the case.

"If not, we're heading for town," she said, as if every decision was hers to make. "It's a good thing I drove—we can stretch him out in my gig."

Panic made him deny the need.

"There's nothing broken . . . surely he isn't hurt that badly," he said.

"But he may be," she said stubbornly. "I'll go on ahead and get my canteen. Maybe cool water will bring him to."

Rafe held Juanito a little closer as he walked to the gig.

Why did he feel suddenly lonesome to the bone the instant she hurried on ahead?

Maybe because he needed help. From anywhere. He had disturbed his son's life in every way, and now he might have let him get injured for life.

He reached the gig and laid Juanito on the seat in the shade of its top. Maddie found her water jug, removed the top, and started pouring water over a handkerchief.

"Open his shirt," she said authoritatively.

She bathed Juan's face, his neck and chest, his arms and hands, talking to him softly all the while.

"Come on, Juanito, open your eyes and tell us where it hurts," she said. "Come on, now, wake up."

After a little more of that, he obediently opened his eyes.

Rafe gritted his teeth. He hadn't even thought to talk to him.

The child looked at both of them, but he wasn't quite focused.

He moaned.

"*Mi cabeza* . . . head . . . hurts," he said, and closed his eyes again.

Gently, Madeleine felt through his thick hair.

"He's got a big knot," she said.

Rafe reached around her.

"Here, let me feel it."

Her deft fingers guided his and he felt the knot that was rising on the back of his son's head.

"I'll get the horses tied on here," he said quickly. "Let's get him back to town."

She nodded agreement and started climbing in beside Juanito.

"There, there," she murmured. "It'll be better soon.

"I think it's just a pump knot," she said, with that same assurance she'd had when she ordered his shirt opened. "Don't worry too much."

Rafe threw a look at her over his shoulder as he ran toward the horses.

"You sure blow hot and cold, Maddie. How come you're worried about me all of a sudden?"

"Because I'm worried to death myself," she said. "And I know it must be even worse for you as his parent."

He jogged back, leading the horses, and quickly

tied them to the back of the gig. Then he stepped up into the driver's seat. "I can tell that you love him a lot, though."

She was silent, wetting the cloth again and running it over Juanito's pale face.

Rafe picked up the lines, clucked to Dolly, and started off at a good clip. The roughness of the ranch road jostled Maddie's shoulder against his.

"This lane needs some work," he muttered, hardly able to take his eyes off Juanito enough to look ahead. "I've got to hire a crew for this place."

It was a tight fit, the three of them in the small gig. Madeleine's scent came to him as it had the night before, that old, familiar combination of magnolia sweetness and lemon tartness.

"I know you love him, too, Rafe," she said, at last. "And I'm sorry for those hateful things I said to you. I take them all back."

Shock coursed through him. And a strange elation.

Which was stupid. Taking back what she'd said didn't make any real difference in anything.

"No," he said, "you were right. The minute I rode out of Los Pinos with him, I knew I was making a mistake that would ruin his life."

"What? No, you weren't!"

She shifted Juanito to cradle his head more securely in the hollow of her shoulder.

"Don't be polite," Rafe snapped. "You were

right the first time. I nearly got him killed today. I'm no kind of father."

"Rafe!" she said sharply. "You're sounding as if you're the one who got hit on the head."

He turned to meet her burning blue gaze.

"You're an *inexperienced* kind of father."

"Yet you've never had a child and you knew to watch him."

"He fascinates me," she said. "I like to watch him. And I certainly never expected any danger in that pasture, either."

How did this happen? How the hell did they keep coming together in these brief moments, when they hated each other so?

He looked at Juanito, whose eyelids were fluttering. Madeleine followed his gaze, and began talking to the boy again while applying her handkerchief-and-water cure. He opened his eyes.

"Donde 'stá?"

"You're on your way to town," Maddie told him. "How're you feeling?"

Rafe felt a huge weight roll off his heart. If only Juanito would be all right!

Madeleine stayed busy with Juanito, talking to him and pointing things out along the road to keep him from closing his eyes again.

Halfway to town, she asked, "You're headed for a doctor?"

"Yeah. I'd feel better about it."

"Me, too."

There it was again, that warm feeling that came when they agreed.

And Juanito was going to keep pulling them together, because after this, Rafe would never have the heart to forbid him and Maddie to see each other. It was time to get a grip on his emotions, for sure.

They went to Dr. Martin, one of Madeleine's host of friends, who proclaimed Juanito already well on the way to recovery. Then they went to the confectioner's shop for ice to put on the knot, and for ice creams, which Juanito loved. The horses stood outside on the street and waited patiently, the proprietress made a fuss over Juanito's injury, a fairly cool breeze blew in through the windows, and Madeleine leaned back in her chair with a sigh of relief and smiled her contagious smile.

Rafe held it all to his heart.

The two hours just past could've been very, very different.

But regrets were useless now.

Juanito and he were together until the boy was grown. His duty as a father was to do what was best for the child.

Once they were back at Madeleine's and Juanito was brushing down all three horses in the turnout pen, Rafe took Madeleine to the carved Mexican bench beneath her big cottonwood tree. From there, they could see if Juanito seemed to be too tired or faint.

"I don't know how to make his life even halfway normal, much less good," Rafe said slowly, "and I *cannot* be with him during the evenings, even if he agrees to sleep at the Menger Hotel. Would you let him stay here at night?"

"I'd love to have him every night," she said simply. "The daybed is his."

"I hoped you'd be willing," he said wryly. "Since I can't take care of a cat, much less a child."

She had the grace to blush and looked at him very straight.

"I told you I didn't mean what I said. I was so scared and so mad, because in a moment like that, a woman wants a man to take care of the danger."

That admission made her cheeks even pinker.

"And feeling that way made me even angrier, because I'd thought I was past that."

"How so?"

"I'm set on doing without a man from now on."

It sounded like a challenge, but she clearly wasn't flirting. This wasn't the old, coquettish Madeleine.

"Do you think you can?"

"Yes," she said, still giving him that long, steady look from those blue, blue eyes. "If I can fight bulls on my own, I can do anything."

He couldn't resist teasing her a little bit.

"Fighting bulls is usually a rare occurrence. There's more to life, you know."

She turned to look at Juanito, who was working away on Tortilla's coarse haircoat. "Yes. I'm learning fast that there's more to life."

Rafe felt strangely rejected, passed over. Which was perfectly stupid.

"I'll pay you extra for taking care of him, of course."

"It'll be my joy."

"No, I'll double your salary. Believe me, you'll earn it."

"All right. I'll have to buy lots of pancake fixin's."

Then she turned and her eyes burned straight through to his heart.

"All I ask is that you warn me before you ever take him and move on," she said. "It'll break my heart, and I'll have to get ready."

"I will," he said.

And then he shocked himself by making an admission of his own, an admission that made him a stranger to himself.

"I've decided to hang around for a year or two," he said. "Juanito's had enough change for a while."

As soon as he said it he wished he'd held his tongue, because her eyes blazed with a happiness that he didn't want as his responsibility. But he had to have help with his son.

"That's wonderful," she said. "So I'll not

worry about losing him, and we'll take it all one day at a time. All right?"

"Done."

Madeleine turned in front of the small mirror on the door of the armoire for the third time, standing on tiptoe to try to see all of herself. If only Sutton hadn't traded off her full-length Louis XV mirror that tilted! Losing it had nearly killed her, for it was the last piece of furniture she'd managed to keep from her childhood home.

She stepped up closer, cocked her head flirtatiously, and gazed into her own eyes.

Sophie had been right about this hat, which was why Maddie had run back down to Mrs. Bolander's and bought it this morning. The unusual larkspur blue of its ribbon and the small bunch of silk flowers tucked underneath the brim truly did bring out her eyes like nothing else she'd ever worn.

Rafe used to always like her to wear blue.

Her eyes widened. Her heart stood still.

Was that why she had bought the hat? She had told herself it was because she could afford it now, with her salary doubled.

She still could hardly believe that she'd jumped at the chance to take care of Juanito at night. What if Rafe *didn't* stay around for a year or two, as he had said?

Well, life was short and uncertain, and she

had to take her pleasures where and when she could. At least she would have these memories of Juanito when she was old—just as she had her memories of the good times with Rafe.

She looked herself sternly in the eye. Was she so crazy about Juan Rafael because he belonged to Rafe? No, she was not. She would love that little rascal no matter who his father was.

She quickly turned away from her image, went to pick up her pie basket waiting on the kitchen/parlor table, and made straight for the door. She hadn't even remembered Rafe liked blue until right that minute.

No matter, she was not going to care what Rafe thought of her hat or her looks. She was *not*.

She was not going to care what he thought of her ribbon-trimmed pie basket, or whether he bid on it, either.

The fact that the pie was his very favorite, buttermilk chess, had absolutely nothing to do with him. Nothing at all.

As she went through the front room where Charlie was setting type for Monday's paper, she adjusted the basket over her arm so as not to crush the curling blue and lavender streamers cascading from the handle. Lots of people liked the color blue.

But her mind was filled with Rafe as she waved to Charlie and stepped out onto the street.

She'd had to be away this noon when he'd

come by to pick up Juanito. If she'd been there, she'd have found out whether he was still planning to come to the auction or not. Last week, when he had accompanied her to the board meeting for the Bexar County Orphans Home— just to get him acquainted with some more people in town—he had said that he would be coming to this benefit picnic.

He had better keep his word, because otherwise, Juanito would be terribly disappointed and so would she. Already she was getting so attached to the child that she hated to let him go for a minute.

Her heart clutched at the thought.

Oh, dear Lord, let them stay in San Antonio for a *long* time!

She quickened her pace to cross the street, picking up her skirts to keep them out of the dust. It was silly that she'd taken so much care with her appearance and then walked to the auction, but it was a lot of trouble to hitch up the gig to drive the short distance to the river.

And she had needed some time to think, anyway. All week, she'd been so involved with Juanito in the evenings and so immersed in work during the day that she felt scattered inside. Of course, Rafe's coming back from the dead right in the middle of her realizing that Sutton was gone and she was free had been enough to scatter anybody.

She took a long breath and shifted her basket to the other arm.

"Mrs. Calhoun."

Startled, she looked up to see Mr. James Flynn, a prominent merchant who consistently bought far more advertisements in the *Star* than anyone else. He touched the brim of his hat and slowed his pace, but Madeleine quickened hers.

"Mr. Flynn, how nice to see you."

She gave him a smile and tried to hurry on past.

"On your way to the pie auction, I see."

"Yes, indeed. In fact, I'm almost late."

He was a tedious man, that was all there was to it. She felt entirely too jumpy to deal with him now.

"Well, then, I mustn't delay you. I plan to attend, but first I need to go by the bank so I'll have a chance of bidding high enough to win your pie."

She chuckled politely.

"We certainly hope the prices will go that high," she said, edging past him. "It's all for a good cause."

"Exactly," he said.

"I will see you there, then, Mr. Flynn."

"I am looking forward to it, Mrs. Calhoun."

A terrible thought struck her as she moved on—Mr. Flynn was an unattached man, an old bachelor. Pray God that he didn't win her basket! If she had to eat her picnic lunch with him and spend the afternoon with him, she would scream.

She should never have told him to bid high. What if he took that as an invitation?

Lately she felt so unlike herself, somehow, a stranger inside her own skin. Like when she'd hurled all that abuse at Rafe that day at the ranch.

She took a deep breath and walked faster, balancing the basket with her free hand to keep the ribbons from crushing against her skirts. Why should she even think twice about Rafe's feelings, anyway?

Hadn't he done the cruelest thing one person could ever do to another, by letting her think he was dead when he wasn't? He had become as iron-hard a man as she'd ever met, so he ought to be able to take a few hard words.

Waiting on the corner for a farm wagon to pass, she realized that the Menger Hotel stood in the middle of the next block. Rafe and Juanito might be inside, getting ready this very minute to come to the auction.

She smiled, remembering Juanito's promise to buy her basket. He had even helped her make the pie. In the process, it had just slipped out that this was his father's favorite kind, and it had fascinated him anew that she'd known Rafe in the past.

The farm wagon passed, so Maddie stepped out and crossed the street. She found herself walking more slowly as she approached the entrance of the Menger. It was always a busy place, and today was no exception. As the double doors swung open, she glanced inside.

"Maddie!"

She glanced around to see Sophie's carriage slowing in the street beside her. A needless irritation just flew all over her, even though Sophie was her dearest friend.

"Get in here with me, you rascal girl, and hurry up about it," Sophie called, in her Mississippi drawl.

She leaned across the seat to give Maddie her hand. There was no help for it—she'd have to ride with Sophie.

That resentment at even *seeing* her best friend scared her. Here was something else the matter with her that made her feel like a stranger to herself—never, ever before had she not wanted to see Sophie.

She handed in the basket, then climbed up onto the side step.

"What's the matter with you, honey?"

Madeleine smiled. There was no putting anything past Sophie, ever. She saw everything.

And they had never lied to each other, either.

"I don't know," she said, turning to face the person she was closest to in all the world. "I'm just aggravated that you stopped, that's all. I guess I was wanting to walk and be alone."

Sophie smiled and just looked at her.

"There you go! Smiling your sphinx smile. What do you think you know that I don't?"

"I don't think, I *know*," Sophie said. "You wanted to walk and be with *Rafe*, not be alone."

Madeleine threw up both hands in despair.

"Help us all! You are completely out of your mind, Sophie Langston!"

"I have logical reasons for my statement which prove I am perfectly sane."

"Drive on!" Madeleine cried. "Good Lord, are we going to sit here all day?"

Sophie laughed. She picked up her lines and pulled back out into the street.

Still smiling, she ignored Madeleine and began to drive.

"All right," Madeleine finally said. "What are your so-called logical reasons?"

"One," Sophie said, "you are too impatient ever to walk this far when you could drive. Two, I found you directly in front of the Menger Hotel, peering hopefully into the lobby. *Three*, and most telling of all, you were lurking there with your basket on full display, wanting Rafe to know that it was the one to bid on."

Madeleine's little voice of truth agreed with Sophie, but she instantly slammed the door on it.

"That's ridiculous. Juanito knows what my basket looks like."

"Hmm, Juanito," Sophie said thoughtfully.

Then she smiled her most infuriating smile.

"Talk on," she said. "I'm listening."

"I'm not telling you another thing for the rest of our natural lives," Madeleine said. "You'd just twist it into some kind of weapon to use against me."

Sophie's irresistible chuckle made her laugh, too.

"You are such a pouty child, Maddie. How do you ever run a newspaper?"

"Juanito has already seen my finished basket; he even helped me make the pie. So I have no need to display it at all."

"Umm-hm." Sophie pretended to be very serious about her driving.

"And besides, I don't even know if Rafe is coming to the auction," Madeleine said quickly.

"Did he pick up Juanito as usual?"

"Well, yes, Charlie said he did. But he's a busy man, Sophie, and he may not care whether Juanito wants to come to the picnic or not."

"I've seen him look at that child," Sophie said. "He cares."

"I know that, but he always says he has to make a living, too."

"I'm not *even* going to talk about this anymore," Sophie said. "All I want to speculate about is how high he'll go to get your basket."

She looked at Madeleine.

"For Juanito's sake, of course. Letting Juanito do the bidding."

Madeleine made a face at her.

"I'm not *even* going to talk about this any more," she said, throwing Sophie's own words back at her.

"I'd think a man who could pay a premium price for that lot at the corner of Travis and Commerce could go right through the roof on a bid, if need be."

An inexplicable excitement shot through Madeleine's blood.

"What? How do you know he's bought that lot?"

"Duncan heard it somewhere."

"So we don't know whether it's true."

"Duncan does, or he wouldn't have told me," Sophie said lightly. "My husband knows I can't keep a secret from you and you might print it in the paper, so it had better be right."

"Oh," Madeleine blurted, "maybe he *is* going to stay!"

Her tone came out so hopeful, that she tried again, indignant this time.

"Surely he won't stay in San Antonio!"

"You never know," Sophie said softly, and turned off onto the road that ran down to the river. "Madeleine, you just never know."

Some other ladies of the San Antonio Orphans Home Benefit Society were already there in the lush shade of the live oaks, laying out the food they'd brought atop tables covered with crisp white cloths, and arranging the perishable dishes and crocks in tubs of ice. A few of their children were helping and others were playing games.

Audra Tarrant's son, Elmer, who was eight, came running to Madeleine's side of the buggy.

"My mama said you have a new boy," he called. "Where is he?"

With an unfamiliar thrill, she realized he was talking about Juanito.

"He's not exactly mine," she said, "at least, not all the time."

"Where is he?"

"I think he'll be along soon."

"All right. We can get our peppermints then."

She smiled as Elmer ran away. He had come to expect the peppermints she always carried.

But she felt a little break in her heartbeat, too. How could she let herself pretend like that? Juanito wasn't hers at all.

Chapter 8

~~~~~

Madeleine slipped her basket handle over her arm to free both hands to balance the long silver tray of teacakes Sophie had made. Sophie herself carried the carefully packed wooden box that held the centerpiece of the whole picnic: the heavy crystal-covered cake stand crowned with Sophie's famous version of Lane cake.

Madeleine forced a smile for the auction chairperson, Mrs. Bell, who was coming out from behind the beautiful white-clothed tables to meet them, but her mind and heart were suddenly raging in turmoil. She loved Juanito, but was she also beginning to feel something toward Rafe besides the terrible hurt and resentment at letting her believe that he was dead? Was that one reason she'd let Elmer think of Juanito as hers?

Sophie was uncanny at reading people, and she knew Madeleine better than anyone else in the whole world.

But this time Sophie had to be wrong. That strange shock that had come with the news that Rafe had bought a lot in town was just surprise. That was all.

If it *was* hope, it was hope that Juanito would be around for a long, long while.

"It's about time you two ladies arrived," Mrs. Bell declared, as she took the silver tray to lighten Maddie's load. "We need some beautiful desserts for that auction table."

"We have a good crowd already, don't we?" Sophie said.

"Oh, we're going to make enough money to buy a whole library for the Home! And there're lots more people on the way."

Madeleine couldn't resist throwing a quick glance toward the road that ran beside the picnic grounds. Then she made herself try to forget Juanito and Rafe and get into the spirit of the occasion.

"I'll circulate with one of the donation pails," she said gaily. "That way, I can see who all's here."

Sophie threw her a significant look.

"And visit with everybody," Madeleine added, giving her a firm look right back.

She set her basket on the table for the supper auction, and picked up a small pail from the stack on another table. It'd do her good to get away from Sophie for a little while. Sophie who, for once in her life, was wrong.

However, as she walked toward a large group of men and women talking at the edge of the river, she cast one more quick glance toward the newly arriving vehicles and horses.

"Well, well, if it isn't the beautiful Mrs. Madeleine Calhoun!"

She turned to see Big Jim Thompson heading straight for her. He wore a broad smile.

"Hello, Mr. Thompson."

"How're you coming with your bucket of money, there? Got it full yet?"

He walked up to her and peered down into the shining, empty pail.

"I'm just getting started," she said, smiling at the horrified face he made. "There's plenty of room for a large contribution from the Golden King."

He began reaching for his wallet.

"Good, good. The Golden King would be happy to oblige."

"I might even be moved to write another editorial about your extremely deep pockets when it comes to the good life in this city," she teased.

Laughing and joking with her, he took out a whole handful of gold double eagles, each worth twenty dollars, and dropped them with a flourish into her container. The amount astounded her.

"Oh, thank you so much! I can't wait to show Mrs. Bell. We'll be able to buy many more books than we expected."

"Be sure and give me credit," he said lightly; "sometimes I'm not sure Mrs. Bell approves of me."

She laughed.

"Maybe it's your profession she doesn't quite condone."

He grinned mischievously, for all the world like a naughty little boy.

"Maybe so."

"You pose a real dilemma for some of the ladies in this town, you know."

He raised one brow and eyed her suggestively.

"Oh? And might I ask what is the nature of this dilemma? And might you be one of the ladies of whom we speak?"

She chuckled.

"Well, I'm sure there're several different kinds of dilemmas about you among the female population of San Antonio, but I was thinking of the contradiction—approval of your cultural activities and disapproval of your profession."

He shrugged, still smiling.

"I can only hope that the approval will win out," he said.

"I'll be sure to spread the word of your contribution," she said.

"Nobody but you, Miss Maddie," he said in his booming voice, "could bring out my generosity. Why, if that'd been anybody else passing the plate around, I'd have . . ."

"Given just as much, and you know it," she said, flashing him a flirtatious smile.

"Not true, and *you* know it," he countered. "You're one of the special people in this town, Miss Madeleine, and you're special to me."

"Only because I write such wildly complimentary editorials about you, Mr. Thompson. Admit it."

He grinned.

"You'd be special to me if you ran a livery stable instead of a newspaper," he said. "But since you *do* write such kindly words about me and we've been friends for so long, we need to drop the formalities. Please call me Jim."

Madeleine didn't have a chance to reply.

"Jim, you're a prince of a fellow, and I, for one, will think of you every time I even pass by the livery stable."

It was Rafe's voice, jovial as could be.

She whirled to see him behind her, Juanito at his side like a small shadow. Immediately she went to greet the child, trying to ignore the fact that Rafe looked even more well tailored and well pressed than Big Jim and a hundred times more handsome.

Trying to ignore the fact that the one quick

glance he'd given her had been sharp and hard to read.

Juanito slipped to her side and she put her arm around his shoulders when she straightened up from hugging him. Big Jim's cheeks seemed to have reddened more.

"Aigner!" he boomed, loudly enough to attract several people's attention as he slapped Rafe on the back. "Glad you're here, just in case I have anybody try to run me down."

He laughed heartily as he held out his hand to Rafe, but something in his voice betrayed that he was still a bit embarrassed.

"Glad to help; just let me know if you need me," Rafe said lightly.

That edge was still there in his tone.

And she heard it in Big Jim's, too, when he spoke again.

"Better put your money in the pot, there, Aigner," he said, nodding at Madeleine's pail. "I'm expecting to see a glowing testimonial to me in print for my contribution. Miss Maddie might write something good about you, too."

"Well, she might," Rafe said. "But I'm saving my money for the pie auction. I'm on a limited budget since I got into the real estate market."

Now there was more edge to his voice.

"I heard about that," Big Jim said.

"I heard that you did," Rafe answered.

The two men stared at each other. A shadow might have passed through Big Jim's eyes,

Madeleine couldn't be sure, but his smile stayed the same. Rafe wasn't smiling.

"Miss Maddie! Is this your new boy?"

Elmer was running up to them, and all of them turned.

"Yes, this is Juanito. Juanito, this is Elmer. Elmer's mother is a friend of mine."

The two boys studied each other solemnly.

"Are you a Mexican?" Elmer said.

Madeleine's blood froze. Why hadn't she thought of this?

Juanito broke into a smile.

"*Mexicano*," he said, with a sudden smile. "*Sí.*"

"Did you ever see Cortinas?"

Juanito shook his head.

Elmer studied him a minute more.

"Come on," he said, and gestured impatiently with his hand. "We've got a terrapin race."

Juanito looked at Madeleine, who looked at Rafe, who nodded. Elmer and Juanito ran off together.

"That boy run your errands and set up your tables for his keep?" Big Jim said.

Rafe looked a hole through him.

"That boy is my son," he said, his voice low and dangerous. "His name is Juan Rafael Aigner, and I'm taking this occasion to introduce him to the good people of San Antonio."

Big Jim seemed to tense in surprise but he kept his gambler's face.

"Good idea, good idea," he said, his gaze

fixed on Juanito's retreating back. "Perfect day for it. Fine-looking lad."

"Thank you," Rafe said. "I'm very proud of him."

"Well, now, I see a man I need to talk to over there," Jim said, moving away. "Come by the Golden King any time."

"Thanks," Rafe said. "I'm at the Menger."

"I'll have to drop in," said Jim.

He tipped his flat-crowned hat to Madeleine.

"Miss Maddie, I'll see you soon."

He added a wink to the promise.

"Good-bye, Jim," she said. "I'll be at my desk, writing about today's contributions."

"Oh," he said, with exaggerated disappointment. "I was thinking, perhaps, a piece about only me."

She smiled back.

"I'll consider it."

When he was gone, Rafe turned to her, his autumn-colored eyes bleak as winter.

"Why the hell hadn't I thought of it, Maddie?" he burst out. "Why the *hell* can't I do anything right for him?"

Madeleine gave a quick glance around.

"Come over here," she said.

She led the way to a grove of tall live oaks alongside the river.

"You *did* think of it," she said. "You just wouldn't admit it to yourself. That's one reason you threw such a fit about him sleeping with the horses. People would think he's your servant.

"*I'm* the one who never thought of it. He's your son, these people he's meeting are my friends, nobody's been bothered by it since he's been here . . ."

He didn't even hear her.

"I've got some kind of willful blindness," he said. "We were several miles outside of Los Pinos before I saw that I'm repeating my father's mistakes."

"Juanito is not a mistake," she said, turning on him savagely. "And neither are you."

"I didn't mean that," he said through gritted teeth. "I meant waiting until a boy is nine years old and then jerking him away from his language, his culture, his home, and everybody he ever knew."

"That's not a mistake, either," she snapped, her heart full of fire. "Don't you think a child needs his parents? Don't you know that's more important than anything else?"

"At least my father had the power to give me a place in the community," he said. "Nobody ever walked up to me and asked if I was Choctaw."

"No, it was not socially acceptable to mention that fact, but everybody knew you were," she said. "After they got used to it and got to know you, it didn't make one bit of difference. You were Raphael Aigner, Prince of New Orleans."

"Because my father and his father had been powers in the city forever. I don't have a city. I can't do that for Juanito."

"That's just as well," she said. "It wasn't good for you. It may be what ruined you."

"*What?*"

She couldn't help smiling at the look on his face.

"Think about it, Rafe. Being Prince made you the man you are today."

"What do you mean by that?" he growled.

"It made you think you can control everything," she said. "And you can't. You can't decide what prejudices people have or what they do with them."

He scowled at her.

"I can decide not to bring my son into a situation where he's not treated right," he snapped.

"He hasn't been mistreated here and I don't think he will be. Elmer was just looking for factual information."

"And he was curious about a famous bandit. It took Elmer about one second to connect Juanito's looks, Mexico, and Cheno Cortinas. I didn't even think about how wild the feelings are against Mexicans when I brought Juanito to Texas."

"He's only a little boy and I don't think anyone'll be hostile to him simply because he's from Mexico. If they are, we'll just have to teach him to deal with it. Together, we can handle it."

He didn't hear her.

"I've brought him to Texas right when Cortinas' constant raids are whipping up anti-
Mexican sentiment; I nearly let him get killed
out at the ranch—I'm not competent to take care
of him. You said it yourself, Maddie."

The look he gave her pierced her heart.

"I *told* you I was terrified, Rafe," she cried. "It
was only fear that made me lash out. I didn't
mean what I said—I was scared to death for
him."

*And for myself. I was trying to drive you away
from me. What if I should fall in love with you again?*

That thought came out of nowhere. It slashed
through her and left her shaky inside.

Because it was a real wish, she knew that
without doubt.

She had been trying to drive Rafe away from
her that day, but somehow, instead, she had
agreed to help with his child. She had tied herself to him.

Desperate to get away from that revelation,
she turned away and started back toward the
picnic.

"Let's go see how Juanito's getting along," she
said quickly.

Rafe immediately followed. "Do you really
think Juanito will be accepted all right, Maddie?"

"He's over there right now playing with a
bunch of little boys, see? He's already *been* accepted."

She turned to give him a reassuring smile. He held her gaze for a long moment, searching her eyes so earnestly he reminded her of Juanito.

It made her want to reach out her hand and stroke the side of his face. He was so afraid he couldn't be a good father, and she had made it worse out there at the ranch.

But she had made it better now; she read that in his eyes, too.

"He wanted to bid on my basket and it'll soon be time for the auction," she said gently. "We'd better go."

She turned and started back toward the crowd again. *She* had better go before she did something incredibly foolish.

"Since when did little boys start bidding on ladies' baskets?"

Rafe was walking right behind her.

"Since I said it might be lots more fun to have supper with a boy than with a grown man," she said teasingly.

To her surprise, he entered into her attempt to lighten the mood.

"Oh? And how are these boys going to pay the bids they make?"

Her spirits lifted.

"We ladies will slip them a few dollars, of course. Anything to save us from the tedium of such company as . . ."

She threw him a teasing glance.

". . . Well, as some gentlemen I could name."

He reached ahead of her and held back a low tree branch so she could pass by. It was almost as if he'd put his arm around her shoulders and she felt an unbidden thrill.

She hurried on ahead. All she had to do was not get too close to him and she'd forget any ideas about wanting him again.

"So now I'm tedious as well as incompetent at child-tending," he said, in a mock-hurt tone.

"I did not name you, Rafe," she said, throwing the words over her shoulder as she gave him a quick glance. "That's your own assessment of yourself."

"Name the tedious person you were thinking of, then," he said, teasing her as he used to do in the old days.

He came up beside her as they left the shelter of the trees for the grassy park.

"Quickly, before you can make something up."

She leaned toward him, standing on tiptoe to reach his ear, although no one was close enough to overhear.

"James Flynn."

"Who's that?"

"The owner of Flynn Mercantile. Have you ever traded there?"

"I bought Juanito some clothes at Flynn's, but I didn't see one tedious man in the whole store."

She laughed.

"You wouldn't recognize one if you saw one."

He pretended to wipe his brow with great relief.

"Thank goodness. If it's true that it takes one to know one, then I'm not tedious."

"And you've been worried sick that you were."

His low laughter sounded a lot like it used to.

Sophie came hurrying toward them out of the crowd gathered near the tables of food.

"Thank goodness! I've been looking all over for you two," she said. "We've already auctioned three baskets—we've got to do them all and serve this food while we still have ice."

She took Madeleine's arm and threw her a teasing, questioning look. Madeleine ignored it.

"Where's Juanito? He wants to bid on my basket."

"Right over there. Elmer's begging his mama for money so he can bid, too."

Rafe stared at Madeleine.

"You were serious? You really gave Juan Rafael money to bid on your basket?"

"Of course. Why not? He was so taken with the whole idea, and I really would prefer him to any other supper companion."

"Does he know which basket?"

"He helped me trim it."

"He may need more money," he said, and abruptly left them.

"I only wish I weren't married so I could've

made a pie for the supper auction," Sophie said. "Maybe Elmer would've bought mine."

She watched Rafe until he was out of earshot.

"Now, tell me," she said, "what were you two doing back there?"

"He was ravishing my body," Madeleine said. "It was the most shocking thing that ever happened to me."

"*Mad-die . . .*"

"Hush, Sophie. And take that look off your face. Rafe will never come courting me again, and I wouldn't accept his attentions if he tried. We were talking about Juanito."

"Hmm," Sophie said. "Umm-humm."

"And take that tone out of your voice."

Madeleine managed to find a spot behind a table—safely between two other board members—serving fried chicken. Sophie followed her and tugged on her arm.

"There," she said, "your famous basket."

The auctioneer, Ford Ripley, husband of the president of the board for the Home, held Madeleine's basket high over his head so everyone could see it. The curling blue ribbons danced around his hand and brushed his hat. The flowers on the handle gleamed whitely in the shade.

"Here's a pretty one," he shouted, "with an aroma that'll make your mouth water. 'Buttermilk chess' it says, right here on the tag."

"Five dollars," Big Jim Thompson said, holding up his hand with a flourish. "A gold half eagle."

A ripple of excitement ran through the crowd.

"Ten!" called James Flynn.

"Highest bid so far," Mr. Ripley said approvingly. "It's for a good cause, folks. Remember that."

"Fifteen dollars!"

That bid came in a male voice Madeleine couldn't identify.

"You're gonna have to beat the suitors off with a stick, Miss Madeleine," Ford Ripley cried. "Let's get serious about this, gentlemen. A beautiful lady and a beautiful pie basket. That's worth some money, you bet!"

"One . . . double eagle."

It was Juanito, his Spanish accent clear in his light boy's voice.

Madeleine looked for him. Rafe had lifted him to the tailgate of a wagon and was standing beside him. Both of them were looking at her.

Big Jim's heavy, booming voice came again; Flynn's light, reedy one; two other bidders; and then Juanito's penetrating young one. Mr. Ripley urged the bidders to stay in and go even higher.

Sophie, of course, was delighted.

"Look at this, Maddie," she whispered, "you're the belle of the picnic! Oh, it's so exciting. I hadn't realized Big Jim felt this way about you."

Madeleine was stunned.

"Me, neither. I don't think he means it as courtship. It's a good cause and he's a good man."

"A good man who has already, this very day, given a small fortune to your good cause."

Madeleine made a face at her, but Sophie was irrepressible once she got started teasing someone.

"I think he really is interested in you, Maddie."

"I'm just thankful James Flynn dropped out," Madeleine said, to try to distract her.

Sophie ignored that.

"One hun-dred dol-lar," Juanito announced, from his lofty perch.

Beside him, Rafe turned to look directly at Big Jim. So did everyone else.

"They're both rich," Sophie whispered. "This could go on all the way to a thousand dollars or even more, until sunset, when they have to get back to town to their games."

"I hope not," Madeleine said. "Much as the Society can use the money, this is driving me to distraction. Poor little Juanito just *has* to win! I could wring Jim's neck!"

But Big Jim eyed Rafe and then Juanito thoughtfully. He turned and glanced around at the crowd.

"Well, it looks as if we're the only two left in the bidding, young man," he boomed. "And you've been quite a stayer, Juan Rafael Aigner. I'm going to reward that by letting you have it for a hundred dollars."

Juanito stared at him, his eyes huge in his little face.

"What do you say to that?" Big Jim asked, as if he were catechizing him on his manners.

"Muy bien, señor," Juanito said loud and clear, in a tone just as adult as Big Jim's.

The whole crowd burst into laughter and cheers.

Even from a distance, Madeleine could see Jim's cheeks grow flushed again.

"Very well," he said. "At supper, will you give my regards to Miss Madeleine?"

Juanito looked at him carefully, clearly trying to figure out what he had said. Finally, he nodded his assent.

Everyone applauded.

Big Jim saluted Madeleine with a brief tip of his flat-crowned gambler's hat and faded into the crowd.

"Sold!" Ford Ripley shouted. "For one hundred dollars!"

He banged down his gavel, set the blue-beribboned basket at the front of the table, and motioned to Juanito to come and pick it up.

"That's the most any basket has brought here, today, friends. So let's have another hundred-dollar basket! This here yellow one looks like it to me."

"So," Sophie said wryly, as Ford held the next basket up for all to see, "you're having supper with *Juanito,* which was your plan all along."

Madeleine gave her a beatific smile.

"Sophie, my plans always work out, so don't start making any of your own for me."

"Mine's working out, too," she replied, escorting Madeleine forward to meet Juanito. He seemed shy but eager to trade the stack of double eagles he held with both hands for the basket and his supper companion. "Because you'll have no choice but to ask Rafe to join you."

"Sophie, you are an incurable romantic. Just because I loved Rafe ten years ago doesn't mean I could ever love him again. Just the opposite, after the way he deceived me."

"We never know ahead of time what anything means in this life," Sophie said cryptically.

Juanito, his face shining with pride and the basket on his arm, led Madeleine straight to Rafe, who escorted them both through the buffet line for some supper to go with the pie. Several people jovially congratulated Juan, who answered with slight, shy smiles. Clearly, he was enjoying this.

Until they carried their filled plates past the podium, where Elmer was bidding on the yellow-trimmed creation now on the block. Juanito stopped short and turned to look at his new friend, listening to the rapid bids.

"El-mer has no doub-le eagles," he said, in

English. Then, frowning at Elmer, he switched back to Spanish. *"Donde está su papá?"*

Startled, Rafe stood still and stared at his son. Precariously balancing his full plate in one hand, Juanito lifted his own basket high in salute to Madeleine, then to Rafe. He was grinning all over his usually solemn little face.

"Muchas grácias, mi papá," he said.

The strangest stillness came into Rafe's face and, for a fleeting moment, Madeleine thought she caught a glimpse of extra brightness in his eye.

"De nada, mi hijo."

His voice was gruff, too. It made her smile.

Juanito's asking where Elmer's father was must have touched Rafe in the heart. The innocent assumption, that a boy's father should be there to help him, should do wonders to quiet Rafe's doubts about his decision to bring Juanito from Mexico.

"I'll get that quilt in Sophie's buggy for us to sit on," she said, to give them a minute alone. "Why don't you two go and pick us a good shady spot in the trees?"

She handed her plate to Rafe, picked up her skirts, and ran toward Sophie's vehicle. It was a wonder that she still knew Rafe that well. He had never been open with his feelings and now he'd had ten years of playing poker to learn to hide them even more, yet she could feel the emotions inside him as if they were inside herself.

Well, some of them. She had no idea whether he'd given Juanito so much bidding money because he wanted to beat out Big Jim, or because he took pleasure in making Juanito happy, or . . . because he wanted to spend this time in her company.

Her breath caught in her chest. No, she was not going to think that way, because Rafe had never truly loved her. He would've behaved differently if he had.

Chapter 9

Maddie made her way to the back of Sophie's carriage, where there were two quilts neatly folded. Sophie always went prepared for any eventuality.

But *she* didn't. She certainly hadn't been prepared for that moment of closeness with Rafe back in the trees.

When she found him and Juanito again, they were waiting at a place near the water, where they could sit and look at the river. Juanito hailed her.

"Our hands are full," he called.

"Thank you for that," she called back. "It keeps the ants from eating our food."

That made him laugh and Rafe smile, and the occasion took on an even more festive air.

Madeleine spread the quilt on the grass, then persuaded Juanito to relinquish the basket long enough to eat his dinner before cutting the pie. Tilda Ramsey and her daughters came along with pitchers of tea and glasses. Rafe confirmed to Juanito that he must eat his meal before he ate pie.

"It is butter-milk chess," he told his father solemnly. "I like butter-milk."

"But the pie doesn't taste like buttermilk," Rafe said, just as solemnly. "You may not like it at all."

Juanito's horrified expression made them both laugh.

"You'll like it, darling, I know you will," Madeleine said. "I've never yet seen anything sweet that you didn't like."

They made a game of Juanito's tasting new foods. All three of them laughed at his reactions to candied sweet potatoes and pickled beets, neither of which he'd ever tasted before. He loved the sweet potatoes and hated the beets. Rafe and Juanito both talked more than usual, because Rafe teased the two of them about conspiring to get all his money for the Society and not caring whether it made him a pauper, then he drew Juanito out by asking details of the terrapin race.

Finally, Madeleine opened the blue-ribboned basket and took out three of her grandmother's small crystal plates and heavy silver forks.

"Those look familiar," Rafe said.

"I haven't been able to save a whole lot of things from home," Madeleine said, as she lifted out the pie, set it in the middle of the quilt, and laid the silver server beside it. "I have a few more of each of these, and that's about it."

To fight the little twinge of regret that thought always brought her, she said what she always said.

"But it's just as well, for I have no place to put them."

Rafe didn't answer.

She cut a slice of the waxy pie, lifted it onto a plate, added a fork, and handed it to Juanito.

"*Gracias, señor,*" she said, "*por la . . .*"

Her Spanish broke down.

". . . for being my escort."

His eyes, so like Rafe's own, lit up with pleasure.

"*De nada, Señora,*" he said, grinning at being treated like a grownup.

She cut another slice and served it to Rafe. When their eyes met, she saw that his blazed with an impotent anger.

"No place to put your few things," he said tightly. "After the way you were raised. After the life you were used to."

"It's nothing, Rafe," she said calmly, although her heart leapt at his sympathy for her. "Things are nothing. These past ten years must have taught you that, too."

He shrugged and started to speak, but didn't.

Madeleine served herself and then they watched Juanito taste the pie. He took one bite, savored it, dramatically rolled his eyes, and cried, *"Delicioso!"*

Their laughing response to his silliness pleased him almost as much as the pie did. He had almost finished the slice when Elmer ran up to them.

"I didn't win the basket," he said.

"You need dou-ble ea-gles," Juanito said, then finished the last of his pie, and jumped to his feet.

Elmer snatched a piece of fried chicken Juanito had left untouched, and they ran off to play.

"His English has grown, even in a week," Madeleine said, looking after them.

"He already had a few words. His grandmother spoke it brokenly, and Angelina, too— but of course, he never knew her."

Suddenly, she needed to know about her, Juanito's mother, this woman whom Rafe had taken to his bed. She needed to know what his feelings had been for her.

"Were they well-to-do people?"

"Not at all. They picked up English from selling food to visitors from the north side of the river, soldiers stationed at Brownsville, and businessmen who came over to trade. Los Pinos is right on the border."

She took a bite of the pie. It was one of her best.

"They had a restaurant?"

"No, only an open-air stall in the plaza."

Suddenly, as if he had decided to talk about it, he added, "They both were wonderful cooks."

His fork clinked against his plate as he set it down.

When she looked up, he was smiling at her.

"And so are you, Madeleine. May I please have seconds?"

It was truly silly for that to warm her so. Why was it such a satisfaction for a woman to please a man with food?

There was nothing personal in this—a thousand women could make a pie that would make Rafe say those very words. She reached for his plate to serve the second slice.

"Thanks for remembering," he said, his voice very low.

"Remembering what?"

"That this is my favorite kind of pie."

She laughed as she handed the plate back to him.

"Rafe Aigner, how could I ever forget? I only drove Lulie flat crazy for weeks until she taught me to make buttermilk chess exactly the way she did."

He took a big bite and grinned at her. "But I thought you did that because it was *your* favorite."

"You did *not*! You knew I was trying to please you."

He raised one black brow and eyed her mischievously.

"Really? Then I guess this pie means that you still are."

Her face went hot all the way up to the roots of her hair. Never had she been so thankful for a wide brimmed hat.

"How could it? I had no way of knowing who would buy my basket!"

His only answer was that infuriating, teasing chuckle of his that had always driven her mad.

"In that case, why didn't you make apple? That's the favorite of most men."

"Oh? Have you been keeping a tally on your travels, asking every man you meet his favorite kind of pie?"

"It's a well-known fact that apple is the favorite throughout the whole country," he said, and took another bite. "Most men have very predictable taste."

"And you're not like most men," she said dryly.

"Correct. And only you know my favorite pie."

She laughed. This teasing reminded her so much of . . .

She slammed the door on the memories.

"Rafe," she said patiently, "I made buttermilk

chess for a whole host of reasons, not because it's your favorite."

He raised both brows in a comic look of disbelief.

"And what might those reasons be, Miss Maddie?"

She ticked them off on her fingers.

"It isn't messy to serve, it keeps very well, it *is* one of my favorites, and I can make one with one hand tied behind me since I spent so much time and effort learning it."

"Ah," he said, giving her a teasing look, "so when you made it, you did think of me."

She leaned against the tree trunk behind her to return the look.

"Yes," she said. "I did think of you, Rafe. I've thought of you every single day since you came in and told me you owned my newspaper."

He kept on looking at her with that look she remembered so well.

"And before that?"

She held his eyes.

"Before that I only thought of you every single year."

He wouldn't let her look away.

"You have become a very direct woman, Madeleine."

"I know. I like that about myself."

"However, you're lying to me now."

"I didn't want to cause you to have any higher opinion of yourself than you already do over the simple accident that I made your favorite pie for this occasion."

He smiled his old devil-may-care smile.

"I promise to keep my pride in check," he said.

Then he became completely serious. Or he simply put on his poker face.

"I thought of you every single day of every single year of the past ten years," he said. "I've never forgotten you, Madeleine, not for one day or one night."

He sounded so sincere that her heart gave a lurch.

"Surely not," she murmured.

"Surely so."

The old hurt surged through her like a raging river.

"Then why didn't you let me know that you were *alive?*"

"I couldn't have so much as sent you a letter without following it in person and tearing apart your happy home."

He meant it. He meant every word. He let her see that truth in his eyes.

"If you had only known what kind of home it was."

"All I knew was that you had married somebody else while, every single night and every single day, I had been imagining you waiting for me."

Neither one of them moved.

"I kept seeing you in my arms on the levee that day," he went on, "with the blazing bales of cotton floating so thick in the harbor that they covered the water, with the Yankee devils at the door."

Her eyes filled.

"I kept feeling that dreadful need to protect you from the end of the world," he said. "I kept hearing myself beg you to come to Texas and marry me and you saying no."

She couldn't even blink the tears away.

"I was desperate," he said. "I even thought of kidnapping you, but I knew if I did, it would kill your love for me."

Her heart stopped.

"I never knew until that minute that any man could love any woman that much."

She searched his eyes and knew it was so. He had truly loved her then.

"Even a woman who said no because she had to run her father's newspaper, for God's sake. With the city burning around her ears."

"My papa had nobody else in the world," she said. "His health was failing. With no more than fifteen minutes to make the decision and without benefit of clergy—which would have killed him on the spot—I couldn't leave him, Rafe."

She challenged him with a look.

"Surely you can see that."

"Now I can. But back then I was a wild boy,

even if I was twenty-five years old. I couldn't see it then."

She held the look.

"So can you forgive me?"

"For not going with me the day New Orleans fell, yes."

Hot anger flashed through her.

"What else are you holding against me? What else have you charged me guilty for, every night and every day of these last ten years?"

"What I told you before: for not waiting until the war ended, to see if I came back."

The heat in her blood turned to ice.

"I truly believed you were dead."

Wearily, she leaned forward to gather the dishes, then wrapped the linen towel around what was left of the pie.

"I truly believed I loved Sutton, too, and that he loved me. My papa had died, all my girl-friends had gone away for the duration, the boys had been killed in the war. I was desperately lonely."

"But you had your precious newspaper to keep you busy."

She looked up at him.

"I loved running the *Times*, yes. It was my first taste of accomplishment and I could lose myself in it."

She tucked the remains of the pie back into the basket.

"And I love publishing the *Star*, too. My work has saved my sanity many a time, especially when I first realized Sutton didn't love me."

"You still loved him?" he asked gently.

"I thought I did. Looking back, I don't know if I ever really loved him."

With her fork, she scraped the last crumbs of crust onto the grass for the birds and stacked the crystal plates in the basket beside the pie.

"Or you, either. Now it seems to me that if I had, I would've gone with you anyway, and let my heart lead my mind."

She looked up to see that he was handing her his fork. Her fingers closed around the stem, barely touching his.

"But I must have loved you. I grieved so hard for you that I made myself sick, Rafe. I thought I would die."

He looked straight into her soul.

"I'm sorry for that," he said softly. "I'm so sorry, Maddie."

She blinked to hide her tears, hating the sorrow that filled her—sorrow for both of them at how their lives had gone—and took the fork.

"You did love me then," he said, even more quietly, "and I loved you. But we were foolish kids who didn't know the world we were in."

Rafe watched her stack the dinner plates that belonged to the Society.

"Let's bury the past," he said suddenly. "I

wasn't fair to you a minute ago, probably because I've held onto my anger for so long. I'm truly not blaming you, still, for not waiting until the end of the war to see if I survived. That's unreasonable."

Madeleine smiled tremulously.

"And if there was ever a word to describe *you*, Rafe Aigner, it's reasonable."

He grinned back.

"I've mellowed in my older days."

Her heart was beating three times as fast as usual. The sensuous curve of his lips, the look in his amber eyes sent a trembling thrill through her body.

He wanted to let go of the past.

What was he thinking? Were these little moments of closeness drawing him to her, too?

Suddenly, any glimmer of a future was too much to think about.

"I'd like to let the past go," she said, "except that I need to know something about Juanito's mother."

Did that sound as if *she* were thinking of a future for them?

"Since I'm going to be helping to take care of him," she added quickly.

Rafe nodded. He stretched out on the quilt and propped his head on his hand as she leaned back against the tree trunk.

"Her name was Angelina," he said. "I went to

her for comfort when I returned to Mexico after finding you married, and we had a few weeks together. Soon after that I went to jail."

"When did you know about Juanito?"

"Not until he was nearly two. His grandmother came to tell me about him right before my release at the end of the war."

"And Angelina?"

"She died birthing him. She lived only long enough to name him Juan Rafael."

Juan Rafael. For his father.

"As soon as the Mexicans released me, I went to Señora Ruiz' house. I sat and stared at him, trying to believe he was real."

Madeleine imagined Juanito as a baby, round faced and plump. A baby sitting on Rafe's lap.

"I don't know how you ever left him."

His dark face paled.

"I couldn't take him from the only mother he'd ever known," he snapped. "And I couldn't take care of him. I was traveling all the time, trying to make a living."

He stared at her with a look she couldn't quite read. Gambling was hard on a person, hard on the spirit. Gambling for a living had changed him.

Not to mention how war could change a man.

"Raphael Aigner," she said quietly, "Prince of New Orleans. Making a living. It's hard to wrap my mind around."

That mollified him.

"Madeleine Cottrell, the Belle of New Orleans," he said. "You've had to make a living, too."

"You were right when you said that back then we didn't know the world we were in."

He grinned, almost his old grin.

"You never expected me to work for a living?"

"No," she said. "That's almost as hard to imagine as your being a father."

A father to another woman's child. I imagined many times your being a father to mine.

"I'm not much of one. Half the time I don't know what to do with him."

"I think raising a child must be mostly trial and error."

"You seem to know what to do, though. He sleeps inside at your house but not at the hotel."

His voice held a tinge of wistfulness that stabbed her heart.

She shook her head, smiling a little to try to cheer him.

"He slept inside the first time because of you, Rafe. Because he was worried about *you*. Why can't you understand that?"

"Because he thought I was some kind of hero," he said. "It was only what I did, it wasn't me."

"No," she said, with exaggerated patience, "it was because you are his father and he loves you."

"That won't wash," he growled.

She knew him well, though. There was a hint

of hope somewhere under his gruffness. He wanted to believe that Juanito loved him.

"Why do you say that?"

"Because I've been his father for nine years. I've gone to see him at least twice in every one of those years. He still refused to sleep under the same roof with me until I saved your buddy Big Jim from getting blindsided into next week."

"No. He kept his distance until you treated him differently."

"No, I didn't."

"You did, and you didn't even know it. When we ran out there into the street to you, you smiled a big welcome at him. You were glad to see him, and you showed more emotion than usual. And you needed help, instead of being invincible."

She fixed him with a sharp stare to drive home her point.

"You weren't scared to give him a hug then, Rafe, and you weren't hesitant to accept his help."

"But I'm always glad to see him."

"He may not know that. You have a strong habit of hiding your feelings, since you've been playing poker for so many years. He wants to be with his father. He's also grateful to you. How about that sweet word of thanks he gave you for the double eagles?"

He scowled but she caught the quick longing

in his eyes. Only for a moment, and then he erased it.

Quickly, with that grace that she'd always loved to watch, he sat up and crossed his legs Indian style. He reached out and broke off a stem of grass to play with, keeping his eyes on it.

"Madeleine, if I took him to the Menger with me tonight, I'd bet that same amount of double eagles he would not sleep in my suite."

"You don't need to worry about that now. What you need to be concerned about is much more important than where Juanito sleeps."

He glanced up.

"What are you talking about?"

"One of the laws of life. I may not have mellowed in *my* old age, but I like to think that I've grown wiser."

"And what is it that you know, Wise Woman?"

"A person only gets the love he or she allows," she said. "Sutton was perfect proof of that."

He stared at her.

"Rafe, let that little boy love you."

"Mi Lena, mi Lena!"

She turned to see Juanito and Elmer running toward them. They came straight to her.

"Some . . . time, *con su permiso*, Elmer can stay the night? With us? We can make . . . camp . . . outside? Near the stable?"

Rafe cleared his throat, but he didn't speak.

Madeleine glanced at him but she ignored his blackening look.

"Maybe," she said. "You'll have to ask Elmer's mother and I'll talk to your father. Or you two could make a pallet on the floor, if you want."

"Maybe if it rains," Elmer said judiciously.

"Maybe if it not rain," Juanito said.

"We'll go find my mama," Elmer announced, and they ran off to talk to Audra.

Madeleine turned to meet Rafe's steady gaze. For once he openly let his feelings show in his eyes—feelings that were rapidly lightening from angry disagreement to wonder.

"I would've said absolutely not," he said, "because if he starts sleeping in the stables again, we're back in the same embarrassing mess."

That sent anger surging through her.

"Your son is a whole lot more important than your reputation, Rafe."

"Have *you* thought of the fact that my reputation puts the clothes on his back and food in his mouth? That it will pay for his education?"

He didn't sound very upset, though.

"You did the right thing, Maddie," he said, "and when the time comes, I know you can keep them in the house. Or at least keep Juanito from going back to sleeping with the horses entirely.

Women seem to know how to raise children— they're meant for it. That's how you always know what to say and do with Juanito."

Shock replaced her anger. He hadn't asked for her help with his son because she was Madeleine; it was just because she was a woman.

Was that what all this burying the hatchet had been about?

Because she was the handiest woman around? The woman he had a hold over because he owned her home and her business?

She opened her mouth to challenge him, then closed it again. He owned Juanito, too, and he could take him away from her with one word.

"I . . . I need to help Sophie and the others," she said, choking on the words.

She scrambled to her feet and fled, longing to be alone and hidden among the trees along the river.

What had she done; oh, dear God, what had she done? She had fallen deeply in love with the child she should've had sense enough to stay away from.

Hurrying through the crowd, she deflected greetings with a hurried wave and a smile, though her face felt as if it would break when she moved it.

She ran into the trees, wanting to dart down the bank and throw herself into the water to douse the fires raging inside her. Then she had a thought that turned the flames to ice, and she suddenly stopped.

Why did she care so much *why* Rafe had asked her to help him with his son? Why did she care whether he thought of her just as a competent woman or as his first love, the woman he'd been crazy about, Madeleine Cottrell?

Chapter 10

"Saddle them both," Rafe said, and then realized he'd be leading the scruffy little mustang right through the middle of town.

But somehow, he didn't care what anyone thought of his horseflesh today. And he didn't care whether Big Jim Thompson had turned their bidding war over Maddie's pie into a very public generous gift to a little boy from the big pompous ass. He hadn't cared about that or anything else Big Jim did or said all week long.

He hardly knew himself lately.

Turning away from the door of the livery, he paced up and down in front of it. All week long, he had hosted only two games. The rest of the time he'd been tending to ranch business; hiring a crew, ordering supplies, furniture, and equipment; and buying more cattle in preparation for sending a herd north on the Western Trail.

If he didn't get a handle on himself, he'd be out of gaming entirely before he even knew what had happened—and God knew he couldn't make a living as a rancher. Good thing he'd been able to hire Clayton Lee as foreman.

Juanito would greatly enjoy seeing Lee's men push the herd onto the trailhead at Bandera. He'd ask Madeleine to go, too, because she and Juanito needed to become even more attached to each other in case he needed to leave Juanito in San Antonio and go sit in on a big game elsewhere. He might be able to win enough by hitting the really big games only a few days a month and staying on the ranch the rest of the time.

"Here's your horses."

The livery man's helper held Beau and the mustang—both saddled, well groomed, and shining from Juanito's daily ministrations. As Rafe took the reins, he noticed that Hobbs, the owner, stood watching from the shadows.

"I'll be gone three days or more," he called to him, as he tied Tortilla to his saddle ring and mounted Beau. "Have your boy strip my stalls, scrub out the water buckets, and put down all new bedding."

Hobbs just stood there. Finally, he raised one hand in reluctant assent.

How stupid could the man be, practically insulting a steady customer?

Rafe laid the rein against Beau's neck and rode out into the street. He didn't care if he'd offended Hobbs. If a man had to be told how to take care of his business, he deserved to be offended.

Big Jim Thompson was another one. He knew how to take care of his own business, but he wanted his to be the only business in town. Scooter, the boy who swept out the Golden King, had told somebody that Big Jim was furious to hear that Rafe had bought that town lot.

Rafe sat back and let Beau slow to a walk through the midday bustle of the plaza. He ought to build a gaming house that would put Big Jim's to shame. That would set his place in the community and start to carve out a respected position for Juanito.

He smiled. He could keep Thompson worried for ages that he'd do just that, and he'd bought the lot just to torture his rival. If Thompson had half a brain, he'd realize that Rafe never stayed in any town for even one year.

His heart sank. Why had he poured all this money into the ranch? He couldn't stay here—settling down just wasn't in him.

And he had been stupid to let Madeleine and Juanito anywhere near each other. The boy had fallen in love with her and the feeling clearly was mutual.

The biggest mistake of all he'd made as a father—except for bringing Juanito with him—was taking him to Madeleine's house at night. That, and listening to the lecture she gave him at the picnic.

He turned his mind away from the echo of her words. No sense in letting Juanito get attached to him, no matter what she said, no matter how much Rafe might like that. Getting too close to his son would only hurt the boy, because he was sure to disappoint Juan.

Well, Madeleine had better love that boy as much as she seemed to do, because she might be all he had to depend on one day if fate suddenly took Rafe down the road. But who could know whether she was sincere? Maybe she was only trying to ensure her hold on her precious *Star.*

The thought shamed him immediately.

For ten endless years he had told himself that she had only pretended to return his love in those long-ago days, that she'd deliberately broken his heart. Or, at best, that she was a shallow, silly girl who hadn't known the nature of love and the suffering it carried.

Since their talk at the picnic, he knew different. He had to admit that he had now seen with his own eyes and heard with his own ears the agony that she, too, had gone through since that awful day when New Orleans fell.

There, on that quilt by the river, she had

seemed like the girl she'd been then . . . except for the knowing way she had with Juanito, like a woman who was a mother.

His thoughts honed in on their target question. Why had Madeleine been so strangely standoffish since the pie auction? Half the time when he went to pick up Juanito at noon, the boy was helping Charlie or brushing Dolly, and Madeleine was out. Or she was in her rooms, hard at work writing an article.

If he didn't know better, he'd think he had made her angry or offered some affront that day at the charity auction.

When *he* was the one who should be offended. Hadn't she lectured him as if he were an errant schoolboy?

You get the love you allow.

If he were honest with himself, he had to admit that deep down, he did want Juan Rafael to love him. He had realized that on that first evening they had camped out together on the way from Los Pinos to San Antonio.

They had ridden until almost sundown and were several miles across the Rio Grande into Texas, when Rafe called a halt and made camp beside a small stream. They dismounted and unsaddled, then Rafe took the halter from his pack, slipped off Beau's bridle, and gave it to Juanito to hold until he could slip the halter onto Beau's beautiful black head.

By then, he'd grown so accustomed to the si-

lence between them that it shocked him when
Juanito spoke.

"*Señor*? May I lead him to water?" he had
said. "*Por favor?*"

Rafe whirled around to see the child clutching
the leadrope with both hands while he tried to
shrug the bridle awkwardly onto his shoulder to
carry it.

"Don't call me *señor.*"

It came out sharper than he'd intended.

Juanito was so busy with the tack that he
didn't answer. One of the looped reins fell off his
shoulder and he struggled with it one-handed
while never loosening his grip on the rope with
the other.

"Here," Rafe said. "I'll take it."

He tried to think what the boy usually called
him, and realized he'd never given him a title
before. On his visits, he had talked mostly to the
grandmother.

As Rafe slid the leather straps from his son's
small shoulder, Beau nudged the boy with his
soft nose. Juanito's thin body relaxed a little. His
eyes glowed.

"You can lead him to water if you'll stay out of
the river," Rafe said, and he was suddenly assailed again by that irrational fear he'd felt that
morning.

Juanito nodded and turned his cheek to
Beau's muzzle.

"Call me *Papá*," Rafe blurted, and at that moment he ached to hear the word.

"*Sí, Papá.*"

Tears sprang to Rafe's eyes. Juan Rafael started for the river, walking beside Beau's shoulder instead of directly in front of him, exactly as Rafe had taught him to do with the long-lost pony.

At that moment he had known that, whatever the cost, he wanted, he *needed* the boy to love him. What he didn't know now was whether he could allow it.

To get his mind off that, he looked around. It was only a short distance to the lot he'd bought, so he might as well ride by and look at it. Maybe someone would see him and mention it to Thompson.

Smooching Beau to a trot, he turned and headed that way, stopping across the street so he could view the whole space. It was a corner lot, which was good; the two streets that formed the intersection were busy ones.

He would hate to tear down the old white stone building on it, though, for it had real charm and would make a good shop. The agent had told him it had been built as a market for produce, hence the wide porch and tables set beneath the branches of the three huge old trees on the site. He wouldn't want to cut them down, either, and they were spaced wrong to try to use a design where the building enclosed a patio or courtyard.

Rafe gave an involuntary grunt of alarm that made Beau lay his ears back.

Here he was, seriously considering an idea that was totally insane. If he was feeling some kind of strange nesting instinct now that he had Juanito, if he had to have his own place, he should build one that would travel on a railroad flat car like the saloons people moved around from cattle town to cattle town in Kansas. The restlessness that had driven him ever since the war would never let him stay in one place, much less one with Madeleine in it.

Resolutely, he kissed to Beau, turned his back on the lot, and rode toward the newspaper offices to find Juanito. He had to get a handle on himself. He'd bought that lot just to needle Jim Thompson, not to really *build* his own place.

If he ever did, though, he'd create a gaming hall that'd throw Thompson's into the shade. He'd build three stories and have every gaming room, billiard hall, bar and dining hall open onto tiered galleries, overlooking a lush garden. He'd feature musical concerts and bring in chefs from New Orleans. He'd use marble and lace and gold appointments that would make the reporter who had said San Antonians were in ecstasy over the beauty of the Golden King wrack his brain for stronger sentiments.

He would call it the Choctaw Club in honor of his mother and his Indian heritage.

He stopped in front of the rickety offices of the *Star* and sat his saddle for a moment.

This would be the perfect spot for the gaming hall. Nothing of real charm or value on the premises, the big live oak trees were in the right place to be included in the gardens, the lot was bigger, and it was only a block or two away from the gaming district of town. The offices and living quarters, as well as the little stable in the back, all needed to be pulled down and replaced anyway.

He wouldn't have to stay in it all the time. He'd have to hire a top-notch staff for an establishment that large, in any case, and then he could still travel. He could leave Juanito with Madeleine and the Choctaw Club to his employees.

He stared at the little building with its big *Star* sign as he dismounted. Juanito and Madeleine were inside, probably either in her living quarters or the stable. He smiled, thinking about Juanito prattling away every day when he came for him, telling all about *"mi Lena"* and the food she gave him and the books she read to him and the English she was teaching him. Madeleine and horses were the two most important things in the life of the son he had taken from his home to no home at all.

What good was that for a child? Sleeping in

one place, eating in another, hanging around a livery stable, having no chores, no dog, nothing to do in a suite of hotel rooms?

That must've been in the back of his mind the whole time he was outfitting the ranch. But they couldn't stay out there all the time, either; he had to make a living.

An impulsive resolution poured into him as he tied Beau to the rail. A man had to control his feelings, and it was time he got a handle on his. Nothing was going to drive Rafael Aigner—not restlessness or anything else. He had to do what was best for Juanito, and here the boy had a friend in Elmer. Boys this age needed friends. If he hadn't had Trey Metairie when his father first took him from the village into town, he couldn't have survived.

Besides, here Juanito and Madeleine could be attached to each other without dragging him into it. In San Antonio he didn't *have* to spend time with her and be reminded of the past; he would simply be her landlord and she could give Juanito the love he needed.

Building his own gaming hall would keep him amused for a while, though. It would take at least a year to build and furnish it.

After that, he'd run it for a few months and then turn it over to somebody like Toby Dresden, who used to run the Silver Elephant in Kansas City. In fact, he'd send a telegram and find out whether he could get Toby himself.

Rafe strode across the sidewalk and opened the door, his mind made up.

"Madeleine!"

She didn't answer. The outer office stood empty.

The living quarters, too. So they must be in the stable, as he'd suspected. He crossed the kitchen and opened the back door.

They were on their knees beside the stable, their backs to him, apparently searching for something.

"What've you lost?"

He crossed the wide yard as they turned to look at him.

"Nothing, *Papá*! We plant peppers," Juanito said, in English.

"You might as well quit now," Rafe said. "I've decided to do something else with this place, and we'll need to tear the stable down."

Juanito's eyes widened as he stared at him. Madeleine jumped to her feet.

"What do you mean, something else?"

She brushed at her hair and left a charming streak of dirt across her pink cheek. That hadn't changed. Anger always pinkened her cheeks.

"Building a gaming hall," he said. "I'm going to move the *Star* to Commerce and Sepulveda."

You would have thought he'd threatened to set fire to the entire establishment.

"No!" Madeleine cried. "You can't!"

"I own both locations."

She met him head on.

"And that gives you the right to tear down my stable and uproot my bougainvilleas and cut down my trees? And our new peppers?"

Juanito looked at him with such horror it made him even more irritated, although he felt sure the boy didn't understand every word they were saying. He did, however, know "our new peppers."

And he knew that his Lena was upset and angry.

"Good Lord, Maddie, be sensible," Rafe snapped. "You can plant some more."

"Not trees. I'd be long dead before they grew this big."

"The other place has big trees. Three of them."

"I don't like that neighborhood. And that's not a big enough building for the press and my living quarters. I can't afford to rent a room, Rafe."

His temper flared.

"Put a rental allowance into your budget."

"What if I don't make a profit and end up with nothing after three years of hard, hard work?"

"Work harder during those years. Make *sure* you make a profit."

Fire flashed in her blue eyes.

"Easy for you to say! There's no way to make sure I make a profit, and you know it. That's why we've ended up in this deal."

He took a step closer.

"We didn't have to end up in this deal at all," he said. "I could've thrown you out on your pretty backside the minute I walked in that door."

"Ra-afe!"

Maddie covered her mouth with her hand and stared at him as if he were the most shocking man on earth. It was a socially unacceptable remark, all right, but she was acting like an innocent maiden.

"I cannot *believe* you said that."

She threw a significant glance in Juanito's direction, then took a step toward Rafe, making a gesture that beckoned him even closer. He ignored it. Already, for some insane reason or for no reason at all, or because of the dirt on her face, he was aching to touch her, wanting to kiss her full, rosy lips, slightly parted in shock.

"Don't worry. Juanito won't be running around all over San Antonio shouting 'your pretty backside.' "

"Well, I certainly hope not! He doesn't need to be hearing such things. And from his own father, too!"

"Oh, quit acting like my maiden Aunt Trudy," he snapped.

She came a step closer.

"Hush and listen to me," she said, very low.

Did she think she could change his mind by whispering in his ear? She couldn't, but she might make him kiss her right in front of his son.

"A man can be pushed only so far, Maddie," he growled. "After that, a woman has to use persuasion."

The words surprised him as much as they did her. He watched her eyes grow wider and then take on the old glint of humor that made them even bluer.

She gave him that straight look of hers.

"Are you making an implication of some kind?" she said archly.

"What kind did you have in mind?"

She smiled.

"Rafe, I would never have expected this from you."

"This what?"

"This attempted extortion of personal favors in a business arrangement."

He smiled and touched the brim of his hat with exaggerated gallantry. She had always made him smile at the most unexpected times. It was one of the things he'd loved best about being with her. But she didn't need to think it would help her get her way now.

"I'm sorry to disappoint you, ma'am, but you've misread me. I'm not bargaining, I'm telling you what I've decided to do."

"Well, can't you consider my opinion before you make a decision?"

She tossed her hair back flirtatiously and smiled at him.

"Is this good enough persuasion?"

"No. I've made up my mind."

She eyed him narrowly.

"Oh. I see. You're just trying to show me who's boss around here. You want me to know I have to do what you say."

"You do. But what I'm doing is announcing a business decision. That's all."

She searched his face as if she'd find a secret written there.

"Is this a game?"

"No."

"If you went through with this plan—let's just say *if*—would I have to pay the moving expenses for the *Star*?"

"Of course. That would figure into your budget."

"Not fair. That wasn't part of our agreement."

She crossed her arms beneath her high, full breasts and tucked her dirt-stained hands into the crooks of her elbows, then lifted her chin to stare at him defiantly.

He had to cross his arms to keep from reaching out to brush the dirt from her smooth, smooth skin. And more.

All he could think was how much he wanted to kiss her again, as he'd done in this stable yard before.

"Madeleine," he said, "you know as well as I do that life isn't fair."

"Rafe," she said, "you know as well as I do that *you are*."

That stopped him cold.

"Isn't that the reputation you have?" she said. "That you never cheat?"

"Madeleine, we're talking about two completely different things."

"No, we're not. It's not *life* proposing to move me out of my home—it's you."

Her lack of logic sent exasperation shooting through him. Then she cut her eyes at Juanito, who was hesitantly approaching them, and he followed her glance. The stricken look on the child's face sent guilt rushing through him.

"Then write an editorial about it," he said, putting his arm around Juanito's shoulders. "I came by here to tell you how it's going to be and to pick up my son."

He turned to Juanito, whose big eyes were filled with worry.

"It's all right," he said, in Spanish. "We're going to the ranch."

"*Y mi Lena?*"

"*Sí,*" Madeleine said, before Rafe could answer. "*Yo, también.*"

He whipped around to look at her again.

"Who invited you?"

"Juanito."

"I'm the father."

"And you're the one who said a woman has to use persuasion," she said. "I'm going with you."

"That's not persuasion, that's horning in."

"Which is necessary," she said firmly. "I have to horn in to get to where I can use persuasion."

Damn! He didn't need this. But her blue eyes sparked with determination and the curve of her lips brought the taste of their last hard, hot kiss to his tongue.

That kiss. Its memory was as intense as if it'd happened yesterday instead of days in the past.

All that kind of feeling between them should be gone. Dead. He *was* losing his mind. He certainly didn't want her under the same roof with him all night. He didn't need her at all!

"Maddie," he said urgently, "we're not coming back for a day or two—maybe three. I'm having supplies delivered to set up the house."

"I have the time. Charlie can manage the paper."

He had a brilliant thought.

"But it'd ruin your reputation," he said triumphantly, "and that would affect your business. Way out there on the ranch for three or four nights alone with me, why, that would . . ."

She interrupted firmly. "We won't be alone with Juanito there."

He reached deep for more patience and made himself speak calmly.

"Madeleine, remember you have to make a profit. You don't want your advertisers to take their dollars away."

"They won't," she said confidently. "Everyone knows I have a second job as Juanito's nanny. No one will think a thing about it."

"That's ridiculous! You know how people like to talk."

"Rafe," she said patiently, "people have talked about me from the day I started publishing the *Star*. I run around all over the country by myself getting stories, I go into men's offices and places of business alone and sell advertising; I attend meetings where I'm the only woman."

She smiled. "Being a nanny puts me a notch up with the prim-and-proper set."

Rafe caught a glimpse of Juanito's worried face, his big eyes looking from one of them to the other, and he knew the battle was lost. The boy wanted her to go with them.

He might even be afraid without her there to protect him from unexpected dangers. The thought stabbed Rafe right in the gut.

"All right," he sighed.

Unfortunately, giving in didn't feel as bad as he'd feared. Something deep within him was almost glad Madeleine was going, and that gave him a scare he tried not to think about.

"Let me wash my hands and gather up a few things," she said, and started for the back door. "I'll leave a note for Charlie, too."

Suddenly he couldn't resist teasing her a little.

"I don't know. Maybe you ought to stay here and work on trying to make a profit."

She turned and made a face at him as if she were still seventeen years old.

"*Going to the ranch* is the way I'll make a profit," she said. "The reason I'm going is to talk you out of this new idea of yours—not because you're so handsome and debonair that I can't resist you."

Her eyes sent out that spark of challenge that he'd never been able to resist.

"I'm a grown up woman, now, Rafe, in case you haven't noticed."

I noticed. You were a beautiful girl, but you're a woman who's one in a million. A woman who makes a man ache to get his hands on you.

She turned and ran to the door, then turned back as she opened it.

"Rafe, would you mind harnessing my horse? I'd hate to hold y'all up, and you could have it done by the time I'm ready to go."

"I will do it!" Juanito cried, his face glowing as he looked after her.

He ran back to the peppers, poured the last of the water in the jar onto their roots, then ran for the stable door.

Rafe stared after him, then went to pull the gig out of the shed. Suddenly he was taken with a lighthearted feeling he hardly recognized. It felt like they were all going on a picnic, or to the horseraces. It felt like the three of them together hadn't a care in the world.

Juanito seemed to feel the same way; he was

whistling tunelessly as he led the mare out of the stable and backed her up between the shafts. Rafe slipped the bridle onto the mare's head.

"She is beautiful, no, *Papá*?"

Rafe thought of Madeleine. "Yes, son, she is."

"Dol-ly," Juanito crooned. "Dol-ly."

Juanito was stroking the mare's neck, looking at her slightly-swaybacked self with his whole face full of love. He'd been talking about the mare.

Rafe, foolishly, had still been thinking about Madeleine. He was in more trouble than he'd thought.

He opened his mouth to correct himself, to say the mare was not a particularly beautiful horse, but he let his words stand. Later today, out at the ranch, he would give Juanito some lessons in conformation, or at least point out some beautiful horses to start training his eye.

That thought gave a little lift to his heart. If they never were able to talk about much else, he and Juanito would always have the inexhaustible subject of horses.

Come to think of it, that was another example of family history repeating itself. He'd never been closer to his own father than at the stables or the racecourse.

Juanito needed only a few suggestions to be able to put all the pieces of the harness on where they needed to be and fasten it together. They had it done when Madeleine came out of the house with a carpetbag in one hand and her reticule in the other.

Rafe smiled proudly as Juan Rafael ran to help her.

Madeleine looked a little pale to him. Maybe she'd thought better of this plan but didn't know how to back out of it without hurting Juanito's feelings.

No. She began laughing and talking with the boy as she always did. She was all right.

He closed his mind against thoughts of her and helped her up into the gig. Juanito made sure her lines were straight and at hand, then Rafe held the mare's head while Juanito put her things into the back.

"All right," she said, lifting the lines, "my outriders can mount up for our trip to . . . what's the name of the new ranch?"

"We must find one," Juanito cried, as he ran to Tortilla and excitedly scrambled up into the saddle. "We talk about it now!"

She invariably knew what to say to make the boy happy.

Rafe went to Beau and stuck the toe of his boot into the stirrup. He had to remember he was spending time with her only for the good of his child.

Driving down the road, Madeleine forced her mind onto the new name for the ranch, on Juanito's natural seat on a horse, Dolly's haircoat, which was so much better since Juanito had been brushing her for hours every day— anything but the terrifying letter. When it crackled in her pocket, she even let herself turn to Rafe for distraction and watched him astride Beau. He had to be the best horseman she'd ever known—he cut such a dashing figure on the sleek black stallion that it took her breath away.

That meant nothing, of course, since any woman in the world couldn't help but have the same reaction.

She took a deep, long breath and steadied her hands on the lines. If she let her fear and anger show, Juanito would be upset—he had taught her that children were as adept as horses at picking up on moods.

"What do you think, Rafe, about the name?" she called, in an effort to compel her thoughts into another direction. "After all, you're the one who won the ranch."

"*Mi papá* will share with us," Juanito assured her.

That made Rafe smile. Both her outriders dropped back to ride on either side of her gig.

"I haven't given it much thought," Rafe said, "but we do need to decide, since I've bought more cattle and hired some help. Soon they'll need to know a brand."

"You could use the Rafter A or Rocking A or Circle A or any kind of A if you want your initial."

"*Los Tres Amigos!*" Juanito blurted loudly, beaming with pleasure at his brainstorm, gesturing in a circle that included each of them.

Instantly, Rafe's eyes met hers.

Once they had been best friends. Sworn best friends forever. She knew at that moment he had never had another friend like that. Neither had she. Not even Sophie.

They looked deep into each other's eyes as the horses moved them along at the same pace.

Maybe they could be best friends again. It was the man/woman aspect of their relationship that had ruined it all. They could keep that out of it and be only platonic friends. Couldn't they?

He smiled at her in the old, knowing way that meant they were secret conspirators against the world.

"*Papá?*"

Juanito's voice was eager.

"*Los Tres Amigos* is perfect," Rafe said, and finally broke the look between him and Madeleine to glance at his happy son.

Juanito's eyes met Madeleine's and he raised his fist, as if, together, they'd fought a long battle to victory.

"What will be the brand?" Rafe asked him.

It took only a second before Juanito drew the numeral 3 in the air.

"*Tres,*" he said.

Then he drew an invisible circle around the three.

"Perfect again!" Rafe and Madeleine said.

With a happy shout of victory, Juanito sent Tortilla plunging ahead. Rafe's gaze followed him.

Madeleine's heart went into a painful clutch.

"Don't let him get out of our sight! Go after him, Rafe!"

Rafe looked at her, puzzled.

"He knows the way. It's not far to the ranch," he said.

She looked ahead. Juanito and the little buckskin mare had disappeared from her sight.

"You can't tie him to your apron strings, Maddie," Rafe said, "a boy has to have his freedom."

"Rafe, please . . ."

He looked at her. She couldn't bear to look at him but she felt his piercing stare.

"I couldn't tell you with him here," she said hurriedly, reaching into her pocket, "but you have to see this. Then you'll know why I'm worried."

Her hand shook as she pulled out the crumpled piece of paper. She held it up to him, but she couldn't wait any longer to have help in carrying this awful burden.

"Mrs. Calhoun," she quoted. "Who do you think you are to bring a Mexican into the wrong part of town? That was a disgrace, him playing with the white children at the pie auction. It's wrong, him staying with you at night."

Her voice broke from the weight of her un-shed tears.

"Damn! Cortinas is doing more damage than thieving and killing," Rafe growled, and read the rest aloud: "If you're so crazy about him, send him back across the river. Get him out of danger. Anything can happen to him and some-thing will."

"Lowdown, yellow-bellied coward," he growled. "Don't worry, Maddie. The kind who won't sign his name is all talk and no action."

But his eyes searched for Juanito up ahead as he crushed the letter in his big fist.

"Where'd you find this?"

"On the floor of the office, held down by a rock."

"Today? Just before we left?"

"Yes. Right in the middle of the room in front of the door."

"I'd just walked through it," he said. "I hadn't been outside five minutes. He knew I was there."

"That was . . . action, and not talk," she said. "For him to come in and leave this when he knew we were both there."

She looked at him and demanded with her eyes that he admit to that truth.

His jaw hardened; his whole face turned to stone.

"Whoever the son-of-a-bitch is," he said, "I

will cut his heart out and throw it to the coyotes if he so much as lays a finger on my son."

He set his heels to Beau and thundered after the child.

Madeleine's heart left her body to go with him.

Rafe might still be dressed in fine clothes, but the suave Prince of New Orleans was gone. In his place rode a Choctaw warrior, fierce as the ones who fought to the death at Horseshoe Bend.

And she was dreadfully afraid she would fall in love with him again.

Chapter 11

They both were waiting for her at the lane to the ranch house. A sigh of relief released the breath Maddie hadn't known she was holding, and Rafe's gaze met hers as if in affirmation that Juanito was safe.

"*Mi Lena!*" he called. "Where have you been?"

"Coming as fast as I could. Dolly's been at a long trot the whole time."

"Then you need a faster horse," Juanito announced. "My papa will give you one."

"Hey, now, wait a minute," Rafe said, teasing him. "Did I say that?"

"No, but we agree, no? Papa?"

Juanito's little voice sounded so sweet, only the biggest ogre on earth could resist him.

"I suppose," Rafe said thoughtfully, as Made-

leine drove up to join them, "if you'll do a lot of
chores, Juanito, to pay the purchase price for your
Lena's new horse. A fast one costs many, many
dollars."

Madeleine and Rafe stifled their smiles and
watched Juanito's face for signs of dismay.

There were none. He was thinking it over, but
he was willing to do whatever it took.

"The new remuda," he said. "They are already paid the price, no, Papa? It has a fast one,
Papa?"

She could see Rafe wanted to laugh but he
didn't because Juanito was so perfectly serious.

Madeleine smiled.

"Thank you, Juanito. I accept. I love a fast
horse. But what shall we do with Dolly?"

"Let her be *abuela por Tortilla.*"

Madeleine and Rafe exchanged an involuntary glance. Juanito had never mentioned his
grandmother.

"Or *su mamá.*"

They stared at him.

"But what work would Dolly do if she became
Tortilla's mama and I drove a fast horse?" Maddie asked.

Juanito smiled indulgently.

"Sleep beside her in the stable," he said. "I
moved to your house."

That made a knot in Madeleine's throat that
threatened to block her voice. He was thinking

of her as his mama, and that was a line of thought she could never take.

"Good idea," she finally said, and drove past Tortilla and Beau into the lane. "Come on, let's go pick out my new horse."

The ranch house and barn had become a real headquarters since her last visit, and Madeleine looked around in disbelief as she drove into the yard. This was obviously already a working ranch now, and the first thought that popped into her mind was that Rafe must be planning to stay. Why else would he bring in more cattle, have at least twenty new horses in the big corral by the barn, and hire a dozen hands or more?

Not to mention his plan to build a gaming palace in town. How could she bear for him to be around all the time? But how could she bear it if he wasn't?

There were three men in the corral riding the new horses, there was one bent over a firepit near the bunkhouse tending two black pots hanging from an iron frame, and one hammering at a repair on the side of the barn. Two more came pounding on horseback out of the trees and down the side of the hill where Juanito had been injured.

He and Rafe rode up beside her gig when she pulled Dolly to a stop.

"Come," Juanito said, as comfortable as if all this activity were the result of his orders and no one else's, "we go to see these horses."

He dismounted.

"Choose the ones you think might be fastest," Rafe said indulgently, "and I'll be there in a minute."

Juanito came to help Madeleine step down.

"Think we can pick the best ones?" she said.

"*Sí*," he said, with such endearing confidence that she wanted to hug him, "you and I, we are horse partners."

She couldn't resist teasing him a little.

"Does that mean we both have to do the chores to pay for my horse?"

He grinned.

"You clean the barn," he said. "I carry the wood for the cooking."

She grinned back and pulled his hat down over his eyes.

"Then you do the cooking, too," she said.

"No! I don't know about making pancakes."

"Maybe we'll have to do without pancakes, then."

He pushed back his hat and looked up at her with such a horrified expression that she had to laugh.

"There's the cook, over there by the bunkhouse," she said. "Go ask him if he can make pancakes."

But Juanito forgot all about pancakes when one of the cowboys came out of the corral leading a bay horse that stepped along so proudly it made people look twice. The man nodded shyly and tipped his hat to Madeleine and Juanito, then went on to put the mare in another pen where three others were waiting.

Juanito stopped and turned to watch them.

"Think is fast, *mi Lena?*"

The bay followed the cowboy into the pen, but when he turned her loose, she bucked for three or four jumps and then ran around the inside of the fence at a quick clip.

"She may be fast," she said, "but I think she's more skittish than I want."

Juanito chuckled as if he were the adult and she the child.

"I'll take the bucks out of her for you," he said, and led her the rest of the way to the corral fence. "I won't let her hurt you, *mi Lena.*"

Madeleine's eyes filled and she ached to hug the boy, but she knew it would embarrass him terribly, in front of these men. Juanito might think that his advanced age of nine years made him too old for that.

"*Gracias,*" she said, swallowing hard. "*Muchas gracias, Juanito.*"

"*De nada,*" he said carelessly.

He climbed up onto the fence to look at all the other choices, his face aglow at such a miraculous situation.

She stood to one side of him and peered over

the unpeeled logs. God help her, if they left San
Antonio, it would break her heart. She wouldn't
even be able to put out a newspaper, much less
make it a profitable one.

When Rafe joined them, she was thankful he
stood on the other side of Juanito. Right now, at
this moment, she could not bear to also be close
to him and not touch or be touched.

She straightened her shoulders and stared
blindly through the bars of the fence. Maybe this
emotion tearing her apart was only that—a longing to be touched. It had been a long time since
she had lain with Sutton, after all, and he had
said she was an unusually passionate woman.
At the beginning. When she had thought she
loved him.

Helplessly, she dug her nails into the rail.
How was she ever to know what the truth was,
if she couldn't trust her own senses when it
came to a man?

Despite his pleasure in watching her and
Juanito look at the horses he'd bought from the
Crossbars Ranch next door, and listening to
them talk to the cowboys about each one, Rafe
felt sharp discomfort at Madeleine's intense concentration in choosing one to try. It must be pity,
he decided, because she'd had only the old nag,
Dolly, for so long that even these mediocre
mounts made her eyes light up.

Or was it guilt because he'd taken away

everything else she owned in that poker game in Goliad?

Surely it wasn't that. He had a ranch to support now and a gaming hall to build, and it was no time to have regrets about his profession.

"Race!"

He turned toward the sound of Juanito's voice.

His new hands were getting up a match race, now that they knew somebody was interested in speed. He tried to think about his workers instead of Madeleine and Juanito. They seemed like a good, solid bunch, and he'd gotten them through sheer luck—they had quit their employer farther west in a body over an insult to one of them, and this ranch was the first place they'd stopped to ask for new jobs. He was glad he'd been here at the ranch when they rode up.

Actually, he'd been out here almost every day since that first visit. It was almost beginning to feel like home.

Los Tres Amigos.

The name made him smile. Juanito surely was crazy about his Lena. Maybe, with that Mexican-hater in town, they should just stay out here.

The anonymous letter was enough to make the hair on his neck stand up. He really did wish none of them ever had to go back to town— Madeleine might be in danger, too.

He looked at her. She seemed to have forgotten all about everything except the horses.

"La baya," Juanito said, proclaiming his choice for winner. It was the bay mare who'd bucked when they turned her into the catch pen, brought back at the boy's request.

The cowboys were pitting their choice against her—a gray gelding with a long, slender body.

"Sí," Madeleine said, *"la baya."*

Rafe smiled. She and his son bore an uncanny resemblance at that moment, their faces still and intent as they waited to see what the horses could do.

The two cowboys rode up to a line drawn in the sand outside the corral and sat, horses dancing, until their buddy standing at the fence brought his hat sweeping down.

"Go!"

They flew past their audience on pounding hooves, floating in the cloud of dust they created. In a flash they were gone, all the way to the corner post of the hillside pasture. The dust finally cleared, and then they could see the rider on the bay mare waving his hat in the air.

"Bay mare!" yelled the man posted at the finish line.

Juanito grabbed Madeleine around the waist and they danced up and down, whooping and laughing and congratulating each other; then they whirled and took Rafe into their circle, making him laugh, too.

Madeleine wore the flower-trimmed, wide-brimmed hat she had worn to the pie auction and he couldn't help but look again—and again—to see how those ribbons exactly matched her blue eyes. She had to be the most beautiful woman he had ever seen and just the sight of her and of Juan Rafael with such smiles on their faces lifted his heart.

"So," he said, with pretended sternness, "how much are you willing to pay for the bay mare, Juanito?"

"I will let you borrow her," Juan Rafael said, without missing a beat. "You can make some money betting on her, *Papá*."

That drew a great laugh from the cowboys watching from the fence.

"That boy's too smart for you, Boss," one of them called to Rafe, "and him nothin' but a yearling yet. Don't bet the limit with him, even if he ain't grown up."

"I won't," Rafe called back, laughing with them. "You're right about that."

But a funny sensation took over his stomach and he felt a strange heaviness at envisioning Juan Rafael following in his profession. Gambling made a man hard-edged and hopeless, somehow. Maybe because there was always another chance to lose.

And that was the biggest reason of all that he couldn't be a decent father to his wonderful boy. Even though gambling was held to be a perfectly acceptable profession by all but the worst religious fanatics and temperance preachers, and although settled, successful gamblers like Big Jim were pillars of their towns.

"Stay here, *mi Lena*," Juanito said to Madeleine. "I get to know her."

He ran off to see the bay mare up close.

Rafe watched Madeleine tousle his hair as he left her. The boy was crazy about her and the feeling was mutual. If he had a shred of decency in him, he'd leave Juanito with her, get out of San Antonio, and just send money from wherever he went. They'd both be better off.

And so would he. The unfamiliar emotions pulling at him were multiplying by the moment.

Madeleine grabbed his arm.

"Oh! I just remembered! He promised to take the bucks out of her for me," she said, her beautiful face turned up to his, her black hair shining like jet in the sun. "Stop him, Rafe. Don't let him get on her and get hurt."

The cowboy who'd ridden the bay to victory was grinning at Juanito's eagerness as he dismounted.

"Hey, Button. You think you wanna ride this one?"

"*Sí!*"

"Better hold onto your hat," he said, handing the reins to the boy.

Rafe's heart gave a resounding thump. But

Juanito would never forgive him if he treated him like a child in front of the cowboys.

Madeleine was straining toward Juanito, desperate to protect him, squeezing Rafe's arm harder.

"Hold on," he said, and covered her hand with his. "Let's see what happens."

The cowboy stood there, talking with Juanito while Madeleine's long, slender fingers burned into Rafe's arm.

"*Ra-afe*," she said. "Don't let that child get hurt!"

"He'll not get on until she knows him, is what I'm guessing," he murmured. "Tortilla was a little devil with me, but Juanito made medicine with her awhile and she never bucked with him."

"How did he do it?"

"Who knows? But when I rode her out of Goliad it was touch and go for a long way, yet when I let him on her, she turned into a lamb."

Madeleine dropped her hand but she never took her eyes from Juanito.

"If he tries to mount right now, I'm going to interfere," she said tightly, in a tone too low for the nearby cowboys to overhear. "It may be your place, but if you won't do it, I will."

"No, you won't, Maddie. Rotten father or not, I know what I'm doing here."

He could only pray that he was right. All he

knew was that it'd be wrong to take away Juanito's pride, especially when he was going to be living and riding with these men.

Madeleine flashed him a fiery blue glance, half anger, half fear.

"I overreacted when I said you weren't a good father. I know now that you do love him. I just think that . . ."

"Did you ever think that a boy has his pride, just like a man?" he said. "These cowboys have just bragged on Juanito's wit and made him feel ten feet tall. He'll need that and more respect if he starts hearing people call him 'wetback' and 'pepperbelly' and 'dirty Mexican.' "

She looked from Juanito to him with tears in her eyes.

"If anyone hurts Juanito with words like that, I personally will cut his heart out and throw it to the coyotes before you can."

Her fierceness made him smile a little.

"Think you're faster than I am, huh?"

She almost smiled back.

"I know I am."

He couldn't keep from touching her—just because he needed to try to distract her. He put his hand on her shoulder and it felt as if it belonged there, cradling her. Maddie was tall and strong, but her bones were delicate beneath his fingers.

"It's all right, Maddie," he said. "I'm watching him."

She quit wringing her hands but she didn't quit worrying.

"I don't want you to watch him, I want you to tell him to let one of these men ride that mare for a week, no, for a month, before he gets on her."

"Do you really?"

He looked down at her, very straight.

She shook her head in defeat. "No. I know you're right. I just can't stand it."

She kept looking at him instead of at Juanito.

"He's only getting acquainted with her," he said.

"She bucked all the way around that pen when they turned her loose awhile ago."

"I know. And Juan Rafael knows that, too."

"Tortilla and this bay are two different horses."

"Yes, but every horse Juanito meets treats him right."

She made as if to move out from under his hand, but then stood still. Her full lips were slightly parted and she appeared to be thinking it over.

Resolutely, she turned and looked at Juanito.

The mare was standing quietly, her rider had gone back to his friends, who were busily paying up and collecting their bets on the race, and Juan Rafael was making a new friend. Totally oblivious to everything and everybody else, he was touching the mare all over, rubbing his hands down her legs and picking up her feet, apparently talking to her the whole time.

While they watched, he took out the pocketknife Rafe had given him and removed something from one hoof. The bay mare swung her head around and looked at him but she didn't try to pull her foot away.

Juan Rafael folded the knife and returned it to his pocket, and then, with a last caress of the mare's pretty face, he threw himself lightly onto her back. She responded to his hands as soon as he used the reins, and he loped her out from the corral in a wide circle that would take in the bunkhouse and the cook fire.

The cook looked up and lifted his hand in salute; the other cowboys cheered.

Rafe sighed with relief while his heart swelled with pride. It was inherited. His son was an exceptional horseman, just as his father had been.

"He reminds me of your daddy."

Shocked that Maddie had read his mind as she used to do, he looked at her. "Me, too."

"I know I'm too attached to him, but I can't help that now," she said. "All I can think about is that horrid anonymous note and making sure he's safe."

"I know."

"I wish we could keep him out here at the ranch all the time."

There she was again, echoing his unspoken longing.

They laughed together in the sweet moment when Juanito came into sight again, peacefully loping the bay mare, and the cook clanged the triangle to call them to eat. He removed the lid of one kettle and the fragrance of smoked meat and spicy sauce drifted out to mingle with the smells of horses, cattle, and dust.

Madeleine tied on her hat as she started toward the fire. "Maybe food will get Juanito off his horse for a few minutes, at least."

"Only if it's pancakes," he said, walking beside her, "and last I heard, it's *your* horse."

She gave him a sideways smile from beneath her hat brim.

"Thanks for the fast horse," she said. "I think. How about if I leave her here until Juanito can gentle her completely for me?"

"Hmm. There'll be a fee—for the gentling, the feed, etc."

She chuckled.

"You're not the one doing the work."

"Ah, but I'm the one paying the bills. Those two wagonloads of furniture and supplies alone that I ordered from James Flynn demand that I find another source of income."

A silence fell between them, a pregnant pause that demanded the thought they both held be spoken aloud. Finally, Madeleine did.

"Sounds like you're planning to settle in on this place. And with your gambling hall . . ."

A little shock ran through him.

"I'm acquiring some properties around here, yes," he said quickly. "But I'll hire people to manage them."

"Oh."

All the new, strange feelings began to roil inside him again. They panicked him, somehow.

"I'm not the settling kind, Maddie."

She only nodded.

He felt a vague need to explain, or to say something else, but he couldn't imagine what. They reached the spot where Juanito was dismounting, preparing to unsaddle the mare.

"Pet her, *mi Lena*," he said. "She will like you."

"I like her, too," Madeleine said, stroking the sweaty neck. "I just don't want her to buck with either of us."

She cupped the velvet nose loosely in her palm, then stroked it, letting the mare breathe in her scent.

"*Mañana*," Juanito said, in a voice so carelessly sure he sounded inviolable. "I ride her again then. Or maybe more today."

Rafe watched them pet on the mare and talk about her as Maddie opened the gate and Juanito turned the mare into the pen again. *Mi Lena*.

He loved her. She loved him. A sudden hollowness came into him, because for one quick instant, he really wished they both loved him.

Foolish, selfish thought. For their sake, it was good that they didn't.

The three of them walked toward the cookfire, Juanito chattering about the mare and her intelligence and her speed.

"You sound like your Grandfather Aigner," Madeleine said to him. "He always used to tell me that his horse was the fastest, no matter who he was running against."

Juanito stopped short, astonished.

"Tu papá?" he asked Rafe.

"Sí. Tu abuelo. He was a good horseman like you. You are like him in that way, and you have the same shape of nose."

He'd never noticed it before but it was true.

Juanito smiled so wide he nearly split his face.

Rafe felt a stab of wonder. He had never thought it would mean so much to the boy to know something about his grandfather, or he would've told him this before. Trust Maddie to know that.

Around the cookfire, where the cook was ladling meat and beans and stewed dried apples onto tin plates and adding hot biscuits on top, the men broke their usual meal time silence with brief, teasing remarks to Juanito—challenges to the bay mare's speed and exaggerated tales of her ability to buck—and Cookie himself joined in. Rafe watched and listened, marveling at his son's new lack of shyness, his confidence, his sense of humor.

At least he had done one thing right: he had

let him ride the mare. And he had kept this place. If trouble came to them in town, this would be safe refuge.

And coming here lured Madeleine away from that eternal newspaper.

He squelched that thought immediately. Madeleine's coming here had nothing to do with him, only with Juanito.

When the men had returned to work and Juanito had gone back to his new love, the bay mare, Madeleine threw her plate into the wreck pan and turned to him.

"Let's go see if the house is clean enough for the furniture," she said. "Do you think those wagons are coming today?"

"Flynn promised them for today. I pushed him on that."

As they crossed the yard, she flashed him that devilish smile of hers.

"Don't get the wrong impression," she said, "I'm not volunteering to clean your house. I really just wanted to get you alone . . ."

"Ah ha," he said, with an exaggerated leer, "I've been hoping you would say that . . ."

"To *talk*," she interrupted firmly.

She couldn't resist a small smile at his sally, though, he noticed.

When they climbed the steps up onto the front porch, she sobered. She stopped before he opened the door and turned to look up at him, her hair lifting, falling, brushing against her beautiful face in the soft breeze. It was cool there, with the wind blowing south to north through the hallway of the house, with the huge old live oak in the yard throwing its shade over them.

"Come on," he said, teasing her, "you'd better get in there and start cleaning."

"I tried to tell you this back at my place," she said, all in a rush, "but I couldn't get a chance without Juanito's overhearing."

He felt a hot, devil's finger of panic touch his spine. Was she changing her mind about helping with the boy? She had said she was becoming too attached.

"Don't tear down the *Star* yet, Rafe. Wait until he's really settled into sleeping inside, will you? It's the only place he feels secure."

The hellish heat spread all through him.

"I am the world's biggest fool," he said, with bitter chagrin. "I should've thought of that. Here I was, thinking I was learning, so proud I'd let him ride that mare, and I never once thought about the sleeping problem."

Her eyes filled with pain. "Rafe," she said softly, "you've made more right decisions for Juanito than wrong ones. Bringing him with you out of Mexico was the first right one and letting him ride the mare was the latest, but there have been many in between."

The words soothed him a little.

And when she took his face into her cool, smooth hands and brought his lips to hers, she set his heart at rest.

Chapter 12

She had only meant to comfort him.

But the instant her lips touched his, the passion to make him believe her turned to passion *for him*. All the years vanished, and he became the old Rafe she loved.

His strong arms pulled her to him; his tongue sought hers in affirmation. She gave it, she could not have refused; and he stole her breath, her mind, too, before her heart could beat again. His scent, that perfect mix of cedar and leather and horse and tobacco which always was Rafe's, filled her nostrils.

She thrust her fingers into his crisp, thick hair, then ran them down the side of his neck and around the edge of his ear, and thrilled to his shiver of response. Her arms grew weak with desire and she let them fall to his shoulders and pressed her body even harder against his, as she kissed him even more deeply.

Vaguely, she realized that he was bigger, more solid than before, but then her mind burned away completely in the magic fire of his mouth. She knew nothing but its heat and its sweetness and its deep, tremulous excitement when her tongue twined with his.

She gave a great, shuddering sigh and clung to him as if she had lived only for this feeling all those long years. He cradled her cheek with one of his big hands and they tilted their heads to change the angle of the kiss.

Rafe. My Rafe.

He pressed her even closer, melded her to his hard loins.

An intense longing took her, a craving, an unappeasable hunger that overpowered her. If she didn't have Rafe, she would die.

But hoofbeats, urgent hoofbeats, brought them back into the world and Juanito's yell broke them apart.

"*Papá, mi Lena*, the wagons are coming!"

Juanito pounded past the porch aboard the bay mare. No saddle. His strong brown legs clamped to her sides, he stuck to her back as if glued. He slowed only to call to them again, his eyes shining as he looked back over his shoulder.

"I go to meet them. The supplies for our home!"

Our home.

The words pierced her heart.

Two wagons hove into view, making slow progress up the ranch road behind their four-horse hitches. Each was loaded to capacity, the goods neatly stacked and tied down, but swaying precariously.

Maddie spoke before she thought, so close did she feel to him at that moment. Her heart was beating so hard she could almost hear it.

"Well, Rambler," she said, "looks to me like you're about to settle down."

He gave her a rueful grin and put his hand on her shoulder as they stood together, hips barely touching, watching Juanito and the mare fly down the lane.

"Just because I've bought a plethora of household plunder, two herds of cattle and a fine remuda of horses, and brought them here?" he asked ironically.

"Right," she said wryly. "But I forgot you plan to hire a manager."

"I do," he said. "But I'll stay around San Antonio for Juanito's sake for a year or two. He needs to be a little older before we move on."

Madeleine walked out from under his hand.

At the edge of the porch, she leaned against a post and watched the wagons come, Juanito riding a circle around them while he stared curiously at their contents.

A year or two. Before we move on.

Why should those words hit her so hard? She had never really believed he would stay.

She didn't want him to stay. Not if she couldn't keep from kissing him at the slightest provocation, knowing full well that it meant nothing at all.

Juanito finished his perusal of the wagons and headed the bay mare straight for the house.

"We have beds!" he shouted. "Like the hotel!"

"The one at your house is the only bed he's ever had of his own," Rafe said, at her elbow.

He had followed her without making a sound, but her whole body had felt his nearness before he spoke.

"And it's not really a bed," she said, "without a head- or footboard."

"Growing up, all he had was a pallet," Rafe said. "And I—"

"Don't start feeling guilty all over again," Madeleine interrupted firmly. "His grandmother always loved him, and so did you. That's much more important than a bedstead."

She felt his steady gaze on her face but she wouldn't let herself turn to meet his eyes. In spite of all, she was liable to kiss him again if she looked at him.

Juanito slowed the mare as he rode up to the porch.

"There is a stove, too, *mi Lena*," he said, grinning mischievously. "So you can make a buttermilk pie."

She grinned back at him.

"After you've chopped the wood and built me a fire."

Juan looked so startled that she and Rafe both laughed.

"First, I must ride your horse," Juanito said solemnly, full of wounded dignity. "That takes much time."

They laughed again.

"Son," Rafe said, "you're a real cowboy. Cowboys never want to do any work they can't do from the back of a horse."

"Should I let you ride into my . . ." Madeleine bit her tongue and corrected herself, ". . . into the kitchen? Would that make it easier to carry in the wood and build the fire?"

Such a ridiculous idea made Juanito smile.

"Maybe not," he said. "*La baya* would be learning one bad habit."

The lead wagon reached the end of the lane and rumbled into the yard.

"Well, Cowboy," Rafe said, "here's your bed. Better tell 'em which room is yours."

Juanito's eyes grew huge.

"My room? Mine?"

"You bet," Rafe said. "All you have to do is pick it out."

"What if he chooses the living room?" Madeleine murmured, as Juanito bailed off the mare and tied her to a tree. "Or the big bedroom?"

Rafe laughed. Then, with a straight look, he said, "You know better than that, Miss Lena. Think about it."

She looked into his amber eyes—eyes that sparked with mischief, eyes that looked right into her mind as if he knew every idea in it already.

"Whoa!" shouted the teamster and brought his team to a halt near the porch. "Mr. Aigner?"

Rafe didn't even glance at him.

For a moment all Madeleine could do was feel the thrill of this long, intimate look she shared with Rafe, which felt even stronger somehow than the kiss. Then, without one conscious thought, she knew. As surely as if he had spoken the words, she read the thought in his eyes.

"Of course," she said, "he'll choose that little lean-to bedroom in the back . . ."

Together they finished the sentence, ". . . Because its window looks out on the horsepen."

Rafe gave her a quick, affirming nod and warmed her heart with his crooked smile that never failed to make her heart lift. Then he turned to the men waiting on the high wagonseats. He invited them to get down for a cold drink of water from the well, sent Juanito to bring some of the cowboys to help unload the furniture, and then walked to the wide screen door and held it open for Madeleine.

"Fit the house out, Maddie," he said. "Tell 'em where to put all this plunder I've bought."

Plunder I've bought. None of this belonged to her; she needed to remember that.

"I don't live here, Rafe."

The words came out tart and brisk. She needed to stay outside and not get involved in arranging this house.

But she walked ahead of him in spite of herself, into the middle of the big, square living room with its welcoming stone hearth, and wide windows looking out onto the gallery and the old rose bushes in the side yard. It was a wonderful room in its honest, rough way. With all this space and light, it would be marvelous when furnished with the right things.

"So fitting out a house is woman's work, like child-tending?" she said, trying to work up an indignation strong enough to hold the rest of her feelings at bay.

"No, Maddie," he drawled, in his dark velvet voice. "I've never been in a home as peaceful as the one you made for your father."

That answer disarmed her entirely. *Peaceful.*

Like her, Rafe had known very little peace in these past ten years.

Why shouldn't she let herself enjoy this? Why shouldn't she forget everything else and live in this moment?

"Rafe," she said, turning to fix him with her

best solemn stare, "you must promise me one thing as I make this house fit for human habitation: my word is law. I am not to be contradicted or overruled."

He laughed that infectious low laugh of his, his eyes warm as sunshine.

"I don't care a whit where anything goes," he said. "Have at it, Miss Madeleine."

He went off to see to the stove pipe for the kitchen, but when Juanito ran in ahead of the first load of furniture, Rafe stepped back into the parlor.

"Which room have you chosen, son?"

Juanito slowed only a little on his way to his own domain.

"The little one, Papa. *Por los caballos.*"

Rafe's quick glance caught Madeleine's. He grinned.

"*Por los caballos?* Do you plan to bring them in to share your bed?"

Juanito halted and frowned at him.

"No. I sleep at the barn sometimes."

Then he was gone.

"Sometimes," Rafe repeated. "Well, that's progress. I knew the minute that was out of my mouth that I shouldn't have mentioned sharing beds with horses."

Madeleine laughed.

"The real progress is that you can joke about it," she said, teasing him. "I don't know if you realize it, but there for a while you were really touchy on the subject, Rafe."

Rafe pretended to scowl.

"You imagined that," he said, and made her laugh again.

"Mr. Aigner, where d'ye want this here chiffarobe?"

Rafe turned and made an expansive gesture toward Madeleine.

"You'll have to ask the lady," he said. "I'm in charge of the stove pipe."

Madeleine looked at the oak chest of drawers balanced between the two teamsters. The golden wood was gorgeous, and even with it slanted sideways, she could see that the large piece of furniture was exactly like this house—beautifully plain and built to last.

"In the big bedroom," she said. "This way."

It seemed that the whole crew came in to help unload the wagons, and they kept Madeleine so busy deciding which room would be right for each piece, and then charming them into moving things when she changed her mind about the exact location of the chests and beds and even a china cabinet, that soon it seemed to her that Rafe had bought enough furniture for two houses. But when the teamsters had declared the wagons empty and had driven off toward town, while Rafe and Juanito were out at the horse corral, seeing to a cow pony that had come up lame, she walked slowly through the rooms and realized that there were still several other items needed to make her vision of the home at Los Tres Amigos come to life.

More comfortable seating for the sitting room, for one thing. Did Rafe think that he was the only person who'd ever want to sit in there?

She shook her head in wry amusement while she walked through the room again, loving the way the sunlight slanted through the windows. Instead of stopping in the kitchen to get on with unpacking all the boxes and barrels of supplies, she drifted out onto the back porch and just stood for a moment, taking in the beauty of the hills behind the house and the inviting, tree-dotted stretch of lane that led to the road. This was a beautiful place, and now it was coming to life with men and horses working the bawling cattle.

And with her making a home out of the house. Quick tears stung her eyes and she turned to busy herself—to arrange the bucket for drinking water, a dipper, and a wash pan on the rough porch table that obviously had been there as long as the house had stood. These would mostly be for Rafe and Juanito. The cowboys wouldn't be coming into the house to eat.

In fact, Juanito and Rafe might be eating at the cookfire with them most of the time. When they did use this kitchen, who would be cooking for them?

Suddenly, a wish squeezed her heart like an

importunate hand. *She* wanted to cook for them. *She* wanted to be with them every single time they came to the ranch.

Surely she wasn't, absolutely she wasn't falling in love with Rafe again. Surely not.

To banish the thought, she ran down the steps, around the house, and began picking the roses that were the farthest gone in bloom. She'd float them in water in the middle of the table to enjoy while she got into the wooden boxes and crates of kitchen things and put them all in their places.

Rafe had dashed up the back porch steps, knocked the dust off his clothes with his hat, bent over the wash basin, splashed water on his face, and destroyed the stack of neatly folded towels beside the porch railing before he realized that he was hurrying to have a little bit of time alone with Madeleine. He stared off into the distance while he dried his face and smoothed his hair.

Well, that didn't necessarily mean anything. It wasn't that he'd bought his household goods to try to please her, or anything like that, although he thought he'd done a pretty good job of it for his first time ever. It was just that Madeleine had always possessed exceptionally good taste, so it was only natural that he'd be interested in her opinion of his choices.

He trying to create a home for Juanito. This had nothing to do with him and Madeleine.

"Maddie?" he said, as he opened the screen door into the kitchen.

"In here."

He stopped short just inside the kitchen.

The place looked entirely different. There was no separate dining room in the small house, yet now there seemed to be—the west end of the long kitchen held the plain chairs and rectangular oak table he'd bought. In its center sat a crockery bowl filled with roses.

He took in their fragrance on a deep, involuntary breath, then walked slowly around the boxes and crates and into the sitting room. Madeleine was there, busily moving one end, then the other, of the spindle-backed deacon's bench across the floor.

"Call one of the men to help you with that," he said sharply, crossing the room in three strides. "What are you *doing*, Maddie?"

"Rearranging the chairs . . ."

She straightened up and looked at him, amusement in her eyes.

". . . What few we have here. Rafe, do you realize that you only bought one comfortable chair? Are you not expecting company ever to sit with you—maybe in the winter, at the fire?"

Taken aback, he stared around the room.

"There are the rockers," he said defensively.

She had placed them on the opposite side of the hearth from his chair.

"Yes. They're comfortable enough. This bench

isn't, but it'll have to do for now. The wing-backed armchair—which I assume you bought for yourself—is the only upholstered piece here."

He recovered.

"Flynn had more. I'll send a wagon to town."

"*Papá, mi Lena!*"

The sound of the back screen door closing muffled Juanito's next words. A scuffing noise followed. As Rafe and Madeleine started for the kitchen, Juanito appeared in the doorway, half carrying, half dragging the silver-trimmed saddle that had once belonged to Sutton Calhoun.

"Son! That belongs in the barn . . ."

Juanito stopped, stepped on the faded buffalo-striped horse blanket trailing along the floor, and nearly dropped it all.

"But *Papá*," he said, his huge eyes seeking Rafe's, "I take it to my room where I have my bed."

"Saddles and horse blankets belong in the tack room," Rafe said. "In the barn."

Juanito didn't exactly defy him but he didn't move toward the barn, either. They stood there, eyes locked.

"When you go to the barn, tell Clayton that I need to send a man to town with the wagon."

Nothing.

To gain more time, he tried to think of something else to say.

"And be sure to watch out for snakes, like

Clayton warned us. He said they're really bad this year."

Still no movement and no answer.

His anger started to rise.

"Juan Rafael . . ."

Madeleine touched his arm. He hadn't even known when she crossed the room.

"It's his first room of his own," she murmured. "He wants all his treasures in it."

The strangest mix of feelings ran through Rafe: gratitude for her wisdom, anger at himself, and irritation toward Juanito, who had not only interrupted his time with Madeleine but had brought such a problem in the first place. Also intense aggravation that he'd not been as clever as he'd thought about furnishing the house, much less about learning to be a father.

He cleared his throat, wishing he could clear his mind as easily.

"All right," he said, "how about a deal? Take your saddle to your room, and then put this smelly old blanket in the barn and give my message to Clayton."

He was rewarded with a look of pure delight from Juanito and another from Madeleine.

"It's a deal, *Papá*!"

They managed to shake on it without Juanito's dropping the saddle entirely.

"Need some help?"

"No, *gracias, Papá*. I can do it."

The child let the blanket fall and took the saddle toward his room.

"Good job, *Papá*," Madeleine said softly.

"Thanks to you."

"I was thinking about the stinky saddle blanket in the house, too, so I'm grateful for your quickness."

Suddenly he felt better. Much better.

Juanito ran back through and scooped up the blanket.

"Tell Clayton I need somebody to go and come back before dark," Rafe said.

Juanito lifted a hand to show that he'd heard and never slowed down. He was out the back door in a heartbeat.

"Now," he said expansively, turning to Madeleine. "Is there anything else we need besides more comfortable furniture for the softies among us?"

She gave him that blinding, blazing smile that turned his knees to water.

"Dish towels," she said. "I haven't been able to find a single one in those boxes. Lemon oil to make this beautiful furniture shine. Oil for the lamps because, most likely, the sun will go down sometime this evening."

He held her gaze and smiled right back at her. *This beautiful furniture.*

"We'll make a list," he said. "I know I bought some paper."

* * *

That evening, despite the heat, he built a small fire in the hearth.

"Madeleine! Juanito! Come in here for a little while."

They came out of Juanito's room, laughing together about something.

"What's so funny?"

"The footboard of the bed makes a perfect saddle rack," she said. "Isn't it amazing how useful furniture can be?"

"It is," he said, settling into his chair and lighting a cheroot. "Why don't you all try these other chairs and see if they're useful, too?"

Madeleine took the wing chair that matched his and Juanito stretched out prone on the matching sofa. He fanned his face with his hand and grinned at Rafe.

"It is cold?" he said.

"I only wanted to see if the chimney would draw," Rafe said.

"Oh," Madeleine said solemnly, "I was wondering."

"The windows are open," Rafe said, just as seriously.

"*Muchas gracias,*" Juanito said gravely.

They all looked at each other and then burst out laughing at their mutual silliness.

Rafe puffed on his cheroot and wondered what was happening to him. He didn't feel like his usual self at all. He felt absolutely no desire to be anyplace on the face of the earth except exactly where he was sitting in his new easy chair in front of the unnecessary fire that burned in his new hearth.

Like a far too complacent man.

That feeling stayed with him almost all the next day. Juanito had slept late in his new bed, and Madeleine had done the same in Rafe's. Rafe, in his sleeping bag on the sitting room floor, had waked with the dawn and had gone out into the relatively cool early-morning air to walk over his place and get acquainted with how it looked at that time of day.

He also wanted time alone to savor this miraculous slice of time when both the people he loved most were safe under his roof. For he did love Madeleine, as a friend.

Well, he was attracted to her as a man, too, of course, but what male wouldn't be? He *did* frequently look at her luscious mouth and want to kiss her; the slightest brush of her hand against his or even a whiff of her scent *did* arouse him; but they could never have things back the way they used to be.

That was what he must remember. This was ten years later. Madeleine Cottrell was Madeleine Calhoun now and she had changed a great deal.

As had he. When they had loved each other

so—or thought they did—they had hardly been more than children. Life had proved that.

The breeze blew from the south, though, and a rooster crowed from somewhere across the hills, and the sunrise broke crimson and golden across the sky. Now was the only time a person ever had, and he'd learned long ago how foolish it was to mourn the past or plan the future. Now was glorious, and before the heat took the day, Madeleine should come out and touch the morning.

He turned and trotted toward the house, slowing only to scoop up a some gravel in his hand. Better not to go in and wake her—the sight of her sleeping with her mass of black hair framing her flawless face on the pillow and maybe the bedclothes in disarray, maybe leaving a leg bare, or . . .

Rafe forced his mind away from the images it was creating and threw the gravel at the window screen of his bedroom, which was above his head since it was on the downhill side of the house.

"Maddie," he called softly, approaching slowly to stand under the window, just as he used to do beneath her second-story bedroom when she was seventeen. "Maddie, are you there?"

A moment later her tousled head appeared.

"Rafe?"

Her incredulous tone made him smile.

Then she laughed that throaty, lazy chuckle of hers that never failed to make his blood run hot.

"Rafe," she drawled, sleepily pushing her hair out of her eyes, "do you have any idea how old we are now? You needn't worry about waking up my daddy."

"I'm trying not to wake Juanito," he said, in a loud stage whisper. "He's worse than your daddy about keeping an eye on us."

She laughed again.

"Come on out, Maddie," he called softly. "Come see the sunrise. It'll soon be gone."

"Wait until I get my shoes," she said. "There are too many sticker burrs out there."

"Be quiet, very quiet."

One more tantalizing chuckle and then she was gone. Rafe stuck his hands in his pockets and strolled to the big cottonwood tree in the front yard to wait.

He grinned to himself. Madeleine had changed in many ways, but not in her thirst for adventure. Never, whether it'd been midnight or sunup, had she refused one of his nocturnal summons.

He'd take her down to the pond in his pasture across the road, he decided. It was the only pretty body of water left in the country during this dry weather, since it was fed by an underground spring. They could sit on the bank and talk for a while before Juanito got up to start his usual whirlwind day.

At last, he heard her light footsteps cross the gallery and he turned to see her running down the sloping front yard.

"Rafe Aigner, you'd better have a great excursion planned if you're getting me up this early," she called. "I could barely open my eyes enough to find my clothes."

"You didn't have to get dressed," he said, as he went to meet her. "In fact, I prefer your peach silk wrapper."

"The last time I stepped out of the house in it you kissed me senseless," she said saucily. "I couldn't take that chance."

"Just because you're wearing a dress and you're not barefoot doesn't mean I won't do it again."

She held out her hand to him and he took it.

"That's why I'm keeping you at arm's length, *monsieur*," she said. "I don't trust you for a minute."

"Well, then, trust me to show you the dawn," he said. "I'm taking you to the shores of a romantic lake where you can see the sun come up in the sky and the water at the same time."

She smiled as they strolled across the road.

"You sound like a Texan for sure," she said. "In Louisiana, that's not a lake, it's a puddle."

"You have to admit it's a Texas-sized sunrise,

though," he said, letting himself take one deep, long look into her blue, blue eyes.

"I do admit that much," she said, looking back at him so long that they almost walked into the fence and missed the gate completely.

"I may not know a lake from a puddle, but I do know when the sun comes up," he said, teasing her with his voice and his smile.

"I wish we'd brought our fishing poles," Maddie said mischievously. "Then we'd have an excuse to stay out here at your puddle all morning and Juanito could cook our breakfast."

"We'll cut some poles when we get there," he said, "and when Juanito comes out to see our catch, we'll send him back to the kitchen. I want to see if he's learned anything from seeing you make pancakes for him by the dozens."

"Oh, Rafe, no," she said, laughing. "I don't want to clean up the kitchen after that child tries pancakes."

Rafe was looking into her eyes again, watching their color change from almost-purple to bluebonnet blue, when the whir-r-ring rattle erupted right at their feet. Or was it echoing off the scattered rocks?

His heart froze but his eyes moved and he saw it instantly, tan and white among the tan and white rocks.

"A rattlesnake! Watch out!"

But she'd already taken that next step and her

skirts swirled over the snake. In a blur of motion and terrifying sound, Rafe grabbed her by the waist and pulled her to him, trying to jerk her away from the danger. Too late.

Maddie screamed.

"It bit me! Rafe!"

He swept her off her feet and crushed her to his thundering heart. His blood pounded in his head, in his legs, and roared in his ears as he held Maddie off the ground and bent to look for the snake. Instinctively he stomped at the snake's head with his boot before it could coil again, and by pure luck—or pure desperation—he hit it dead-on the first try.

"No!" she cried. "Rafe, it'll bite you, too—"

"Quiet!" he roared, taken suddenly by such terror for her that it threatened to unman him completely.

He was was already turning, striding toward the big live oak beside the gate, his mind racing, trying to think what to do first. He had to stop the poison as much as he could.

Now. He couldn't even take time to get to the house.

Silently, he cursed. There he'd been, right beside her, close enough to touch, and he had let her walk into disaster! He hadn't been watching their path or the ground around them; he had forgotten snakes existed until he'd heard the rattle, in spite of what he'd told Juanito, in spite of

Clayton's warning. What an idiot he was—calling her out of her bed to take her on a walk to get snakebit!

"Where did it hit you?"

"M-my leg," she whispered.

Her face had gone chalky white, her eyes wide with fear.

He kicked through the grass growing beneath the big tree and knelt. His breath didn't want to come and his insides had gone cold and still. He made his arms move—he had to let her go if he wanted to help her.

"No varmints here," he said, forcing steadiness into his voice. "I'm going to set you down, Maddie. Do not move. *Do not move.*"

He was talking to himself as much as to her. It seemed he was moving slowly as molasses, it seemed an hour had flown by already. The poison would be surging through her veins.

She made a motion as if to cling to him.

"No. The less your muscles constrict, the less the poison spreads. My Choctaw grandfather always told me that."

She stilled.

He put her down carefully, then he pulled up her skirt. On her ankle, two red fang marks had made a glancing blow. Not too deep, but they'd drawn blood and that was all that mattered.

"You need a tourniquet."

He pulled a silk glad rag out of his pocket,

folded it in half and rolled it quickly, whipped it around her lower thigh, and tied it tight.

She was precious beyond belief and he might be losing her.

He reached for his small pocket knife and flicked it open with one hand. "I'm going to cut the wound now and suck out what venom I can."

He swiftly drew the blade across her creamy skin. Once. Twice, to make a cross.

He watched the crimson blood well up against the whiteness of her skin and prayed that the snake's glancing blow had delivered very little venom. Then he bent to the wound, drew her blood into his mouth and spat it out.

As he repeated the actions a few more times, Maddie sat still and quiet. She didn't even lift her arms to put them around his neck when he picked her up.

He held her, hard against his heart, and began to run.

Chapter 13

"**J**uanito!" Rafe bellowed, as they crossed the front yard. "Son! Wake up and come help me."

Juan Rafael appeared on the gallery, obviously already awake. He let the screen door swing shut behind him and stared at them, horrified.

Then he was running down the steps and Rafe's heart was breaking yet again, which he would've sworn to be utterly impossible. The boy's eyes, huge with fear, were filling with tears.

"*Mi Lena*, what is wrong? What has happened to you?"

Rafe allowed himself one look at her face and saw tears there, too.

247

"A rattlesnake bit her," he said. "She mustn't move, son, don't touch her."

He ran past Juanito and up the steps.

Juanito followed, a catch in his voice when he spoke.

"*Papá*, what can we do? You call me to help you. What to do?"

Rafe looked down at him.

"First get some boots on," he said. "And your leather gloves."

Juanito ran through the door ahead of them, crossed the sitting room, and flew into his bedroom. Rafe strode toward the bigger bedroom.

He thought his heart would come out of his chest as he laid Madeleine down. She was very pale, she was sweating, her eyes were huge, and her gaze rested on his so trustingly that another frisson of fear went through him. She believed he could save her life. He was her only hope.

Dear God.

"Rafe," she said haltingly, "I feel sick."

A cold hand clutched his stomach.

"He only got you with a glancing blow," he said, with much more cheerfulness than he felt. "Hang your leg off the bed, don't move it, and let me release your tourniquet."

Rafe untied the knot, let the blood flow briefly, then began to tighten it again. Juanito ran out of his room and into Rafe's. He stared at Madeleine, then tore his gaze away and fixed it on Rafe.

"The snake poison is making her sick," he

said, barely able to speak past the cracking of his voice. "*Papá*, can I talk to her? Is *mi Lena* going to die, *Papá*?"

"No, sugar, I'm not going to die," Maddie said softly. "Don't worry, Juanito."

The child broke into heartrending sobs, tears running down his cheeks unchecked. He couldn't even move, apparently. A galling helplessness filled Rafe's throat, which already felt too tight for words to escape it.

This responsibility was overwhelming—both Maddie and Juanito were helplessly looking to him. How could he know what to do?

Juanito turned desperately toward Maddie and started to approach her bed. His weeping was growing wilder. Any minute now, he could become hysterical.

"It's all right, sweetie," Maddie said. Heavier sweat was breaking out on her brow, though her face filled with worry for Juanito. "Don't cry so. Don't worry."

Rafe set his jaw. Maddie couldn't help him with the boy now, and any agitation would make her pulse beat faster and the poison spread more. He shouldn't have let the child come in here in the first place.

"Son."

Rafe grasped Juan Rafael by the shoulders and turned him around.

The child's whole body began to shake and he covered his face with his gloved hands.

"Juan Rafael," Rafe said, "I know you're tough. You're tough enough to stop your tears and help me now, aren't you? You have to help me help Lena. Will you do that?"

Juanito nodded vigorously, still sobbing, and dropped his hands so that his teary eyes could meet Rafe's.

Rafe tightened his grip and held the child up straighter until he felt the slender little body take its own weight.

"You know jimson weed, don't you? Stinkweed? The one Clayton showed us that will poison the horses and cattle?"

Juanito nodded again and wiped at his tears with the back of his hand.

"It's medicine for snake poison. Take a pan from the kitchen and go fill it with leaves from the jimson weed plants with the biggest flowers," Rafe said. "Watch out for snakes."

He dropped his hands and Juanito was off, running out the open door with a backward glance to see his Lena one more time. His bootheels drummed on the wooden floor of the sitting room and then the screened door slammed.

Rafe glanced at Maddie's face and his heart sank all over again. She looked half-dead. No wonder Juanito had run as if his feet had wings.

Tears sprang to his own eyes. Juanito loved Maddie so much, as much as if she were the birth mother he had never known. What had he done, bringing these two together with less thought than he'd give to a poker hand? Juanito was too young to learn that loving someone could break your heart.

"Relax as much as you can, Maddie," he murmured. "Keep your breathing slow and shallow, and keep your leg still."

She gave him a weak smile. Her lips were nearly as pale as her face.

"I hope he'll be all right . . ."

The love between them went both ways. Maddie was in for a broken heart, too, whenever the time came for him and Juanito to move on.

If Maddie didn't leave them today. Forever.

The thought pierced the wall he'd thrown up around his heart the minute she was bitten.

"He'll be careful," he said flatly. "He's determined to bring the medicine back to you, so he'll keep a sharp eye out."

He tore his gaze from hers before she could see his concern and strode to the washstand in the corner.

"Let me get a cool cloth for your face," he said, "and then I'll go find the mortar and pestle. It'll only take Juanito a minute, because that weed's all over the south pasture."

"Do I have to drink a tea of it?"

Her petulant tone made him laugh.

"No whining, now. You sound like a little kid dreading her medicine," he said, wringing out the washcloth.

She laughed, too. His heart lifted a little.

"I never whine," she said, trying to return the teasing with a tone of mock righteousness. "I'm just thinking I've had enough poison for one day."

He went to her bedside and, careful of her leg, bent to sponge her face and hands.

"That's right," he said, "so I'll make you a poultice instead of a tea. Now, don't talk anymore."

He folded the cloth and laid it across her forehead, and could hardly take his hand away. A terrible longing filled him, a fierce need to hold her, to kiss some color into her pale lips and more strength into her body.

He looked deep into her eyes.

"I'll be right back," he said. "Don't move."

"In the pie safe," she said, so low he could barely hear her. "The mortar and . . ."

"I'll find it," he said. "Maddie, stop talking. And don't worry—that'll make your heart beat faster."

The rest of that horrible day went by in a blur to him. Maddie passed out during those few seconds he was gone, and he had to fight panic every minute, every hour after that. He loosened and tightened the tourniquet, crushed the jimson weed leaves, bound poultices to her wound, and tried to comfort Juanito while panicky thoughts ran in his head. They turned his heart to ice and his hands to ineffectual stumps. They threatened to obsess him so that he couldn't think what to do to calm his son.

Finally, he sent Juanito to a neighboring ranch where Cookie said they could buy chickens and eggs and milk to make soup and custards for Maddie when she got better. Thinking of the evil anonymous letter, Rafe sent Cookie along, too.

Waiting for them to return, waiting for Maddie to come to herself, waiting for time to loosen the tourniquet and change the poultice—waiting was all that gave shape to the hours as they dragged by. Finally, at dusk, with Juanito helping Cookie at the bunkhouse and the cowboys at the barn, the only thing he was still waiting for was Maddie's return to consciousness.

Scared to his very bones, he paced back and forth from her bedside to the sitting room windows where he could look out at the sunset and, if he turned, still see her bed. Her skin was growing hotter with fever. Soon he'd have to bathe her all over, if the blackberry leaf tea that he'd forced between her lips didn't bring it down.

The sky flamed red with a sundown that reflected in the window glass like living fire. He couldn't bear to look at it.

And he couldn't bear to return to Maddie, lying white as death on his bed. He dropped into the easy chair where he'd sat in such unbelievable contentment less than twenty-four hours before.

With Maddie and Juanito around him. With a

warm glow in the grate that had made this place seem a home.

Now the fireplace held only black ashes, and the house felt empty as the prairie in winter.

"Juanito!"

He started to his feet. Maddie's voice!

"Juanito, come out of there, that horse kicks like a mule!"

Delirium. He needed to get back in there and fight the fever.

For one long heartbeat, though, he stood still, waiting . . . surprised at his own hope that once, just once, she would call, *"Rafe."*

"Rafe?"

Madeleine's mouth felt too stiff to form a word, but she said it again.

"Rafe!"

She just knew those were his hands that had been touching her, cooling her skin.

"I'm here, Maddie, right here."

He sounded happy. She opened her eyes and saw that he was smiling as he bent over her. The breeze was blowing in through the window and it ruffled his hair.

"I love the way your hair curls down on your forehead," she said.

Her voice sounded so faint she could hardly hear it herself.

He laughed. She could see the amber light in his eyes by the glow from the lamp on the table.

"Why are you so happy?"

"Because you're too strong for a rattlesnake to kill."

It all came flooding back to her then, and she struggled to sit up.

"Here, now, whoa," Rafe said. "Not so fast. You've had a high fever and you're bound to be weak."

"My sheets are damp," she said, as he placed a pillow behind her and helped raise her head.

"I've been bathing you all night."

She glanced down, realizing that she wore nothing but her thin cotton shift, the pale blue dimity one.

"Who undressed me?"

"I did," he drawled, "and I would've taken advantage of you if you hadn't been out of your head."

Boldly he looked into her eyes, teasing her, yet searching, too, to know how she truly fared. He sat down on the side of her bed and brushed her hair back from her face.

"Always the gentleman," she teased in return. Surprised at how hard it was to speak above a whisper, she went on, "Southern gentleman. That's what I've always heard about Rafe Aigner . . ."

She tried to give him her most wicked smile, but she barely had the strength.

". . . That is, when people aren't telling me what a renegade you are."

Though he smiled back at her, his eyes showed worry, too. He scooped her up into his arms, threw the quilt from the foot of the bed over his shoulders and her, and stood up.

"I don't want you to get chilled," he said, "but Dr. Aigner believes you need some fresh air."

She let him cuddle her against his broad chest as he would a child, and she leaned into it, helpless not to because it felt so solid and safe. And so sensual she could swoon. Pathetically weak as she was, a flame of desire kindled deep inside her.

"I'm sorry I missed being there for the bathing," she whispered, as he carried her through the dark sitting room to the front door.

Shameless. One snake bite had made her completely shameless—and reckless, besides. Anything more than a kiss with him would destroy her forever.

"So am I," he whispered back. "It would've been a lot more interesting if you had participated."

He carried her out into the early morning, where the air felt fresh and a little bit cool on her face. She snuggled closer to him, fitted her cheek into the hollow of his shoulder and her palm against his chest. Rafe wrapped his arms more tightly around her.

The old porch swing hanging across the corner moved gently back and forth as he sat down and held her in his lap.

"It's a good thing you're holding me," she murmured. "I don't think I have the strength to sit up on my own."

"You'll be back to normal in a day or two," he said. "I won't keep you out here long, but you need to see the sunrise, Maddie."

"Since I lived through the night?" she said lightly.

"Yes."

The simple word, flatly spoken, hung in the air between them like a blessing. Like a thanksgiving. Maddie tried to imagine the hours just past, the hours she couldn't remember.

"You took off my tourniquet?"

"When the poultices began to work."

"That's what's on my ankle?"

"Right. I'll make a new one soon."

"I'll help you," she said.

He laughed. "You'll be lucky to sit up in bed later today."

"I'm tougher than you think," she said, but she hardly had the energy to get the words out.

"I know you can do anything," he said wryly. "But your fever didn't break until about an hour ago. I thought you could cool off out here and then go back to bed."

She was too weak to hold up her head and too weak to hold her tongue.

"How can I ever cool off sitting in your lap?" she said, and turned her face up to his, her cheek moving against his chest in a slow caress.

He bent his head and kissed her, a sweet, short kiss so heartfelt that it brought tears to her eyes.

"Just you wait until you're well," he whispered. "I'm claiming more and longer kisses then."

"I'd never be well if it weren't for you," she whispered in return. "Rafe, you saved my life."

"And now it belongs to me," he said, teasing her. "You'll have to serve me and do everything I say."

"That's nothing new. You already own my home and my business, where I'm working for you every day and raising your child besides."

"Always the writer," he said. "Always exaggerating. Maddie, I can't believe a word you say. I've got to watch you every minute."

Suddenly he grew still and quiet. He swung them back and forth before he spoke again.

"But I was too late. I'm so sorry I wasn't watching more closely when you stepped on the snake."

She used the last of her strength to raise her head and look up at him.

"Rafe, please. Don't think you're responsible for that. I'm a grown woman who can watch her own path. I'm the one who should've been watching where I stepped."

He looked into her eyes for a long minute, then shook his head and smiled before he dropped a kiss onto the top of her head. She let the weakness take her and her body melted against his.

All her strength was gone, she could not move or talk, sleep was about to take her, yet she was filled with the delicious contentment of a child burrowing beneath a fantasy tent made of a blanket and two chairs in her own safe room. Cozy in Rafe's arms, wrapped with him in the soft quilt and the new morning, all she wanted at that moment was never to leave his arms, never to leave this very spot where they sat waiting for the golden dawn light to reach them.

Madeleine awoke to the smell of something burning, a feeling of terrible thirst, and the sound of Rafe and Juanito arguing.

"Ask Cookie, *Papá*," Juanito said. "The chicken soup, it does not have milk."

"It would make it richer."

"*Mi abuela* not put in milk, no. Use *agua* and *chiles* instead."

"Maybe that was because she didn't have any milk. Maddie's been sick and *chiles* would be too much . . ."

"The tortillas!" Juanito shrieked. "Fire!"

"No," Rafe thundered, "stay back! Let me do it."

Bootheels clattered on the floor, water poured, a pot or pan clanged against another and water splashed.

"It go in the stove!" Juanito wailed. "The fire will go out! The soup *por mi Lena!*"

"It'd be worse if the house burned down around her ears," Rafe growled. "Didn't I tell you to watch those tortillas?"

"*Sí,* but the soup . . ."

Madeleine took in a deep breath, gathered all her strength and called, "Rafe! Juanito! Help me!"

At first she thought they didn't hear, but a moment of shocked silence fell. Then Juanito came bursting into her room with Rafe close behind.

"*Mi Lena!* You sleep all the day!"

"Maddie! How do you feel?"

A staggering joy flashed through her at the sight of them together.

"Thirsty," she said, her voice rasping in her dry throat.

Both of them spun on their heels and rushed back toward the kitchen, bumping into each other in the doorway.

"Cool water," Juanito said.

"Don't take time to go to the well," Rafe said. "Here, this is cool enough."

In a heartbeat they were back at her bedside, Juanito bearing an overflowing tin cup full of water. He used both hands to give it to her, spilling some on the sheet. Shakily, she took it and drank.

"We're making chicken soup, too," Rafe said, as eagerly as if he were the same age as Juanito.

"The chicken is cooked but we don't know what else to add."

Madeleine drank some more water to hide the smile creeping onto her face.

"*Papá* want to put milk," Juanito said, then tactfully waited.

Rafe waited, too, his expression as intent and hopeful as his son's. They might as well be two little boys desperate for the resolution of a dispute, and she couldn't bear to disappoint either of them.

To gain time, she handed her empty cup back to Juanito.

"Thank you, Juanito," she said. "I was so thirsty I could barely call out for water."

"Well?" Rafe demanded. "I clearly recall that Lulie made a thick chicken soup with milk and cheese. Isn't that right?"

He was so earnest about it that Madeleine could hardly keep a straight face.

"That's one way to make it," she said slowly, "but my stomach might be better off right now with a very plain, light broth."

Juanito and Rafe looked at each other, both victorious.

"No milk," Juanito said.

"No chiles," Rafe said, "and we don't have cheese, anyway."

"Anything to get some food in her," they said, speaking at the same time.

Madeleine smiled. For Juanito to pick it up,

Rafe must've said that phrase a dozen times while they were cooking.

"Maybe I could come into the kitchen," she suggested, "and have my soup in there."

Rafe frowned doubtfully but she added, "I'd really like to get out of this bed for a while."

Both males went into immediate action. They brought her water to wash her face, and a fresh shift and a wrapper, then moved an armchair and a footstool into the kitchen, and, when she was ready, Rafe carried her to it. It thrilled her to realize that although she was still weak, the long sleep had given her a lot of strength.

"I can sit alone and feed myself," she said, once they'd settled her in the chair and propped up her foot with a fresh poultice bound to it.

"So that must mean that you're a *big* baby, at least a year old," Rafe teased her.

"I have more years than you, *mi Lena*," Juanito said, entering into the joking as he took another tin cup from the pie safe, "so you must do as I say."

"And what do you say, *mi Juanito?*"

"Eat all your soup and tortillas," he said firmly, as he went to the stove and ladled some of the chicken and broth into the mug while Rafe stood near him unobtrusively watching, "so you'll grow big and strong."

The three of them laughed together and the room filled with a sweet warmth. Madeleine savored the sensation as she began to eat her soup.

At that moment she didn't have enough strength to banish the errant thought that this felt more like home than anyplace she'd been since New Orleans.

After Juanito and Rafael had cleaned up the mess they'd made putting out the flames of the burning tortilla, they ate, too, and washed the dishes. Madeleine leaned back and watched them, enjoying the easy rapport between father and son. She had helped bring about some of that, and that gave her a great deal of satisfaction.

It would be disastrous falling in love with Rafe again, but she really didn't think that she was. The time would come when she'd have to part from both of them, and when it did, she could remember this moment and the difference she'd made in their lives. That would help her through it.

Yes, that was the way she'd look at this whole situation from now on. She'd concentrate on the relationship between the two of them, and build a little wall around her own heart to protect it. Hadn't loving Rafe nearly killed her the first time? She would be very careful to preserve a little distance between them.

When the chores were done, Juanito left them to go see *la baya*.

"Do you feel strong enough to sit in the swing again?" Rafe said.

Madeleine's pulse quickened.

"Yes."

She meant to add that she could sit beside him in the swing this time. She should say that they mustn't kiss again or touch at all. Honestly, she should tell him that she thought she was able to walk, that he needn't carry her to the porch.

But she couldn't get another word out of her mouth because her heart had leapt into her throat.

He was standing over her, ready to pick her up again. He swept her up into the incredible strength of his arms, and strode through the sitting room, and out the front door.

His chambray shirt, wet from Juanito's enthusiastic help with the dishwashing chores, soaked through her thin garments in an instant. The heat of his skin clung to hers, the feel of it so intimate that it was more than a caress. Fast as lightning they melded.

This time, it was darkness that enveloped them instead of the quilt, and the air was still full of the heat of the day. That must be the reason she hardly could breathe.

Rafe sat down in the swing, but he gave no indication that he intended to let her out of his arms.

Put me down, Rafe. I need to sit away from you a little.

Her treacherous mouth and hands moved without her direction.

"I think you got more dishwater on your shirt than Juanito did," she said.

Her fingers went to the top button of his chambray shirt, just above the middle of his powerful chest. It slipped from its buttonhole.

Rafe pretended not to notice.

"That child is wild with water," he said. "I didn't expect to survive cleaning the tortilla mess off the floor, either."

Her hands slipped down to the next button. It gave way.

"You know," she said, "this shirt is soaking the only fresh wrapper I have with me."

"You know," he said, "I think you should finish what you're doing there and then I'll take it off."

She pushed it back off his shoulders and off down his arms.

"Rafe . . ." she said.

But he kissed her then, crushed her mouth with his and kissed away the rest of her words, so that in an instant she'd forgotten what they had ever been. He traced the seam of her lips with the tip of his tongue and then thrust it inside her mouth to lay claim to every bit of it.

She ran her hands over the smooth, hard muscles of his chest and his shoulders and his arms, she felt their shapes with her fingers and traced their power with her palms. He cupped her breast in his hand and cradled it, kneading its hard tip with his thumb.

Madeleine curled one arm around his neck and kissed him back. The hard shaft of his manhood thrust against her thigh, and heat crackled through her blood like a wildfire.

They could make love just this one time. She had almost died, hadn't she? They could be separated at any second, forever. One time, and she could live on that memory for the rest of her life.

She was a strong woman now. She could make love with Rafe one time and not fall in love with him again.

Dimly, somewhere at a great distance, a screened door slammed. She couldn't take her mouth from Rafe's, she couldn't bear to let him take his hand from her breast—but that noise had been the back door.

Juanito! She could hear him now, running through the house.

They pulled apart as the front door squeaked on its hinges.

Maddie felt bereft beyond belief. And scared.

Because at that moment, she knew that it wasn't the kitchen or the sitting room or this swing where she was really at home.

It was in Rafe's arms.

Chapter 14

Madeleine picked up her pen and put it down again. She shuffled the pages of the article she'd written about Marlyse Borden, the singer who was presently performing at Big Jim Thompson's Golden King. And then, since she couldn't even read this morning, much less write, she replaced them carefully on the corner of her big desk—underneath the pretty rock Juanito had found in the garden for her.

She smiled. That child was a wonder and there was no other word for him.

But thinking about him and his father was the major reason she couldn't work. She stood up and paced to the window; paced back again.

A year or two. Only for a year or two.

What would she do then?

She set her jaw and paced to the window again. What she would do *now* was the more urgent question.

The answer was work. Work had saved her before and it could save her again.

But she stared out the window and didn't see a thing, her mind was so full of Rafe and Juanito.

Every nerve in her skin prickling, she turned and marched to her desk.

Dear Lord, she had to work. Sutton had left her homeless and nearly penniless and Rafe had given her a chance to get it back, and here she was, about to lose it all again.

Just as she was losing Rafe again.

That thought made her clench her jaw to keep back the tears. It actually made her heart hurt.

Why couldn't she keep from wanting him? She used to believe she had gotten over him completely, so why couldn't she have gone on that way, instead of worrying that she'd never stopped loving him in all these years?

That was probably a totally wrong conclusion. She was imagining some kind of wonderful fantasy about the past because seeing Rafe alive again had been such a shock. That horrid anti-Mexican letter threatening Juanito had been another shock.

Unable to make herself sit down, she turned on her heel and paced to the window again. But her heart lifted a little with this new theory.

Yes, it was *Juanito* she loved, not Rafe. Which was a relief because, sure as the sun had come up that morning, Rafe did not love her.

In spite of kissing her so passionately that it had set her blood on fire that first time standing on the porch, a moment later he had stood right there touching her, actually *touching* her, and talked without turning a hair about leaving San Antonio a year from now.

Rafe could not love her and kiss her that way and the next instant show no emotion in saying that to her. He had truly grown hard and heartless if he'd had no reaction at all to that wild kiss.

Yet then—and later, in the swing in the dark—he'd certainly held her and kissed her as if he felt as much passion as she did.

Maybe, in ten years of playing poker, he'd just learned to hide his feelings even better than she'd thought. Or his feelings had been so false he'd turned them off in an instant.

How could she have tied herself to him for three years? She should've mopped floors first, or tried writing dime novels for a living.

She paced to the window again and stood looking out, not seeing a single thing except Rafe's beautiful chiseled profile as he'd stood beside her watching those wagons bring furniture and food and sheets and towels and dishes to his house. *His* house.

Oh, how much easier it would be if she'd never kissed him at all! It was the irony of her life—she'd been trying to comfort him that first time. But she'd kissed him again, and plunged herself into misery.

The well-remembered taste of his lips, that sweet, cedary flavor that tied her to the earth somehow, that was what had done her in. That was what had made her keep on kissing him instead of moving away.

She must be on her guard against such foolish behavior on the trip to Bandera tomorrow.

She could get through the next three days without doing anything personal with Rafe; she could even keep their conversations impersonal. The only reason she was going with them to the trailhead was for Juanito's safety, in case there was any reason Rafe might have to be away from him.

Of course, she did have a second reason for going to Bandera: her work. She would write an article—assuming she could keep her mind on the words—describing the excitement of beginning a long, dangerous trail drive that would stretch from South Texas all the way to Kansas.

At the window again, her eyes suddenly focused on something familiar. She looked again and had to smile.

Sophie, dressed to the nines, and wearing a hat Madeleine didn't remember having seen before, was hurrying across the street toward the *Star* with an air of important purpose. Thank goodness. Sophie could get her out of this slough of obsession and back on track—she'd never had a problem that Sophie couldn't put directly into a clear perspective.

It'd be irritating, of course, to have to admit that Sophie had been right to sense something in the air between her and Rafe, but when she explained there would never be anything to come of it, that'd stop Sophie's meddling once and for all. But she wouldn't tell her about the kisses. She wanted to keep those memories to herself.

She gasped and clapped her hand over her heart. Sophie was so intent on reaching the door to the *Star* that she almost let a fancy carriage run her over. She jerked her skirts free of its wheels, shook her fist at the driver, and ran the rest of the way to Madeleine's door.

"Well," Madeleine greeted her. "For someone who looks like a picture in *Godey's Lady's Book,* you don't behave in a very ladylike fashion."

"No time for niceties," Sophie said, gasping for breath. "Where's Charlie?"

"Over at the café. I'm hurt; I thought you came to see me."

"I did, you ninny. Is anybody else here?"

"You did come to see me but you want somebody else?"

It amazed her that she could suddenly find

herself in such better spirits just by being reminded that she had a friend who would stand by her, no matter how mixed up and confused she might be.

A very exasperated friend, at this moment. That made her smile, since it was usually Sophie who exasperated *her* to distraction.

"I swear to you, Madeleine Calhoun, if you don't answer me this minute, I can't be responsible for my actions."

"No one else is here. It's just you and me. Any secret you wish to tell will be forever safe."

Sophie turned and crossed the room into the hall that led to Madeleine's living quarters.

"I need coffee," she said, "hot and strong, and I need it now."

Madeleine followed her.

"I'm not serving coffee, tea, water, or mulberry wine until I know why you need it."

Sophie ripped off her new hat and threw it down on the narrow divan that had become Juanito's bed. Madeleine went to fill the kettle with water.

"I may have been *wrong!*" she cried. "Can you believe it? I've *never* been wrong about a man's character before. Never! Ever!"

"I swear to you, Sophie Langston," Madeleine said, mimicking her friend's drawl, "if you don't tell me your secret this minute, I can't be responsible for my actions."

"The sad thing is, it's no secret," Sophie said,

coming to stand right in front of her, "I've heard it in two places this very morning."

"What?"

"That Rafe has connections to Cheno Cortinas."

Madeleine dropped the kettle onto the stove top with a thud. She stared at Sophie while she tried to comprehend.

"Cortinas? The bandit? Why would anyone say such a crazy thing?"

"I don't know."

"Who would spread such lies?" Madeleine demanded.

"I don't know where it started, but everybody's talking about it. I heard it at Mrs. Bolander's. Then I went by Duncan's office and he'd heard it, too. It's all over town."

"It can't be true. Rafe's no thief, no killer— Cortinas and his men show no mercy."

"It's been ten years since you knew him, Maddie, remember that. You said he's changed a lot since then."

"He has. But he hasn't turned into an outlaw or a traitor to his own kind."

Sophie looked at her strangely. Steadily.

"What?"

"His own kind, Maddie, includes his son."

She felt the blood drain from her face. Was this more of the work of the anonymous-letter writer? This would put Juanito into even more danger.

"You said he spent a long time in Mexico during the war," Sophie said, clearly troubled. "Maybe Cortinas was in the same jail . . ."

"Hush!"

Madeleine turned back to her task and went to the cupboard for the coffee.

"I can't believe you're taking this seriously, Sophie. I never thought you would be so eager to believe a vicious anonymous rumor."

"I'm not. Maddie, I tell you, I don't believe it. Yet."

Madeleine whirled on her.

"*Yet?*"

"They say there's proof. Some kind of papers or something."

"And who has that proof?"

"I don't know. No one knows."

"Whoever the lowlife is who started this talk ought to be hanged," Madeleine cried. "Rafe's pride alone would not let him be in league with someone like Cortinas."

"It's been ten years since you really knew him."

"He wouldn't do such a thing."

"You said he's changed a lot."

"Not *that* much."

"Listen to me, Maddie. What I really want to tell you is to be careful. Don't go to his ranch anymore. I know I can't persuade you to stop keeping Juanito at night, but stay away from Rafe as much as you can."

Madeleine stared at her.

This was too much, just entirely too much to deal with. Ever since Rafe had walked through her door, her world had been shifting and changing like a picture in a kaleidoscope. Now sensible, practical Sophie was becoming a hysteric.

"What do you think he's going to do to me, Sophie? He's already taken my business and stolen my home and my peace of mind. Are you afraid he'll carry me away as a prize to Mexico?"

Sophie frowned. "No. I'm afraid you'll fall in love with him again and get your heart broken again, and it'll all be my doing because I've been encouraging you to remember how you used to feel. I pushed you together at the pie auction. I . . ."

Madeleine stared into Sophie's huge brown eyes, filled with genuine anguish. Then she started to laugh.

"You are the funniest person I have ever known, Sophie," she said. "And I love you." She threw her arms around her dearest friend.

"I hate to tell you this, honey, but you don't wield an infallible influence, even though you might like to."

Sophie returned the hug, then held her at arm's length to meet her gaze.

"I knew you'd never stopped loving Rafe, though, Maddie—I could hear it every time you talked about him and I could see it from the minute he reappeared. I was fanning those flames even though it was none of my business. If he's become a traitorous desperado . . ."

Madeleine looked at Sophie's pretty, worried face, but instead she saw Rafe's hard, handsome one.

"Those flames are going to burn no matter what you do, Soph," she said. "I can't help being powerfully attracted to him, but I'm not sure if I ever loved him. Your remarks aren't driving my feelings, so don't feel guilty."

"But . . . but, Maddie! He obviously has a lot of money. What if he's not making it all by gaming?"

"Rafe would never be a party to murder or stealing."

With a calmness that amazed her, she made the coffee and then went to sit across the table from Sophie.

"Get ready, Sophie," she said. "Somebody is trying to make Rafe take Juanito away from here because they hate Mexicans. We need to find out who it is."

She told her about the threatening letter. For once, Sophie listened without saying a word until the story was done.

"I'm so sorry, Maddie," she said. "I am so sorry I said what I did about Rafe. Can you forgive me?"

Madeleine smiled at her dear friend as she got up to pour the coffee.

"You were only worried about me and trying to warn me," she said. "But I won't forgive you until you find out—with utmost discretion, of course—who's behind all this."

"Done," Sophie said. "My spies are everywhere. I'll try to have news by the time you get back from Bandera."

Rafe rode along on one side of Juanito, watching Madeleine ride on the other side of him and listening to their familiar chatter. He needed to concentrate on the business ahead of him in Bandera, supplying his men and getting them onto the trail with his newly purchased cattle.

But when it came right down to it, Clayton Brevard would handle most of that, since he'd bossed a trail drive before. The foreman had even promised to find a couple more men for the trail in order to leave two on the Circle Three while the rest of them went north.

Well, he could think about maybe getting into some horse breeding, an idea which had pricked at the back of his mind ever since he won the place. That ought to keep him from constantly tasting Maddie's kiss on his lips and remembering the look in her eyes when she'd taken his face in her hands that day on the front gallery of his house.

That look had seared his soul.

If he were honest with himself, it was that look—and the kisses—making him hunt for a distraction. He couldn't let himself get that close to Maddie again. He *would* not.

"Papa, tell *mi Lena*," Juanito said, turning to Rafe. "This bay mare, I must slow her down more."

"I can ride a fast horse," Madeleine argued passionately, which seemed to delight Juan Rafael. "You've never seen me ride a fast one, Juanito. You're just embarrassed to ride this slowpoke gray you brought me from the ranch."

"Now, now, children," Rafe said, "we have to hold them to a long trot anyway, unless we want to wear them out before we get to Bandera."

Madeleine made a great show of pretending to pout, which sent Juanito into gales of laughter.

"The bay mare is *mine*," she said. "Juanito, you gave her to me yourself. Now, get off and let me have her."

"I gentle her," he said, suddenly solemn and gravely concerned. "You might be hurt if I give her now."

"You're a pair of bad actors," Rafe said, laughing. "Hush and let me tell you what I'm thinking about."

They turned to him expectantly.

This was foolish. He should keep even the thought to himself because it sounded as if he'd truly be settling in on the ranch. He could come back for a couple of months a year, though, and see to the bloodlines.

"I'm thinking about fast horses," he said.

"Maybe a stud from Kentucky to breed to this bay mare here. What if we started a line of running horses? Reckon anybody'd want to buy them?"

Juanito's eyes grew huge.

"We have *lots* of fast horses?"

Just the ecstasy on his face would make every dollar worthwhile.

Rafe nodded.

"In time. Only one each year from this mare, but we could find some other fast ones."

"Yippee-e-e!"

The bay mare gave a start and threatened to run, but Juanito spoke to her and kept her under control, all the while looking at Rafe. Then he broke loose.

"Muchos caballos rápidos!"

He went galloping off ahead in celebration, but soon slowed to a brisk trot.

"I remember what you say," he called back over his shoulder. "I keep you in sight."

"He's so good," Maddie said, as they rode along behind.

"He is."

"Rafe?" Her voice suddenly trembled with tension.

He turned in the saddle to see that her face had paled.

"I heard a terrible rumor," she said quickly. "We must keep an even closer eye on him from now on."

"Tell me."

"Someone's spreading word that you're connected to Cortinas."

His shock was so real that her heart leapt. It thrilled her that she had believed in him before she had proof.

"*Cheno* Cortinas?"

"Yes."

"*What?* How could I be?"

He started to laugh, but only a bitter chuckle escaped from his throat. A cool, thin trickle of dread caressed his spine.

His reputation—that was what the bastard was after. It was his livelihood the bastard was after.

For the space of one heartbeat he felt relief that maybe Juanito wasn't in danger, after all, but the next one brought the truth. If a man would go this far, he would go much farther. Maybe even to the point of hurting the son to drive out the father.

And Big Jim Thompson was the only person who wanted Rafe out of San Antonio, so far as he knew.

Now he had a son to support, a stud horse to buy, a ranch to keep afloat. Good thing he hadn't already started on the casino. Being unable to finish it would've lost him face from San Francisco to Kansas City.

"Rafe?"

Madeleine's voice was full of concern for him.

"That explains a lot of strange behavior and dirty looks I've been getting," he said. "Hobbs, at the livery. Pritchard and Jones, cattle brokers who'd asked for seats at last night's game but didn't show up."

No one would play in his games if they believed this rumor. Texans hated Cortinas with a passion and blamed him—mostly rightly so—for every murdering raid on every ranch from the Rio Grande to the Nueces. Cheno Cortinas was a scourge on the country and the cattle business.

Even people who didn't believe the rumor would hesitate to be seen with him.

He must've looked stricken, because Madeleine spoke very gently again.

"According to Sophie, it's all over town and being taken pretty seriously."

"I can see that now that I look back."

"Fear makes people lose all good sense," she said. "And everybody's scared to death Cortinas will be bold enough to raid this far from the border."

"Idiots."

"I know. But . . ."

He slowed his horse even more, so as not to reach Juanito before they'd finished with the conversation.

"I'm getting to the bottom of this," he said. "Right now. I'm going to put a stop to it."

"Fighting a rumor's like fighting fog," she

said. "It's trying to prove you're innocent, and that's impossible."

"Don't tell me it's impossible!"

"No, now listen here. Sophie's looking into it. She knows everybody in town and she may be able to find out who started it."

"I can save her the trouble. Big Jim started it—but he'll have his tracks covered like a Comanche."

"He wouldn't! Not Jim!"

She might as well have slashed him with a knife.

"You don't know him any better than you know Cortinas. Wake up, Madeleine! You're supposed to be telling the world the truth."

He couldn't keep the bitterness out of his voice and even lost his famous poker face.

"Remember what you said when you chose the *Times* over me? That it was your duty to keep publishing it so you could print every scrap of truth you could get past the Yankees?"

She went white as her blouse.

"If there ever was a time to forget the past, it's now," she snapped.

Then her face softened.

"Rafe, it may be Big Jim. But it may be someone we'd least expect. People have strange, hidden motives sometimes."

He searched her face as if he were searching for his soul.

Did Madeleine doubt him?

Was there the slightest chance that she thought him capable of consorting with a criminal?

No. There was something there that looked almost like . . . love.

He looked away. He was not only losing his handle on his self-control, but hallucinating now, too.

Well, she might not love him, but she loved Juanito and would protect him with her life. That was his main comfort now.

Chapter 15

❦

Bandera was usually a very quiet, small town but it had suddenly come to teeming life. Just the outskirts had been exciting enough, with the two large herds of cattle being held for the trail drive filling the horizon between the road and the cypress trees that lined the river, plus the many vehicles meeting them up and down the road.

But now, riding in the main street of Bandera with Juanito and Rafe, Madeleine felt complete disbelief. Lots of people in San Antonio would be surprised at this transformation, even people who had nothing to do with the cattle business. This had been the staging area for herds going up the Western Trail for a couple of years—she should've written an article about the trailhead before now.

"Juanito, you stay close to me or Lena," Rafe said fiercely.

Juanito turned to him in surprise.

"Porqué, Papá?"

Rafe looked at him, then hesitated, as if he couldn't think what to say.

"There are lots of people in town," Madeleine said. "We don't want you to get lost."

Juanito laughed at that.

"I find you," he said. "I know Papa *y mi Lena* anyplace."

Confidence was a wonderful thing, Madeleine thought. Sometimes.

"We've got to get this business done and put that herd on the trail in the morning at the latest," Rafe said. "There're bound to be a lot more herds coming in soon, with this many people here."

They wound through the crowds in the streets, some dancing to the lively music of a band set up under a shade tree, peddlers driving wagons and buggies filled with goods on display, cowboys headed for the saloons for one last, great good time before months and months of eating dust and rationing water. She had published an interview last December with a drover who'd been up the trail twice—it would've been even more colorful if she'd come see to for herself what things looked like at the start of that trail.

"Let's head for the bank first," Rafe said, "then we'll look for Brevard. He's buying the last of the supplies today."

"Then we go see the remuda?"

Instinctively, Madeleine's gaze met Rafe's and they smiled. Both had thought the child was too caught up in the excitement around him to be listening, but here he was, on his ever-present subject of horses.

That one look made her feel as if they'd touched.

"Yes, and the cattle," Rafe said. "Some of them I bought sight unseen, so I want to see what we're sending all the way to Dodge City."

"Me, too," Juanito said, nodding gravely.

Madeleine shared another smile with Rafe, the two of them like proud parents.

She stifled the thought. Ten long years of a life that had taught her to see reality would stand her in good stead now.

"You'd think it was after sundown, with all this revelry going on," she said.

"You should see the towns on the other end of the trail," Rafe said. "Abilene and Dodge City and all the other shipping points where the cowboys get paid off—it's like midnight twenty-four hours a day."

"Then where did these cowboys get their money?"

"Maybe some of 'em had a little to start with. Others are on credit from their boss."

"But some of them won't be in very good shape to hit the trail."

"That may be good—they'll get some of the rowdiness out of their systems. According to Brevard, some bosses think that'll help 'em settle into one unit for the trail."

"What about our . . . I mean, your men? Is Brevard one of those bosses?"

"No. His men are already a seasoned crew. We're giving no credit and we're keeping them with the herd."

"You all are tough to work for," she said, teasing him.

"Damn straight," he said, frowning fiercely, "and they'd better not forget it."

"Damn straight," Juanito said, also mimicking Rafe's frown.

Madeleine gave Rafe a warning look.

"Son," he said, "you're too young to cuss."

Puzzled, Juanito looked at him for an explanation.

"Cuss?"

"To use curse words."

Still, Juanito didn't understand. He waited.

Madeleine bit her lip to keep from laughing as they swung wide of a freight wagon and rode closer to the rickety buildings with their wooden sidewalks. That saved Rafe from trying to explain.

"Well, hey there, Mr. Rafe Aigner. Ain't seen you since Kansas City!"

It was a trilling, very feminine voice coming from the doorway of a saloon marked Topay's Tavern. The owner of the voice apparently worked there, to judge by her appearance. She wore a very low-cut, quite short dress made of green satin, in addition to a great deal of paint on her face.

She stepped out onto the boardwalk.

Rafe tipped his hat and smiled at her.

"Lou!" he called back, loud enough to be heard over the noise in the street. "Good to see you. How are you?"

Lou opened her mouth to answer, but a man stepped out of the tavern right behind her, grabbed her by the shoulder, jerked her around, and slapped her—hard enough to send her staggering. Shocked, Madeleine stared for a second, then caught a movement in the corner of her eye that she incredulously took as Rafe falling off his horse.

Then she realized that he was on his feet in the street, moving so fast her heart hadn't taken another beat by the time he held the black-suited man by his string tie to smash his fist into his face. The man hit him back.

Lou screamed.

Rafe swayed, widened his stance, hit his opponent with a right, a left, and then both men's fists moved so fast and furiously that she couldn't have said what was happening. The one thing she could see for certain was a cut open across Rafe's cheekbone.

Juanito started climbing off his horse, and Madeleine threw herself off hers and managed to catch him before he scrambled up onto the boards. Rafe and the other man were fighting all over the sidewalk, hitting hard, gasping and grunting and giving no quarter. Their blows slammed each of them in turn against the front wall of the saloon.

Juanito struggled in her arms.

She held him closer and pressed her cheek against his.

"Don't bother your *papá*," she said, "if he looks at you, the man can hit him again."

Then Rafe came surging back from a blow and knocked the man flying out into the street.

Madeleine sank to the ground and pulled Juanito into her lap.

"Not yet," she said, as he struggled again. "He may get up."

But the man lay still.

Rafe stepped off the walk and strode out to stand over him.

"I ought to horsewhip you now, Fullerton," he said, "but I'll settle for running you out of town."

A cheer went up and Madeleine realized that traffic had stopped. Men were pouring out of the saloon and others had gathered in knots on the sidewalk and in the street. A man with a badge pushed his way through.

"What's the trouble here?" he called, looking at Rafe.

Rafe shrugged. His broad chest barely moved up and down beneath his torn shirt—he certainly wasn't heaving for breath after the fight—and his chiseled face showed no emotion at all.

He had never been more appealing to her, and never more fiercely handsome, not even the time he'd escorted her to the Mardi Gras ball dressed to taunt society as the great Choctaw chief Pushmataha. With the blood on his cheek shining and his amber eyes flashing, he turned to face the man wearing the sheriff's star.

"No trouble, Sheriff," he said coolly. "Mr. Fullerton is preparing to leave town."

Fullerton finally rolled onto his side, sat up, and pushed to his feet.

"Fullerton hit a woman, Sheriff," said a man from the sidewalk. "This gentleman was defending her."

The sheriff glared at Fullerton, who swayed a little on his feet.

"Well, then, Fullerton, you heard the man. Get your horse."

Fullerton started walking in the general direction of the saloon.

A man stepped off the sidewalk and walked toward Rafe. Madeleine realized it was Clayton Brevard.

Fullerton stopped short and stared at him.

"How's . . . it . . . feel," Fullerton called to Rafe's foreman in between gasps for more breath, "to work . . . for a . . . greaser-lover, Brevard? I heared yore boss's best amigo jist happens to be ol' Cheno Cortinas."

A sudden silence fell over the street.

Then somebody said, "Cortinas?"

Someone else called, "What are you talking about, Fullerton?"

The atmosphere changed as fast as a cloud passing over the sun.

Clayton stopped in his tracks, wheeled and started toward Fullerton.

The sheriff stepped between them.

"Get your horse, Fullerton," he said. "Next thing you know, somebody's gonna get killed around here."

Rafe's face had become terrible.

He strode straight to Brevard, they spoke for a moment, then he came to Madeleine and Juanito.

"I'm staying in town for a while," he said, dropping onto his haunches to look into their faces. "Clayton's gone to get some of our men to escort you out to the herd."

Madeleine's heart ached to tend the cut on his cheekbone, to find ice for the bruises already rising on his jaw. She longed to stay with him and not let him out of her sight.

But she only nodded.

"Papa," Juanito whispered. "The hurt . . ."

He touched his own cheekbone.

"It'll be all right," Rafe said, much more gently than he'd spoken before. "Don't worry about it, son."

Four men materialized behind him, one of them the cowboy who'd ridden the bay mare in the race.

Rafe stood up and turned around.

"Don't let them out of your sight."

"Right, Boss."

They all nodded and touched their hat brims to greet Madeleine. Dimly she heard the word "Cortinas" repeated somewhere behind her back.

Rafe held out his hand, took Madeleine's trembling one, helped her to her feet, and guided Juanito by the shoulder toward the horses.

"And keep a sharp lookout," Rafe said.

"The sharpest."

He swung Juanito up into his saddle, then held his hands for Madeleine to mount.

"Be careful," he said, and looked deep into her eyes for one heartbeat. "Ride safe."

"We will. Don't worry."

Then he was gone, and his men surrounded her and Juanito and took them out of town. Clayton Brevard stayed with Rafe.

That fact was a solace in a tiny corner of her heart which was searching madly for comfort.

Anything could happen, anything at all.

Fullerton could whip up a frenzy before he left town—if he did leave town peacefully—and someone could notice Rafe's Indian looks and pile one prejudice on top of another. Rafe had probably known Fullerton because he was also a gambler, judging by his dress, but he didn't know anyone else in Bandera to help him, as far as she knew.

She was good at speaking as well as writing; she could help shape people's opinions if a furor sprang to life over the Cortinas rumors. Why, people hated Cortinas so much that anything could happen . . . she tried to shut down her imagination.

Never, in all her life since that terrible day when New Orleans fell, had she felt so torn. She wanted to watch over Juanito, but she *needed* to go to Rafe.

Yet she knew she had no choice. She rode beside Juanito and kept her voice calm and tried to ease his worries about his papa's bleeding cheek.

Once they reached the herd and the two men Brevard had left on watch, a visit to the remuda distracted the boy. He amazed her and the men alike by recognizing nearly every horse in it. They talked with Cookie, the men teased Juanito about his bay mare, and one of them started teaching him how to rope.

The hours passed, second by slow-moving second.

The spring dusk fell and blurred the shapes of the cattle and the horses.

It brightened the colors of the campfire.

The men passed through the line and received their food, then sat around in a silent circle to eat it. Juanito ate a few bites. Madeleine accepted a plate but couldn't bring herself to touch the food.

Then, just as the night herders were mounting up and Juanito was asking her permission to go ride with them, the faint sounds of hoofbeats floated through the air. The two men on guard galloped out to meet them. Cookie and the others still in the light stepped away from the fire. One man went to the back of the wagon and came back with a gun.

"Who goes there?"

The shout was faint and Madeleine strained to hear. They were almost too far away.

"Aigner and Brevard."

Rafe's voice.

Something inside her fell apart and came together at the same time.

They rode to the edge of the circle of firelight and dismounted. Juanito ran to Rafe, who picked him up and hugged him.

Then they started walking, side by side, in step, toward Madeleine. The sight made her smile.

"Everything go all right?"

She could not believe the calm in her voice. Inside, she was still trembling.

"Not bad," Rafe said, and then Cookie brought him a plate.

He ate, teasing Juanito and ruffling his hair, while she sat in silence, so relieved that she felt as if she would never be able to move or make another sound.

One of the nightherders began singing. The plaintive melody floated to them faintly and Juanito turned toward the sound.

"May I ride with them, *Papá*? I can sing, too."

Clayton, standing at the wreck pan where he'd just thrown his dirty plate and utensils, overheard Juanito and chuckled.

"That's what it takes for night herdin', boy," he said. "We don't like to listen to no ear-splittin' caterwaulin' around here."

Rafe's eyes met Madeleine's in the dim light and lingered for a long moment that made her heart beat faster.

Then he turned to Clayton.

"I'll take him with me for an hour or two, Boss," he said. "I need to talk to them boys, anyhow."

"Thanks."

"I'll get him a good night horse."

Rafe turned to Juanito.

"Let the bay mare rest and ride the horse Clayton ropes out for you," he said. "It takes a special horse to be a night horse and we don't know the bay mare that well yet."

Juanito nodded and went to Clayton's side, ready to ride.

Rafe tossed his own plate into the wreck pan with a clatter and went to Madeleine.

"Come on, Maddie, let's take a little walk down by the river," he said. "Stretch our legs a little."

"I'm just glad the good people of Bandera didn't stretch your neck a little," she said.

She took the hand he offered, grateful for the help to stand. Her legs suddenly felt weak and shaky, and Rafe seemed to know it, since he kept holding onto her as they walked away from the fire.

"I could see your thoughts running that direction when you got out of town and left me to my fate."

"*What?* You *made* me get out of town. It was all I could do to go away and leave you!"

He started laughing, and she realized he was teasing her.

"Rafe!"

She pretended to try to pull away, but he kept hold of her hand. His big, callused palm pressed against hers seemed as intimate as a kiss.

It scared her as the kisses had done, and for the same reason. It made her want more and more of this closeness with him. A closeness with nothing between them . . .

Heat surged into her cheeks. This was ridiculous. She forced her mind to the problem that was worrying her sick.

"You'd better not joke about this! That Cortinas rumor about you is lethal, and you know it. People get hysterical at the sound of his name."

His low chuckle told her it pleased him that she cared.

"Tell me this, Warrior Woman. If you'd stayed in town, how were you planning to defend me?"

"With my tongue, I guess."

"Hmm, I'm not sure if a lynch mob has ever been stopped by plain talk."

Suddenly, it was too much—the pain that knifed her with the danger-filled images of his words.

His strong, sure hand enfolding hers, steadying her when the ground got rougher, melding them together in a grip that could never be torn apart, made him seem all-powerful and the two of them together and forever safe. But she knew it wasn't so.

"Let's not talk any more about what could've happened," she blurted. "I've worried about that all afternoon. Just tell me what did happen."

They were crossing the wide, grassy space that lay between the herd and the trees growing tall and thick in the bend of the Medina River. The moon was rising huge and yellow over the edge of the world.

"There was a little more muttering about

Cortinas, but the sheriff asked who wanted to put their faith in anything Fullerton might say, and Jack Burke, the owner of the saloon, said he'd known me for years and would vouch for me anytime. So that was the end of it."

"But the vicious lie is already all over South Texas," she said worriedly.

"So is mesquite," he said, "and there's nothing we can do about either one."

That made her laugh and she clung to his hand so the warm, secure feeling would enfold her. This was a moment out of time that would not come again.

"Lou said to tell you thanks," he said.

"For what? I didn't do anything."

"For not pitching a fit because I defended her in public," he said. "She assumed I'm your . . . man."

An unbidden thrill rushed through Madeleine's veins.

"And what did you tell her?" she asked archly.

He didn't flirt back.

"I let her assume whatever she wanted. I don't explain my life to anyone."

Does that include me?

Of course it did, for he was *not* her man, not anymore. What she had to remember on this balmy moonlit night was that she didn't even know Rafe as a man. Except for a couple of traits that had stayed the same.

"I loved it that you defended Lou," she said. "I felt so sorry for her. Why did Fullerton hit her?"

"Seems he was *her* man, at least for the moment, and jealous to a fault."

"How did you know them?"

He shrugged.

"Oh, he's been a small-timer ever since I've been in the game," he said. "Mostly in Texas, although I've seen him in Kansas City a time or two."

"And Lou?"

"She was a saloon singer years ago."

And he said no more.

Madeleine loved him for that, too. His gallantry extended to women in all walks of life.

"Do you think Fullerton will leave her alone now? Did he leave town?"

"Yes. That sheriff put the fear of God into him, and I promised him a personal reception if he comes back. Lou'll stay in Bandera for a while."

They reached the dappled shade thrown by the tall cypress trees. It drew them into its shifting patterns of moonlight and shadows.

"Don't you feel sheltered in these trees?" he said. "Sometimes, even after all this time, I really miss New Orleans with its lush vegetation and big trees."

"Which is why you're scheming to cut mine down."

She spoke lightly, though, feeling no rancor.

Here, in this magic place with the river running along just down the bank catching bits of the moon on its water, it seemed Rafe could never do such a thing.

"I never said I'd cut them down," he said mildly. "You jumped to that conclusion all on your own, Miss Maddie. I'm planning to build around them."

At that moment, she could hardly remember her trees, to tell the truth. She couldn't quite think what she felt like in their shade or living in her home. Nothing seemed real but Rafe.

"If you say so, I believe you," she said.

She led him faster down the slanting, low hill toward the river, running a little to stay ahead of him.

He followed, laughing a little.

"Would you also believe me if I told you something else?"

"What?" she said breathlessly.

Her mind leapt to an impossible hope, then shied away again.

They'd reached the edge of the grass that grew along the river. Rocks and tangles of roots connected the trees with the river, the water with the earth, but suddenly she didn't want to venture out on them. She stopped at the last minute, clinging to the haven of the trees and the thick grass underfoot. Rafe stood behind her and put his hands on her shoulders.

"Maddie, you looked so scared today when

Fullerton accused me of a connection with Cortinas. Try not to take all this to heart so much—
vicious rumors and anonymous threats don't
necessarily lead to physical attacks."

She twisted around to look up into his face
and reached up to the healing cut on his cheek.
Her hand trembled as she touched the cheekbone above it.

Her voice shook a little bit, too.

"This looks like a physical attack to me."

"Which wasn't caused by the rumors, if you
recall."

He cupped her hand in his, warm and sure.
His eyes wouldn't let hers go, they wouldn't let
her have a single secret.

"How do you know how scared I was?"

Her breath caught in her throat. He'd been
paying attention to her then—he had seen her
feelings and been concerned, even with his enemy at his back and his face cut open.

"I saw the fear in your eyes, Maddie. I know
you."

She opened her hand against his cheek and
his hand held it there. For a moment she
couldn't quite think what she had meant to say.

"You only think you know me, Rafe."

"I know you want me to kiss you right now,"
he said.

She smiled.

"And how do you know that?"

"I see it in your eyes. Your blue, blue eyes."

His hands spanned her waist, hard and strong enough to pick her up and carry her off. His eyes looked into her heart.

It was galloping in her chest like a runaway.

He gathered her to him then, swept her off her feet, and held her wrapped in his arms so tightly she could never fall, took her mouth with his and robbed her of her breath. And her mind. And her heart, forever.

He couldn't get enough of her lips and her tongue and her taste and her feel, and neither could she of his, and she could not think past that moment. She didn't even want to try.

Whatever happened on this once-in-a-lifetime evening, this unforgettable sultry night, when even the breeze stood still in anticipation, would happen. While the faint singing to the cattle floated on the air, bringing with it memories of all the other times Rafe had held her in his arms beside another river, she would live this one moment in time.

He broke the kiss, then, leaving her desperate for more as he lifted her still higher to move his mouth down her throat, burning his brand on her skin again and again with its fire. She arched against him, helpless to do anything more.

Then, wanton as any woman could ever be, she offered her breasts, rubbing them against him, caressing him with the hardening nipples and willing him to touch them. He lifted her higher as he started to lay her down so he could take one into his mouth, ravenous, as heedless of the thin cotton layers of her dress and the shift beneath it as of all the years between them.

Chapter 16

As he laid her down in the sweet-smelling grass and swept open her blouse and camisole, as she felt the sweet heat of his lips and his tongue as he suckled her with no barriers in between, Maddie lost her senses, lost all awareness except that of his mouth on her breast. It became her whole world, her very life, her only pleasure, her only need.

She held his head in both her hands and kept it there until his tongue had whipped the flashing flame inside her into a blaze. But it wasn't enough. Not nearly enough.

She needed his skin on hers, all over, his skin to feed hers. She needed more.

"Rafe . . ."

Her voice barely made a raspy whisper, but he

lifted his head. He left her bereft, his mouth gone.

"No," she whispered, "I mean . . ."

His eyes gleamed hot in the moonlight; their lids were heavy with desire. Then, while his mouth took hers, with his hands he cradled her breasts and thumbed them into ecstasy.

He knew what she meant. Rafe knew her, after all these years.

His tongue twined with hers like a wanderer coming home. Her lips opened to his desperate settling-in with a need so deep she went limp, sinking into their bed of grass while he crushed her against his growing hardness.

At the same moment, they broke apart and began to do away with buttons and ties and boots and clothes. Rafe spread out her riding skirts so he could lay her down again, and she reached up for him.

But he held back, his body broad and hard, the moonlight shining on his coppery skin, handsome as any man ever born.

"Madeleine," he murmured, "you are so beautiful."

Then he was reaching for her—no, he was leaning over her.

"Let me take down your hair, Madeleine," he said, his voice so low and rich that it melted her right into the ground. "I promise not to neglect you while I do."

He brushed the hard peaks of her breasts

against his harder chest. The delicious agony of it made her cry out.

"Rafe, please . . ."

"Soon."

He took a pin from her hair, then another. He bent even closer and pressed his open mouth to the side of her neck, trailed the tip of his tongue along her skin.

She trembled.

"*Rafe*," she said.

He took the next pin from her hair, then the next, so slowly and deliberately that she had to bite her lip to keep from crying out. Now his hands were not touching her anyplace but her hair. How could he do this with her breasts crying out for them?

His marvelous hands.

His incredible mouth.

He finally spread her hair out around her head.

"There," he said.

His heavy-lidded eyes moved over her, all of her, with a look as palpable as a caress, a look as hot as the fires inside her.

Then he came over her, stretched out and took her into his arms, slid his skin against hers the lengths of their bodies.

A long sigh came from her throat, and she wrapped her arms around the solid column of his neck and clung to him for dear life.

Their mouths found each other again and struck sparks.

But it wasn't enough. Not nearly enough.

He slipped one of his long thighs between her own and kissed her chin, her throat, her breast.

All the world stopped, except for the low, slow sound of the river.

And the beating of their hearts, together, rhythmic and joyous as a song.

He came into her as unerringly as the river moved in its bed, melding them into one spirit, one heart, one fire. Madeleine clung to him and welcomed him.

She buried her face in his neck and moved with him into ancient, pounding need, into the swift, untamed passion that she had known forever she could find only with him. It carried her out of herself and into him, taking and giving, bringing them out into the wilds of mindless wonder and holding them together until they finally found a new home of fire and cool peace.

A home where they lay for a long, treasured time, wrapped so closely in each other's arms that nothing but the quiet could come between them.

At dawn, Rafe sat his horse and watched the herd move out onto the Western Trail, with Brevard at its head and the two young hands Clayton had hired the day before on drag. The experienced men were scattered in between. There was a sufficient crew out at the ranch. His business was all in order, everything under control.

Except his emotions. Again. Instinctively, he glanced across at Madeleine, who looked as lovely in the early pink light as if she'd slept in a featherbed for hours.

He should never have given in to his desire, never should have touched her, much less made love with her. As an experienced thirty-five-year-old man, for God's sake, he should've known that one night with her would only make him want a hundred more. A thousand more.

"When will Clay and Cookie and the others be back, *Papá*?"

It took several seconds for him to process the question through his addled, sleep-deprived brain.

"In the fall, Juanito."

Silently, he counted in his head.

"Five or six months. *Setiembre o octubre.*"

He waited, but the boy didn't ask to go with them, not even as the remuda swept past them at a long trot. Of course not. He wouldn't want to go and leave his Lena for such a long time.

Rafe's heart twisted in his chest. He couldn't settle down and stay with Maddie. He couldn't marry her even after dreaming of it all those years. He wasn't fit to be a husband: he wouldn't be able to stick; he'd be on the road and gone before he even knew his own intentions.

And that would break her heart all over again.

He ought to smooch to Beau right this minute and fall in with the boys riding drag and eat dust all the way to Kansas, as punishment for being so damn stupid. Now he had to stay in San Antonio for a few months, at least. He had to get to the source of this rumor mess and straighten it out so that he knew both Madeleine and Juanito would be safe.

He was the biggest fool in all the world. No one else could've managed to get himself trapped into being forced to see Madeleine, undoubtedly the most beautiful woman in the world, every day and not let himself touch her. That was too much punishment, even for all his sins.

Madeleine had barely slept or eaten for two days and two nights when Rafe came striding masterfully into her office, waving sheets of paper covered with his bold, scrawling script. Her quick resentment was entirely attributable to malaise and exhaustion. It had absolutely nothing to do with his withdrawal from her—his colossal standoffishness—ever since they'd returned to San Antonio.

It was an insult to her, as if he were assuming that she'd expect him to marry her now, or to declare his undying devotion or make some other commitment he didn't want to make.

She shouldn't be the least bit surprised or dismayed at his reaction to their lovemaking. She should just take it as the lovely memory it was, which was what she'd intended at the time. Hadn't she already seen that he didn't intend to let anyone love him?

"Put this on the front page," he said brusquely.

He slapped it onto her desk, directly under her nose. Right on top of an editorial she was halfway through revising.

"With a good headline. You can decide what size."

"Well, thank you so much, Mr. Aigner," she said sarcastically, "for giving me permission to do my job."

He threw himself into one of the two leather armchairs in front of her desk so impatiently that it seemed he had no time to sit. However, he folded one long leg, settled his right ankle onto his left knee, and adjusted the crease in his immaculately pressed trousers.

To keep from looking at him any longer, Madeleine glanced down at the pages he'd brought.

"Let me correct myself," she said. "Thank you for actually *doing* my job for me."

"I was under the impression that this is my newspaper."

She looked him straight in the eye.

"Nowhere in our agreement did I give you the right to force me to publish anything."

His sleepy eyes widened.

"You expect me to *pay* to put news in my own paper?"

"Perhaps this isn't news," she said, and frowned down at the article he had given her. "Hmm. 'New Gaming Palace Planned for San Antonio,' you say. That sounds remarkably like an advertisement to me."

He slammed both feet flat to the floor and sat upright.

"It damned well is not! That's a piece of news for this town."

She cocked her head and raised one eyebrow as she stared him down.

"That's for me to decide, as long as I'm editor of the *Star*. Of course, I am at your mercy if you should want to dismiss me from that position."

"What are you talking about, woman?"

"I expect you to get out of my way and let me be the editor of this newspaper. You cannot *order* me to make one single decision as to its contents or its management. Otherwise, you're not giving me a fair chance to take the financial responsibility, make a profit, and earn it back."

He glared at her so hard she thought his neck would snap.

Finally, he spoke, in a deliberately mild tone that clearly strained his voice and his nerves.

"I didn't *order* you, I . . ."

She quoted him. " 'Put this on the front page. With a good headline.' "

He swallowed hard.

"I meant that as a request," he said formally.

"Then I'll read what you've written and I'll report the pertinent points as news if I feel they're sufficiently important."

"Pertinent points! Now, you listen here, Madeleine Cottrell—"

"Unless, of course," she said, "you'd like to buy advertising space and have this masterpiece published in its entirety."

His jaw dropped. He frowned at her so ferociously it made her want to laugh.

She kept her face as expressionless as he would've done in a high-stakes poker game.

He snapped his mouth shut.

She held his stare.

Finally he opened his mouth again.

"How much? For the front page?"

"We don't put advertisements on the front page of the *Star*."

"I want this on the front page. I want it where everyone in town will see it and talk about it."

She glanced at his pages again, as if considering.

"Even if you decide to go the news route with this, I'm afraid it wouldn't rate high enough for Page One."

She looked up and smiled at him sweetly.

"An alternative would be to buy one of our special advertisements with Charlie's own fancy frame around it and extra large type."

Once again, she perused the words in front of her. Rafe had the most beautiful handwriting of any man she'd ever known.

He shoved back his chair, stood up, and plunked a small leather sack down on her desk with a force that jangled the coins inside it.

She looked up to see him towering over her.

"I want every word of that published, exactly the way it is, in your next edition. Inside Charlie's fancy frame. Put nothing else on that page. I want Page Two, if you don't have any rules about that."

He strode toward the door.

"Tell my son I'll be back in an hour."

Then he stopped and turned on his heel.

"What I want you to know, Madeleine," he said, with a jerk of his head toward the pages he'd left her, "is that although I have given a very near date for the destruction of this property, I don't actually intend to start building that soon."

She picked up the pages.

"But that's giving your potential customers a false impression," she said. "Why would you . . ."

"Because this is a ruse, a piece of bait," he snapped. "I intend to see if Big Jim will come out of the shadows to run me out of town if I appear to be settling in his territory permanently."

She took that in.

"So you haven't been able to find out anything about Mr. Anonymous?"

"Not a thing."

"Sophie hasn't, either. She can't believe she's failed."

"Tell her to keep trying." He went out as suddenly as he'd come in.

They were a pair, weren't they? They couldn't even get through one meeting maintaining a formal distance. He might never let her love him, but an everlasting bond connected them, all the same.

Rafe was sitting in the lobby of the Menger having a smoke and a sociable chat with a button drummer from Dallas when the newspapers containing his advertisement were delivered to the hotel desk. While he'd been gone to Bandera, many of his acquaintances had turned definitely cool. The rumor mill had been busy, all right. Now maybe he'd find out who was stoking its fires.

He bode good-bye to the drummer, dropped his money in the bowl and took his paper, then strolled along the hallway to the dining room. Some of the breakfast regulars would be there. Some of them—in fact, most of them—were prominent men of the town who enjoyed a game now and then, and he could observe their reactions to his announcement.

The maitre d' led Rafe to his favorite table in the corner. When the waiter came, he ordered his usual eggs, cured bacon, beaten biscuits, and fruit. He opened the *Star*, approved the look and position of his purchased advertisement, then folded the paper on the table and glanced around the room. Slowly. Five men out of the seven who happened to meet his eye nodded courteously in greeting.

The percentage cheered him. Maybe more people disbelieved the rumors than he'd first thought.

As more businessmen came and went, while he ate his breakfast, he overheard two positive remarks about his prospective new gaming hall and accepted congratulatory remarks from a half-dozen more. He finished his meal and relaxed a little.

Whoever was trying to do him damage might not be so skillful, after all.

But his feeling of well-being lasted only until his last cup of coffee. Footsteps running across the marble floor sounded out in the lobby, accompanied by a shrill, excited stream of unintelligible words, then a hubbub of voices began.

The young messenger, a boy about Juanito's age, paused in the arched doorway into the dining room.

"Cortinas!" he shouted into the room. "Raided

three ranches west of town last night! Them Mexicans, they'll hit here in San Antonio next!"

Then he went clattering off to find a fresh audience to tell the news.

Immediately, clamor filled the room. Several men got up and left, presumably to seek more details. Others came in from the lobby and the street to talk about it after hearing the news.

"They say three people were killed on the ranches," one man said, his voice loud with fear and excitement. "One of them a woman."

He sat down at the table next to Rafe's to talk to Tad Murphy, a businessman who also ate breakfast there every day.

"Murdering bastards," Murphy said. "Any bandits dead?"

"None that I heard of."

Rafe signed his check and pushed back his chair, trying to control the thundering of his heart. All this talk of Cortinas would whip up more anti-Mexican feelings, and that could be bad for Juanito. Fear would multiply, with raids so close.

West of town—*Los Tres Amigos* could've been hit. He would find out as soon as possible, but really, only Juanito mattered. Pray God he and Madeleine hadn't gone out for a morning stroll about town as they sometimes did.

Madeleine would catch hell, too, if that anonymous letter wasn't just a ruse to try to make him leave town.

On his way to the door he caught snatches of talk.

". . . Never dare come into San Antonio, not with the military here . . ."

"That Mexican snake would do anything, dare anything, just to twist the knife . . ."

". . . Doesn't care how many soldiers. *Anything* in San Antone'd be such a feather in his cap . . ."

". . . *Why* can't the Rangers set a trap . . ."

Rafe wasn't more than a few strides from the wide arched doorway into the lobby when Big Jim Thompson appeared in the center of it.

"Aigner," he boomed, his voice loud enough for the whole city to hear. "Congratulations, sir! I hear your ranch escaped Cortinas' raiders last night."

Conversation in the room died instantly. Rafe felt stab of relief that the men he'd hired were safe, then a quick foreboding. Thompson had a hidden purpose here.

"Too bad all your neighbors lost their stock, though," Thompson said, "and some, apparently, lost their lives."

The silence behind Rafe had become enormous.

He stopped walking.

"You know more than I do, Thompson. I haven't heard from my men."

It was true, though; he'd bet the ranch on it. If Big Jim was coming out to make this public spectacle of him, then you could wager your last dime his information was solid. Big Jim Thompson was a *careful* gambler.

And he stood fast in the doorway as if he'd been planted there.

"Oh, you'll hear from 'em and they'll tell you just what I'm saying," he said. "Why do you suppose Cortinas' *bandidos* left your place untouched, while they murdered and rustled their way around the neighborhood?"

Rafe's first urge was to hit him right in the middle of his big, loud mouth, and the second was to ignore him and walk right past. But he might have a chance here, in such a public place, to lessen the impact of the nasty insinuation.

"My guess," he drawled carelessly, "would be lack of plunder. I sent ninety percent of the cattle I owned and a fine remuda up the Western Trail a few days ago."

"*My* first guess," Thompson said, "would be the Spanish name of your place. What is it . . . *Los Tres Amigos?*"

Rafe ignored him and began walking again.

"Way I hear it," Thompson boomed, "it was the Crossbars, the Rafter N, and the old Tobey place that lost the biggest part of their stock. But my sources say the raiders thundered right on past your place."

He smiled broadly.

"Reckon it was the name of the place?"

"Hardly. The name on the sign is the Circle 3."

"Maybe Old Cortinas told 'em the location then," Big Jim said. "Maybe he described it to 'em."

Instantly Rafe's blood boiled.

"Keep making these insinuations about me, Thompson, and you won't be the first man to dig his own grave with his mouth."

It was all he could do not to flatten Thompson on the spot, but that would only make some people think he was upset that Thompson had told the truth.

Rafe strode through the doorway past him and didn't look back.

Looking back never did any good. He had learned that a long time ago.

Madeleine's heart stopped when she glanced up and saw Rafe at her back door. The expression on his face was so terrible she thought danger was imminent, and instantly started for the stable where Juanito was grooming the horses. Rafe stopped her with a gesture and she ran to him instead, desperate to know what was wrong.

"Cortinas has hit the ranches all around ours," he said.

Ours.

But of course, he meant his and Juanito's.

"According to Big Jim, the raiders passed us by completely. He came into the Menger and made a scene announcing that fact to the world. He also emphasized that the ranch has a Spanish name."

Her heart was beating so hard she could barely speak.

"But Rafe, that doesn't prove Big Jim is Anonymous."

He flashed her a look as he started for the barn.

"It proves he's out to get me. Whether my announcement drove him to a public display of that fact, we'll never know."

Madeleine walked beside him, matching him stride for stride with her long legs, trying to think about how to make Rafe safe, keep Juanito safe. Who would turn against them and who would be her loyal friends?

"Did many people at the Menger seem to believe Big Jim's insinuation?"

"I didn't wait to find out. But I wouldn't be surprised if ninety percent of the people in town believe him and take up the cry. They're all in a frenzy, expecting Cortinas to ride into San Antonio any minute now, to slaughter all the Anglos and drive all the horses back across the Rio Grande."

"This couldn't have been planned, though. Unless *he's* in league with Cortinas," she said.

"Big Jim Thompson's just one damned lucky son of a gun. This fell into his lap at exactly the right moment."

"It's still hard for me to believe that he'd be

such a snake as to gallantly let Juanito buy my basket at the pie auction and then turn around and use the child's heritage to incite the whole town against him."

"Believe it."

"Do you think Juanito's truly in danger, now?" It nearly made her heart stop just to say the words out loud.

"Anything can happen when fear takes over," he said. "I don't think Thompson actually wishes Juanito any harm—my gut tells me he's just using this to try to drive me out of town."

"Maybe, until this all passes . . ."

"Never," he snapped. "I can protect my own."

They had reached the stable door.

"What are you going to tell him?" she whispered.

"The truth," he said. "As clearly as I can."

Juanito looked up from currying Tortilla as they came in, and his face lit up with happiness at seeing his *papá*.

"Mi hijo," Rafe said, *"buenos días."*

Juanito responded with a big smile and picked up a soft brush to offer Rafe to use. Laughing, Rafe took off his coat, hung it on a peg by the door, and went to help him work on Tortilla's once-rough coat that now was slick as a seal's. Juanito curried and Rafe came along behind with the brush.

"Mi Lena," Juanito called, "would you like your horse to be pretty, too?"

"Are you hinting for me to get to work?"

He smiled at her pretended indignation.

"Sí. Mucho trabajo aquí."

She went to the tiny tack room for more brushes and to give them a chance to talk. Her stomach felt as if it were tied in a dozen knots and she gathered her supplies slowly with hands that shook. How much would it hurt Juanito if Elmer stopped being his friend?

Evidently, Juanito and Rafe were thinking along the same lines. When she went back out to Dolly's stall, the one next to Tortilla's, they were working in silence. Then Juanito looked up at her.

"Elmer knows I am not bad, like Cortinas."

"Yes," she said, and then stood tongue-tied, helpless to think of a way to prepare the child for any other eventuality.

"We don't know what Elmer's mother and father might think about *me*, though, when they hear the news of the raids," Rafe said calmly. "You know they're the ones who decide what Elmer can do."

Madeleine glanced at him approvingly.

Juanito gave a short, quick nod. His silence might be hiding tears.

She turned back to her work to give him some privacy.

Rafe's voice came again, in a lower tone, a little bit raspy with emotion this time.

"Son, you know, don't you, that I love you? Always? No matter what happens?"

"*Sí.*"

She dropped down on her haunches to curry Dolly's fat belly so as not to intrude.

"I love you, *Papá.*"

Not everything was bleak right now.

If Rafe would let himself accept Juanito's love, it would change his life.

It would change Juanito's, too.

Chapter 17

Four nights later, Rafe made his usual sweep of the stable and Madeleine's back yard, keeping to the shadows, being careful not to get the horses stirred up and nickering. No danger lurked that he could see, and he sensed none. Good. Maybe most of the vitriol would be thrown at him, since there'd been little change in Juanito's and Maddie's lives so far. He moved silently along the wall of the little building to the Commerce Street side and waited until the one rickety wagon in the street had rumbled past.

He stayed out of the glow of the street lamp on the corner and walked swiftly in the building's dark shadow, past the large window and to the door to the office of the *Star*. As he had done each night since Big Jim had publicly accused him of being in league with Cortinas, he used his pick in the lock. Then he slipped inside. Slowly, slowly, he closed the door behind him. The latch made only a tiny click.

He stood still for a moment to make sure nothing had been left out where he'd stumble over it.

The huge room was dark as midnight—which happened to be approximately the time—since the door to the living quarters was closed and the lamp from outside threw only the dimmest glow in through the window.

"You're early."

It was Madeleine's voice, but he startled like a deer anyway, which made him angry.

"What the hell are you *doing*, Maddie?"

She stepped out of the blackest shadow and the faint light from the window glinted off the six-shooter in her hand.

"Waiting to find out who's sneaking into my office."

"Well, you said I'm early. You must've known who it was."

"No. Your arrival has been at one-thirty or two."

It made him so aggravated he wanted to put his fist through the wall.

"So you've known all along and decided to let me make a fool of myself?"

She chuckled a little, that low, sexy laugh deep in her throat that always stirred something in his gut. That irritated him even more.

"I do appreciate your standing guard for us," she said, "but why don't you just knock on the door, Rafe? Or tell me you're coming, and I'll leave it unlocked."

Because I don't trust myself to see you in the middle of the night. To sleep in the same house without being in your bed.

Damn! It was so much easier when she hated him.

"I'm trying to protect your reputation."

"How do you know someone didn't see you come in? You'd have an even faster entry if I were waiting at the door."

That teasing tone with the underlying chuckle made him long to cross the room, take hold of her, and kiss her breathless so she couldn't say another word.

"I'm still plenty fast with a lock pick," he snapped. "I used to be a secret agent, you know."

There—maybe that would make her remember and hate him again.

"Well, I was letting you hone your burglary skills," she said lightly, walking toward him as she put the gun into her pocket, "in case we need to sneak into Big Jim's place and steal those fake documents he's touting."

"Fat lot of good that'd do. People don't even need to see the evidence for themselves. All they want is a way to strike back at Cortinas, a way to keep from feeling quite so vulnerable—and attacking me is it."

He sounded so self-pitying and whiny, he could've kicked himself. Madeleine had thrown him completely off-balance. He had better get a grip.

"Did nobody come to your game tonight? Is that why you're early?"

She dropped into one of the hide-covered armchairs at the edge of the window's light, and with a wave of one slender hand, invited him to take the other. Irritation with her, with himself, with everything, still rankled along his nerve endings, but he couldn't resist the sympathetic companionship she offered.

Truth to tell, he couldn't resist her.

"Four men did come," he said, pulling the other chair a little away from hers and sitting down. "But they weren't prosperous enough— or maybe foolish enough—to last very long."

"So Big Jim's plan is working?"

Cold anger flared again. The very thought of Big Jim Thompson had created a permanent knot in his stomach.

"It is, damn it. And I've got to fight back somehow."

To his surprise, she said nothing, only listened. He hadn't had a confidante for ten years, nor felt the need for one.

"Ninety percent of my acquaintances are cutting me dead, the other ten percent are throwing me doubtful looks and very little conversation. Participation in my games has gone down steadily for the last three nights, and I've had two men confront me to my face," he said. "All I could do was assure them the supposed letters between me and Cortinas and the 'deed' where I give him half the ranch are fakes."

"Did they believe you?"

"Maybe. But with Jim and his friends telling everyone that the real purpose of the Circle 3 is to hold stolen cattle until they can be driven to Mexico, who knows? Next thing you know, they'll have a mob whipped up to ride me out of town on a rail."

He rubbed his hand over his face and loosened his string tie, slid down in the chair, and put his feet up on the edge of her desk.

Madeleine leaned toward him and smiled.

"Rafe, let me make you some tea. Then why don't you go back there and crawl in bed with Juanito? Or I'll make you a pallet in here. You can't spend another night in that position."

He jerked his head around.

"How do you know where I've been sleeping? Have you been standing over there in the shadows every night?"

"No," she said, raising her eyebrows at him archly as her smile turned into her most mischievous grin. "I know because every morning I see the imprint of your pretty backside in my chair."

She laughed at him after she threw his words back at him, laughed right in his face with her beautiful blue eyes sparkling bright in that dim light, and her gorgeous, lush mouth tempting him beyond hope. She stood up to go make the tea.

He grabbed her hand as she started to swish past him.

"You come here to me this minute, Madeleine Cottrell."

Laughing, she let him pull her into his lap.

"Careful," she said, as she slowly, deliberately put her arms around his neck, "remember I'm armed."

"With a mouth that won't quit," he said. "That's your most formidable weapon. But now it has gotten you in trouble."

He couldn't have kept from kissing her at that moment if she had held the gun to his head.

In an instant he'd lost himself in the heat of her, the feel of her in his arms and the taste of her tongue on his. He needed that so badly he would've died to get more.

But it was the way she tightened her arms around his neck and clung to him as she kissed him back that melted all the bones in his body, and the hard coldness in his center where his troubles had been. Where the lone-wolf feeling had been.

Finally Maddie pulled her mouth away.

"Rafe, this is dangerous," she said, "I'll get your tea."

He let her go.

"Forget the tea," he said. "Bring the pallet."

While she was gone, he removed his boots and his coat, tie, and shirt, and padded to the window for another look at their surroundings. The street held no one at that moment. The night-lively part of town wasn't far, but the saloons hadn't closed yet and no one seemed to be headed home.

It looked good to him, this quiet darkness. It wouldn't be a bad way to live, to look out on it every midnight.

He heard Maddie behind him and turned to see her. His heart skipped a beat.

She had changed into the peach-colored silk wrapper she'd worn that early morning in the yard. His hands itched to slide over it . . . there, on the curve of her hip, there, down the slender length of her thigh. To feel the warm softness that was Maddie, his Maddie. Her fragrant flesh that was the sweetest thing ever in this world.

"He's fine, sound asleep as only a little boy can be," she whispered.

That she thought of his son at this moment, thought of him first and made him the most important, brought feelings to Rafe's heart that he couldn't even name.

He could hardly speak.

"Thanks, Maddie."

She lifted the quilt and spread it on the floor. The motion pulled the wrapper loose over her full breasts and he couldn't look away. He couldn't look at anything else, ever.

He prayed she would not move out of the little bit of light.

His fingers ached to peel the cloth away, beautiful shining cloth gleaming in the darkness, covering Madeleine's beautiful shining skin. He had to have his hands on it. His mouth on it.

His voice would barely come out of his throat.

"Madeleine," he said, rasping out the word in a voice he didn't even know. "Madeleine, you were right. This is dangerous."

He moved toward her and saw that she was barefooted, too. She was totally bare beneath that silk. She was his Madeleine, naked for him.

Only for him.

Her task done, she turned to him and opened her arms.

He didn't go into them.

"No," he growled.

He touched his fingertips to the sides of her neck; slowly, he slid his hands up into her hair, set his thumbs beneath her chin and his palms against her cheeks.

He looked deep into her eyes.

"This is what I should've done that time I kissed you in the yard," he said. "This."

She smiled.

He let his hands slide down onto her fine shoulders, let them push the cloth back, let them move along each edge of it, almost to her nipples now. Hard and firm, standing for his touch, they called to him. She moaned.

But he shook his head.

He trailed his fingertips to her waist, and untied the knot of the belt without touching her anywhere else. She caught a deep breath.

"Rafe . . ."

He shook his head, again.

He trailed along the edge of the robe, upward this time, across the soft, ripe swells of her breasts, up to the delicate collarbone, along it to where the wrapper barely clung. He pushed it away and it fell into a pool at her feet.

He cradled her shoulders in his hands.

Her eyes were huge, devouring him, begging him.

Then she reached for the buttons down the front of his pants, and brushed her hand once over his swollen manhood.

"Madeleine," he whispered, for that one touch took his voice away completely.

It almost made him the beggar instead of the king.

She undid the button at his waistband. Then the next one. With each one, she brushed her knuckles against him, a little bit harder each time.

Deliberately, she drew out the torture again and again, but finally it was done.

He took his hands from her and swiftly stepped out of his pants, then kicked them away. She held his gaze with her fathomless eyes.

He took her hand and led her to the quilt. "Now," he whispered, "lie down."

She did as he said, still holding him with her eyes.

Gently, gently, he parted her legs and knelt between them.

"Madeleine."

He looked deep into her eyes a moment longer.

Then he bent and placed a kiss in the middle of her abdomen.

She cried out. "Oh, Rafe!"

She thrust her fingers into his hair and held his head there as if willing the imprint of his lips to stay on her skin.

She lifted him up and brought his mouth to hers. Then she brushed his cheek with her long lashes as she opened her eyes to look at him one more time before she let the lids drift slowly closed.

"Come into me, Rafe."

He did as she said.

She wrapped him tight in her arms, she took him in and held him with her heart.

Rafe woke with a terrified clattering of his heart, from farther down in a sweet, deep sleep than any he had found in years. The tinkling fall of the last pieces of glass woke him completely.

No, it was Maddie, in his arms, her fingers digging into his shoulder, her eyes wide with fear that woke him.

"Somebody broke the window," she said.

"Juanito!" they said together in alarm, and then scrambled up, reaching for clothes.

Rafe got his hands on his pants.

"The glass is all over everything," he said. "Don't move, I'll bring your robe."

He shook out his pants, jammed his legs in, shook out his boots and stepped into them, found his gun, fastened the top pants button, and jammed the weapon into his waistband. Maddie was shaking glass from her robe, then putting it on.

"I told you to wait. Don't step."

"I *can't* wait."

Her voice trembled a little, but now she sounded more angry than scared.

"Here," he said, and swept her up into his arms. "Thank God this door was closed."

"Maybe he didn't hear," she said, her breath warm against his neck.

Opening the door into the hallway, Rafe ran to the kitchen, to the daybed where Juanito lay heedlessly sprawled on his stomach. He snored gently.

"Thank God," Madeleine whispered.

Rafe set her down.

"Put on some shoes," he said. "I'll take a look around outside before we go back into the office."

Not a soul was stirring anywhere. Rafe slowly circled the building in the deep darkness, sensing the air and the space in front of him before he advanced. No one. No one in the stable. But he hadn't expected to find anyone.

From the look and feel of the night, it must be right before dawn. He stood still in the black shadow of a live oak for a minute, breathing deeply, trembling inside like a leaf in the wind. He could feel the last traces of the good sleep leaving his body, his nerves settling from high alertness to their normal state of wariness. He was getting too old for this kind of shock to his system.

For a long time he stood there, staring at the back door to Madeleine's kitchen, visualizing Juanito asleep, his bed against the wall just to the side of the door and Madeleine in her bedroom, getting dressed to face whatever this day would bring.

He couldn't make himself go in. All his warrior instincts were rising deep inside, and he watched the yard and the alley without even being aware what he was doing.

He wanted to protect them. That was all he wanted now.

They lit a lamp and cleaned up the mess together, determined to be finished before Juanito woke. Madeleine made one last try at shielding the boy.

"A fast-moving wagon wheel *could've* thrown a rock hard enough to break the window," she said. "That's the truth, too, Rafe."

"I don't want to scare him, either, Maddie, but sometimes a little scare's a good thing. He needs to take our warnings of danger to heart."

"I know," she said, as she dumped the last batch of trash into the can. "I know you're right. But it makes me so mad, to have to put fear into him like this just when he's feeling secure and happy."

"Me, too," Rafe said absently.

His mind was whirling with questions about how to provide more protection, how to recover his fast-fading reputation so he could continue to support all three of them, how to get to Big Jim somehow and stop this insanity. One thing he would not do was leave San Antonio. He would truly be finished then, and they'd all be poor and therefore powerless.

Madeleine thumped her broom on the floor.

He glanced up to see her staring at him, her face white, her eyes blazing. Two spots of pink blazed high on her cheeks.

"I am going to *get* Big Jim," she said, in the coldest voice he'd ever heard from her. "I am going to make him wish that *he'd* left this town before he ever started this war."

Rafe stared at her, a thrill running through him at the familiarity of Madeleine in one of her furies of indomitable determination.

He almost smiled as sudden, crazy visions flashed before his eyes—Madeleine holding her six-gun to Big Jim's head while she beat him with the handle of her broom, Madeleine storming into the Golden King and, with her broom, knocking all the bottles behind its bar into the floor to flood the place with a river of whiskey, Madeleine personally tarring and feathering Big Jim and forcing him onto her broom handle to be ridden out of town . . .

The way she looked at this moment, she could do anything.

"How are you going to get him?"

"With the power of my pen. Today I am beginning an editorial campaign to match the slanderous one he's begun about you. I'll show him what the word 'insinuation' really means."

Rafe shook his head. She could make things worse very easily; she would surely put herself and Juanito into more danger; she would need more money to keep the *Star* in business with every advertiser she lost; she might even get herself killed if her accusations were too plain. She could never prove him innocent of collusion with Cortinas, so she might as well keep her situation as good as it could be.

But she was Madeleine Cottrell in a state of

high dudgeon, and if he wanted to change her mind, direct confrontation was not the way to do it.

"Better think that over, Maddie," he said. "Your friends will turn their backs on you, if they haven't already, and you'll lose your advertising revenue. I'm telling you this because I've just found it out the hard way—Big Jim's ruthless and he's got this town wrapped around his finger."

"Well, it's fixing to come unwound."

She set her jaw and lifted her chin. It would take a miracle to move her one inch from her path once she had set her mind.

"I have a lot of friends in San Antonio, Rafe."

"I know that," he said gently, "but friends can fall away when public opinion bears down on them. They have businesses to protect and debts to pay, and maybe people of the opposite opinion to live with."

He thought he saw a tiny flicker of doubt flash in her eyes, so he pressed the advantage.

"Think about it, Maddie. We have a deal. You have to make your own way with the *Star* and a profit in three years if you want it back again."

She glared at him but at least she was listening.

"That editorial campaign could do financial damage that three years wouldn't even begin to heal," he said. "It might even put you out of business."

She waited, long enough for him to know that she wasn't just spouting off out of temper, holding his gaze with her fierce one.

"Then so be it."

Every word was a block of ice falling from her lips.

Just as the old Maddie had done, this new one could make him furious in an instant.

"Damn! Are you thinking at all? You'd be penniless! This newspaper means your *life*, Madeleine."

The ice all came to rest on him.

"Don't worry that you'd be obligated to support me, Rafe. You made a fair deal with me. If I don't make a profit, it's not your fault."

"Maddie—"

"Don't 'Maddie' me, Rafe. I wouldn't take any financial help from you if you begged me."

"*Listen* to me, damn it!"

"No! *You* listen to *me*, damn it!"

The color in her cheeks heightened, as did the fire in her eyes.

"I know that a part of you has always believed I chose the *Times* over you that day New Orleans fell. Well, maybe that's true, in a way. Running a newspaper myself was pretty heady stuff for a seventeen-year-old girl."

He felt as if she'd kicked him in the gut.

"But now I'm ten years wiser and I know myself ten years better. I absolutely do not care if I lose this newspaper and my few other pitiful possessions. What's being done to you is a shame and a disgrace, and I intend to fight it with everything that's in me.

"You're a fair man, Rafe, and you're being treated monumentally unfairly. You're an honorable man and you're being treated with reprehensible dishonor. I will not let that happen as long as I have breath in my body."

"Are you telling me that you'd give up your livelihood for the sake of my honor?"

She stared back at him.

"Yes. I *am* giving it up, probably. For you, not just your honor."

"Your newspaper?"

"Yes. My newspaper."

A great feeling of lightness filled his whole body. A joy, a happiness.

She meant it. She would give up the *Star* for him.

"Why, Madeleine?"

She gave him an indulgent look, like one she would give Juanito.

"Because I love you, Rafe. I always have, and I always will."

For the space of a heartbeat, his soul took wing.

She bent over and picked up the bucket full of glass. "And now I'm going to leave so you won't feel constrained to make a reply. I'll see you around noon, as usual."

Rafe never knew how or when he left the office of the *Star*, or how he came to have his shirt on—although without the tail tucked in—and his coat over his arm. Completely uncaring that he looked like a drunk coming home after a hard night in the saloons, he greeted the doorman and walked through the wide double doors of the lobby of the Menger and headed blindly for the stairs.

Chapter 18

⁓ഀ

Sometimes a man has to do something, even if it's wrong.

Rafe had been in that position many times before. He'd made split-second decisions about whether to trust another agent during the war, whether to shoot and at which enemy, whether to surrender or give up his life, whether to hold his ground or vanish into the darkness.

He still made those decisions every day, with every game, every hand that he played.

And now he'd decided to make a very public move against the man who threatened all he held dear. He'd hired two men for the next couple of nights to protect Juanito and Madeleine, but that wasn't enough. He needed to save his reputation, or lose everything he'd worked for these past ten years.

Right now he was fighting for his very life.

Unobtrusively, he noticed admiring glances from each side of the street. He hoped he looked good enough to be seen with Beau, whose black coat gleamed luminously in the sun, the silver on the saddle glittering. He'd taken almost as much care with his own toilet as with Beau's, and had worn his very best hat and boots, not to mention his most expensive summer suit.

He'd decided to stage this confrontation in the late afternoon, when there was still enough light to be seen and there were still quite a few people in the streets and stores.

The more people who saw Beau outside the Golden King and asked why Rafe had gone there, the better. He wished he could head up a whole retinue, like the Pied Piper, just to make sure they had an audience. But he'd dropped a word here and there at the Menger today, so it was likely there'd be plenty of men already inside Big Jim's establishment waiting to see what would happen.

There were. As he turned the corner and trotted down the street toward the big, beautiful gaming palace, he saw that the hitching rail in front of it was full. A valet, dressed in one of the gold-colored uniforms Big Jim favored for his employees, was taking the reins of the next customer's horse.

Rafe smiled.

"Well, old boy," he murmured to Beau, who put his ears back to listen, "if we win this place we'll have to change its name and the color. I favor blue, myself."

That immediately made him think of Madeleine's blue eyes. And her hat with the blue trim. And the blue dress she'd worn to the Mardi Gras ball.

A great longing swept over him, but he closed his heart against it.

No emotion. He would think about Madeleine at another time.

He rode up to the Golden King and swung down with a flourish, then handed the reins and an eagle gold piece to the boy.

"Keep him close by the door and be ready when you hear me whistle," he said. "I shouldn't be long."

The boy looked again at the money gleaming in his hand.

"Yes, sir! I'll have him right here."

It would ruin his whole scene if he had to wait several minutes to make his dramatic departure.

Rafe reset his hat and started up the steps toward the doorman who was holding the door open for him.

"Mr. Aigner, sir. Welcome to the Golden King."

It was obvious from the tone that his arrival was no surprise.

Rafe smiled again.

He gave his hat and another smile to the beautiful woman in the gold silk dress whose job it was to take it.

The huge, high-ceilinged area of the main bar, with its mirrors and shining brass rail and chandeliers and paintings and gleaming mahogany tables, was crowded with men drinking, eating, and talking. The noise lessened considerably when Rafe walked in.

Big Jim was standing at the middle of the bar, his back to the door, talking to someone who was leaning on one elbow and facing the door. Rafe saw the man touch Big Jim's elbow in a signal that Rafe had arrived.

Good. Big Jim wanted this meeting to be public as much as Rafe did.

The Golden King's proprietor turned slowly, pretended to notice and recognize Rafe, then came to greet him, hand outstretched. Rafe stopped where he was.

"Welcome, welcome to the Golden King," Big Jim said.

"I didn't ride over here to shake your hand . . ." *Low-life bastard. Malicious liar.* ". . . Yet," he said.

"Then you must've come to see what a real gaming palace is," Big Jim said, smiling even more broadly as he let his hand fall to his side. "You must want to sample the best before you build your own . . . Choctaw Club, is that the name?"

He put a sneer into the word "Choctaw" that made it a dirty word, but Rafe ignored that.

"Sit down, sit down," Thompson said, gesturing toward a table that Rafe realized he'd kept empty for this purpose. "Sample our food and our drinks. Ask me any questions you want. We can even break out a new deck of cards and have a little game."

Rafe smiled at him.

"As a matter of fact, Thompson, that's exactly what I have in mind."

"Oh?"

Big Jim's eyebrows lifted in a comical fashion, but his eyes held no humor at all.

"Aren't you afraid of getting in where the stakes are too high for your reach?" he said.

Rafe kept smiling.

"No."

"Way I hear it," Big Jim said, "business in your suite over at the Menger has slacked off a little. Maybe you oughtta think twice about throwing down the gauntlet to me."

"I do have a little time on my hands now and then," Rafe drawled. "That's the reason I thought about challenging you to a game or two."

Big Jim turned and gestured toward the empty table.

"I accept," he said. "Have a seat."

"Sorry. I do happen to have a game of my own

this evening, starting within the hour. I'm just here to make some arrangements."

He waited a beat.

"That is, if *you're* not afraid of buying in where the stakes are too high, Big Jim."

A murmur of intensified interest rippled across the room.

Big Jim stiffened.

"Aigner, I feel certain that I can match you dollar for dollar until you're cleaned out."

Rafe opened his hands and turned slowly from side to side, inviting all the onlookers to share his surprise.

"Did everybody hear that?" he said.

A buzz of assent grew into a louder one of pure excitement. This could prove to be a legendary match, and there was no one in the Golden King tonight who was unaware of that.

"Very well," Rafe said. "Here's my proposition. Three games. Twenty-four-hour time limit on each, twenty-four-hour rest in between. Every game stands alone; two thousand to ante up and no limits; we play in a neutral establishment where the proprietor is the bank."

He stopped to look Big Jim over.

"Winner takes two out of three by a margin of a hundred dollars or more."

"For what?"

"The money on the table and the gambling scene in this town."

Big Jim gaped at him. "If you lose two games out of three, you never again gamble in San Antonio."

"That's it. *If* you can beat my take each game by a hundred dollars or more," Rafe replied.

Big Jim thought about it, but he had no real choice because the murmuring had become a groundswell of noise.

"Go on, get him, Jim," someone called from the back of the room.

"Wanta bet?" another voice called. "My money says Aigner can take him."

Poor Big Jim. He still thought there was a hidden catch to this somewhere, but he couldn't find it and time was running out on him.

"Aw, come on, Thompson," somebody called, "don't let him get away with this."

"Ante up, Jim!"

He hesitated for one more heartbeat.

"Done!"

Big Jim said the one word so loudly that it echoed back from the ceiling over the bar.

"*Now* let's shake," said Rafe.

Madeleine threw down her pen and looked out the window at the man Rafe had hired to guard the place, who was loitering outside on the street. He was fairly unobtrusive and he hadn't spoken to her since Rafe had introduced them, but he was bothering her tremendously.

She turned her back on him and put her feet

up in one of the hide-covered chairs. What she needed to do was relax.

Telling Rafe that she loved him hadn't driven him away.

If it had, that was just as well because it meant there was no hope that he'd ever return her love.

Oh, if only she'd kept her feelings to herself! No man liked the pressure of a woman so boldly stating her feelings before any kind of declaration from him.

But she couldn't have kept those words inside, even if she'd known they would drive him away. Life was short and it was becoming more dangerous, and she was taking no chances that, ever again, he wouldn't know exactly how she felt about him.

Tears stung her eyes. Rafe needed her love so badly!

It was going to prove almost impossible, though, for him to let any woman love him— much less the one who had caused him to be so wary of opening his heart to anyone, even his own son.

She wrenched her mind from the subject. Or tried her best to do so.

Sophie and Duncan would be back in a few minutes with Juanito. Thank God she'd sent the other guard with them, in case Rafe dropped by before they returned, although she had no fears that Duncan couldn't handle any trouble that arose.

She smiled. Never mind Duncan, *Sophie* would kill anyone who threatened Juanito with her bare hands.

As a matter of fact, Sophie could tongue lash a person into *wishing* he were dead.

They had only taken him down the street to the ice cream parlor, but at least it would be an outing. The child couldn't sit here all day like a prisoner. She felt like one herself, but she also dreaded to go out in public, if this day had been any indication of what was to come. Her editorial in defense of Rafe and in subtle attack of Big Jim had hit the streets early in the morning, and by noon she had lost James Flynn's advertising and two of her delivery boys.

It had hurt even more, though, that two of the women who served on the board of the Orphans Home with her had sent notes condemning her stance and severing relations with her.

Until the evidence Mr. Thompson holds is proven to be false, one of them had said.

Well, how about Mr. Thompson proving it authentic?

She put her head in her hands. Though she had devastated her entire life in only two days' time, she would not change a single word.

Rafe had fought his way through the first two games with Big Jim using only half his mind, which was the most dangerous way to play poker. During both games, he felt as if he'd stepped off the edge of the earth and become somebody he didn't even know. He had lapses when he forgot to look at his own cards or couldn't remember what had been played and what hadn't, and others when he couldn't remember how much was at stake or decide how much to raise it.

He deserved to lose the whole series. But not just for his lack of concentration in the fight of his professional life—for his lack of response to Madeleine's declaration that she loved him as well.

Madeleine had taken over his mind.

She had opened such a well of feeling inside him, underneath the stone lid he always tried to keep on his emotions, that he was in danger of falling into it. She loved him without expecting anything in return.

Dear God, she was putting her precious newspaper on the line for him!

It was time he got out of town, whether Big Jim beat him in this third game or not. He wasn't meant to be a publisher or a rancher, and he should put some distance between them. It would be best for Madeleine, for he was a natural rambler and was never meant to settle down. How irresponsible was he, when he couldn't keep from making love to her every time he saw her? He could never take responsibility for a wife, as well as a son.

"Front door or back, Mr. Aigner?"

The driver's voice startled him so that it took a minute to grasp the question. Fear stabbed him. He was doing it again—forgetting where he was and what he was about.

"Front," he said shortly. "Why would I go to the back?"

The frustrating thing was, when those first two games were over, he and Jim held winnings within fifty dollars of each other. He had thought he could beat the man soundly in every game, but the cards hadn't fallen that way. Or his mental lollygagging had interfered more than he had realized.

"Because of the crowds, sir."

Rafe leaned out and looked ahead. His heart began a rapid, hard beat.

There must be three hundred people crowding the street, the steps, and the entryway to the hotel. He'd *really* been in another world, not to have noticed the noise.

The Aigner-Thompson games had generated more and more interest with each successive one. Crowds gathered in the streets, at the hotels and saloons, to hear news of the outcome of each hand played. Betting was rampant. Lots of emotion was riding on every card's turn.

His stomach clutched. Was there also a crowd in front of the *Star*? There'd been a couple of anti-Cortinas rallies in the street over there the past week, but the guards he'd hired had assured him they'd been peaceful, just carrying anti-*Star* banners and signs in defense of Big Jim.

But these men were milling around, shouting back and forth, and one knot of about six or eight had started a small fire.

Surely two guards would be enough for Madeleine and Juanito tonight. He'd doubled their salaries to keep them on through the series of games, so they'd surely do double duty if there happened to be any trouble. Tomorrow, though, he'd hire more. This was the last game, and if he won, there'd be a lot of angry friends of Big Jim.

Big Jim had also been courting all the hangers-on with free drinks at the Golden King for several hours a day. That way, he'd have lots of fans to cheer him on.

The driver pulled up in front of the Bexar Hotel, which was the neutral establishment agreed upon. Rafe got out and strode to the foot of the steps through the path that opened for him.

A rough voice shouted from the street.

"Hey, Aigner, where's your buddy, Cortinas?"

Another answered.

"Down in Me-hi-co, a'course! South of the border!"

Rafe climbed the steps slowly, deliberately, refusing to let the ruffians make him hurry.

There'd been anti-Mexican, anti-Cortinas sentiment in the air all week, and most of San Antonio seemed to have judged Rafe guilty as charged. He'd been booed and verbally sniped at as he entered and left both the other games.

"Remember the Alamo!"

A great shout went up and then more jeering followed him in the door.

His whole body was fully alert now.

He stopped in the lobby and summoned a bellboy, scribbled a note of warning, and sent it to Madeleine.

Then, his pride and his reputation on the line, he went in to try for the third time to beat Big Jim's take by one hundred dollars.

Madeleine paced back and forth in front of the window, watching the crowd outside, wishing she could ignore the ugly sight. But she couldn't—it was fascinating, somehow.

The guards were inside now, one here at the front door, one at the back near Juanito. Worn out after a day of playing in the stable with the horses and Elmer, he'd fallen asleep, thank goodness, before the crowd had gathered.

"Ma'am, I'm thinking you might ought to stay away from that window."

"Yes. I will, thank you."

She moved to the side of it and stood behind the curtain.

A couple of people had torches and several had signs saying, DON'T READ THE STAR and MADELEINE TRAITOR CALHOUN. IS SHE A MEXICAN IN DISGUISE?

It felt so strange, almost like watching her own funeral.

The one that made her blood run cold, however, read, SEND THE BOY HOME. WE DON'T WANT HIS KIND HERE.

Inside the Bexar and outside in the street, a great, angry groan went up when they heard the news twenty-four hours after the start of the third game, at ten o'clock the next evening. All the doors stood open, from the lobby throughout the gaming rooms, but the night breeze couldn't reach Rafe for the crush of spectators. Every sound floated to him, though, and after the groan came an expectant silence.

"Yes, twenty dollars difference," the self-important doorman said, first from the door of the room where they played, then from the top of the steps outside. "One double eagle, my friends, separates Aigner's take from Thompson's. Three games ending in a draw."

"We didn't bet on a draw!"

He clapped his hands for silence.

"Wait here. There'll be an announcement shortly."

Inside, Rafe and Big Jim, the only two left at the table, sat and stared at each other. All the former players and as many spectators as could crowd into the room watched and listened.

"What's this announcement, Thompson?"

"Aigner, I know how we can decide this poker

duel once and for all," Big Jim said, "but I want to put the proposition to you the same way you did to me. Right in front of God and everybody."

He got up. "Come with me."

Rafe got up and went, much as it galled him. He had to defend himself, whatever this was.

In the middle of the lobby full of people, Big Jim stopped and turned to Rafe.

"We can prove once and for all who's the best and who will stay to gamble in San Antonio," he said loudly, looking around to be sure he had everyone's attention.

"Get on with it," Rafe snapped.

"A week from today, at the Silver Grove Gambling Palace in Dallas, there's a game that'll separate the men from the boys. Ante up ten thousand dollars to start."

He turned to look at Rafe.

"I'm proposing we both sit in, as long as we have the money, and whichever of us has more take when he folds is declared the winner. What do you say, Aigner?"

Lots of people liked that idea, judging by the excited buzz of voices.

The instant Big Jim had said "Dallas" Rafe's gut had said no. How could he leave town with crowds in front of the *Star* every night? How could he leave Juanito and Madeleine?

"What's the matter, buddy?"

Big Jim was sneering. Loudly.

"Scared you're not good enough?"

On the other hand, how could he let this son-of-a-bitch get away with accusing him of being a criminal and traitor and then a coward on top of it all? He could beat Big Jim, given one more chance.

His reputation would be wiped out by a refusal.

"You're on, Thompson," he said.

Rafe stuck out his hand to seal the bargain.

"One week from today, the Silver Grove in Dallas," he said.

His sharp instincts cut at his gut all the way down the steps. He shouldn't have agreed to it—but he'd had no choice.

Madeleine couldn't even think about going to bed, although she'd have to get up early to hitch Dolly to the delivery wagon and take the papers out. Charlie was still horrified by her doing that herself, but she needed him setting type and running the press, and since Terrence and Lyndol had quit "because she'd gone over the border to the Mexicans," she hadn't been able to hire anyone else. Nobody wanted to work for Madeleine Traitor Calhoun.

Thank God Charlie was so loyal. If he left her, she'd have to shut down.

Pretty soon she'd have to anyway, with so little money coming in.

But she wasn't going to think about that now. She would publish right up until the very day she couldn't buy paper and ink. And every one of those days, she would tell San Antonio and the world around it that Rafe was not a thief or a murderer or the kind of man who would consort with criminals.

She kept looking through the window at the troublemakers milling around out in the street. Somehow it satisfied some need to protect Juanito and herself and her place of business. Her handgun was in her pocket. The guards were out there.

And so was Rafe.

She crossed to her desk, and pushed the clock into the dim light from the streetlamp. It was after eleven. The third game was over. He'd promised to let her know the results as soon as he could.

She moved through the office as confidently as if the lights were on, opened the door, and slipped into the hallway. Rafe would come to the back.

She entered the kitchen and froze in mid-step, her heart in her throat when she saw a man's silhouette in the straight chair by the door. Instantly, though, she knew it was Rafe.

He was sitting near the foot of Juanito's bed, watching him sleep.

He looked up.

"How long have you been here?" she whispered.

He shrugged.

"Awhile."

"Was the guard out there when you came in?"

"He's on the job. He challenged me."

Then, reluctantly, almost wearily, he got up.

"Let's go into the office," he said. "I need to talk to you."

She turned back into the hall and he followed her.

"Aren't you afraid of flying glass in here?" she said, as he closed the door behind them.

He chuckled, that low, rich sound that always warmed her heart.

She wanted to touch him so badly it brought tears to her eyes.

"Madeleine," he said, "I'm going to Dallas in a few days. We've got to make some plans to keep you and Juanito safe."

I'm going to Dallas. You and Juanito.

The words echoed in her head until she could hardly hear the slight grating on the floor as they turned the two hide-covered chairs in front of her desk to face each other. They sat down.

Rafe related the story of the third poker game and Big Jim's challenge. Madeleine tried to take it all in while she worked at calming her racing pulse.

What would she do? How would she bear it; how could she feel safe, with him in Dallas?

The thought jolted her upright. She'd been alone for weeks at a time when Sutton was off somewhere gambling. True, there'd been no angry crowds yelling at her from the street, but she'd taken care of everything perfectly well. She could take care of herself and Juanito.

"... Hire more guards," Rafe was saying, "and have a professional oversee them. I intend to talk to Tol Malloy—you know, he used to be a Ranger ..."

But *he* would be gone. Rafe would be gone.

Chapter 19

"**M**y reputation hangs by this one thread," Rafe was saying. "I have to accept Big Jim's challenge or be labeled a coward as well as a criminal."

She couldn't think of anything to say.

"In this business, my reputation is everything. You understand that, don't you, Maddie?"

His tone—half concern, half irritation—jerked her out of her trance. The last thing she'd ever let him see was her pining over him. If he wasn't going to let anyone love him, he'd have to bear the consequences.

She put on her most brisk manner.

"I certainly do," she said. "You have no choice, Rafe."

She got up from the chair, and staying out of

the light, stood behind the curtain. Though she really didn't think anyone saw her, someone yelled out at that moment.

"Why don't you write about your *amigo* Cortinas, Mrs. Turncoat Calhoun? Tell us where he's gonna hit next."

"Yeah!" came another voice. "That'd help us catch the murderin', rustlin', grease-bellied bastard!"

"*Damn* it!"

Rafe got up and started to the door.

Madeleine ran to him, caught his arm.

"No! There must fifty of them! We're only four, counting the guards."

He turned on his heel.

"I'm going to get hold of Malloy," he said. "I've got a lot to do. There's not enough venom out there tonight for them to work themselves up too much, and the guards are out there. Get some sleep."

"Maybe this'll be the last night," she said. "The poker games are done."

"If Big Jim had beat me, that'd probably be true," he said. "But now I don't know. Lots of 'em had big money down and now they'll have to wait until after Dallas for a winner."

He crossed the room to the hallway door in three long strides, then paused with his hand on the door handle and turned.

"Maddie, the main thing is to keep you two

safe. Don't worry about anything else. If it ends up you've destroyed the *Star* by defending me, I'll keep you clothed and fed. I'll take care of you."

That just flew all over her.

"*I'll* take of me," she said tightly. "I told you I'll not accept charity."

Fury was rising in her, stirring her insides like dust before a tornado.

"I'm not talking charity," he snapped. "I'll need you to take care of Juanito if I lose. If I can't gamble in San Antonio, I'll have to find a new town for us."

Her, too, going along as nanny?

"If you go to Dallas," she said, from between clenched teeth, "you go there to *win*, Rafe Aigner. You're a thousand times the poker player Big Jim Thompson is, and you'd *damn* well better *act* like it!"

He stood still, as if surprised.

Then he chuckled.

"Yes, *ma'am.*"

He opened the door and vanished noiselessly down the hallway.

Madeleine walked back to the chairs where they'd sat, to the chair he'd been in when he pulled her into his lap for that kiss that had started the lovemaking that had turned over her world. She dropped into it and hung her legs over the arm.

The lovemaking that she would never forget.

Which was a lucky thing, because she'd have to live on it for the rest of her life.

She would never want another man's touch, she knew that now with a sure knowledge.

And she would never have Rafe again, because he knew how much she loved him.

He was planning to move away. Even if he didn't know it yet, win or lose in Dallas, he was getting ready to run.

It was after midnight by the time Rafe returned to the Menger—too late to send any telegrams, too late to find out how to contact Malloy, too late to send down for food. He didn't bother to light the lamp, just stripped to his shorts and threw himself on his back on the bed, crossed his arms beneath his head, and stared at the dark ceiling.

He could make some plans, get things set in his mind the way they needed to be for this next week, at least. After that, he didn't know.

If he lost to Thompson in Dallas, he'd have to come back to San Antonio to tell Juanito—and Madeleine—good-bye. He'd have to hire a better foreman to take care of the ranch until Clayton Brevard got back from up north. He'd have to make arrangements for his other properties.

His mind went back to Madeleine and Juanito. Maybe he should take them with him when he went, although surely this anti-Mexican stuff would die down when he left. It came from Big Jim for one purpose only—to get Rafe out of San Antonio.

He caught his breath. What the *hell* was the matter with him? He was thinking about losing as if it were a done deal. He was making plans to leave San Antonio as if he *wanted* to get out of here!

Wasn't this where he'd been trying to make a place for Juanito? Wasn't that the reason he'd put them all through this torment of the last few days?

He might as well have gotten out of town the minute he received the anonymous letter, if he was unknowingly planning to throw this game at the Silver Grove before he even sat down at the table.

You're a thousand times the poker player Big Jim Thompson is, Rafe Aigner, and you had damn well better act like it!

In spite of his panic, he grinned. Madeleine Cottrell had become a plain-talking woman, that was certain.

The other certain thing was that he'd never forgive himself if he did lose in Dallas. His entire position in the gambling profession would be lost, too.

Even worse, he would hate to bring that news to Madeleine.

So he worked on his competitive mental edge, the way he did before every game. He roused his pride and recalled all the insults from Big Jim; he thought of all the high-echelon gamblers he had won fortunes from in the past. He remembered times when he'd called when no one else would have dared, because his instinct had told him what cards the other players held.

Then he pushed all those emotions away to let his mind fill with the cold dispassion that was the second element that always made him the winner.

It served another purpose, too. It kept thoughts of Madeleine away until finally sleep took him.

Madeleine got through the next few days by hook or crook, she never really knew how. She steeled herself every time Rafe came near and she worked herself into exhaustion each day. The best thing was that, even though the hecklers did go away when the poker game series was done, Rafe kept the guards on anyway— from sundown to sunup—so she was able to sleep at night.

As a matter of truth, she craved sleep. It was filled with dreams of Rafe loving her, being at her side. It was the only time she could forget the reality of Rafe preparing to leave her.

Without admitting it even to herself, she was counting the days until he was gone at the same time that she was trying not to think about it. Big Jim had left town the day after Rafe accepted his challenge, and Rafe would be sure to head out soon. Every day, she expected it.

Halfway through the week, Rafe came in the front door to pick up Juanito instead of the back, and found her at her desk.

"Where's my son?"

His abrupt tone irritated her so much that she went on with her proofreading.

"In the stable. And hello to you, too."

"Madeleine. Hello."

He came around and sat on the edge of her desk.

She kept working.

"I'm leaving on the midnight train. I've contracted with Tol Malloy to put two men on this place around the clock."

That made her look up. He looked back with hard eyes that barely saw her. His jaw was set, too.

"Why?"

"Word from the gambler's grapevine. I sent out feelers in all directions and today I got a telegram from Gibson Harris, an old friend of mine in Kansas City."

She waited. He looked past her into the near distance.

She propped her chin on her hand.

"And how is ol' Gib doing these days?"

"What?"

Startled, he looked at her and really saw her this time.

"Gib says there've been whispers around that Big Jim sent for a couple of *cabrones*, real bad men from up around there, and that they left for San Antonio two days ago."

Something in the way he spoke made her feel his fear.

"What do these bad men do, mostly?"

"Fire. Mostly."

Her heart stopped in her breast.

"You think they're coming to burn us out?"

"It'd be a neat way to do it. Jim's gone to Dallas; no one local can brag or confess to someone else local."

She nodded. "No trail would lead back to him."

"Right. What I'm thinking, Maddie, is that you and Juanito should stay with Sophie and Duncan while I'm gone. Tol's men will be with the two of you whereever you are."

"No! I'll not just let them torch my home and my business. It's all I've had for a long time—"

The sudden pity in his eyes made her stop.

She sat up very straight and set her jaw as hard as his.

"It's an excellent idea for Juanito to go to Sophie and Duncan and for him to have a bodyguard. I'll miss him, but I'm not going."

"Maddie, I'd worry so much less—"

"Face it, Rafe," she snapped, pushing back her chair and getting to her feet, "you have no right or reason to worry about me. Isn't that true?"

Quickly, she strode to the window, her blood racing, her breath coming shallow.

"I'll send word to Sophie. I'll get Juanito with her as soon as his bodyguard arrives. When should I expect him?"

"In about an hour."

"Fine. Then, if that's all, I need to get back to work."

"Fine," he snapped, in return. "I'll go tell Juanito good-bye."

She didn't turn around. She didn't hear him leave the room.

But she knew when he was gone.

Rafe packed with great care the clothing just cleaned and pressed by the Menger's laundry, then he carried it to the lobby and sent for Beau. The black would go with him by train to Dallas, since he wouldn't risk appearing at the Silver Grove on an inferior horse. No other mount gave quite the intimidating aspect to Rafe's arrival that Beau did.

When the boy brought Beau into the circle of light outside the front entrance, Rafe tested the cinch, checked the bit, inspected all the tack, and finally buckled the handles of his bag to the saddle. Then he swung aboard.

He would ride the train all night and part of tomorrow, arriving in Dallas in time to register in one of the fine hotels and acclimate himself. He had never felt more keenly ready to take on a tough opponent in his life. The mental conditioning had worked; Big Jim would rue the day.

This trip was absolutely necessary in the larger scheme of things. He would be doing more good for himself, for Juanito, *and* for Madeleine in Dallas than if he stayed here to protect them from harm. Tol and his men were as honest and as tough as they came, and he trusted them implicitly to keep his loved ones safe.

And Maddie *was* his loved one, too. But he loved her too much to ruin her life by asking her to be his wife.

A deep warmth ran through him.

I love you, Rafe.

He banished the elation and joy. From now until the moment he had raked in the last pot and beaten Big Jim, he wasn't going to feel anything. He would be all mind and instinct and focused on one thing only: the game.

But as he rode for the midnight train, he couldn't help but scan the gig and the carriage coming from the direction of the depot. It was too dark to tell anything about them, but the hair rose on the back of his neck. The thugs coming down from Kansas City would be here by now, if Gib's information was correct.

The smell of cinders and steam, the noise of the trains blew toward him, and his feeling of imminent danger intensified.

His hand clenched into a fist at his side.

He had left Maddie and Juanito in good hands. No harm would come to them.

But the fiery impulse to know that for sure stabbed him again.

A train headed north pulled in as they trotted the last few feet to the station yard. He should get Beau to the horse car and get him loaded.

But at the edge of the yard, Rafe turned Beau around and headed back at a long trot.

He knew Madeleine was in her shanty of an office, watching out the window with her gun hidden in her skirts. A professional arsonist would be the last thing she'd see.

And Tol's men were good, but they couldn't be everywhere at once.

And he loved her. He loved Madeleine *more* than he had in the past.

He rode up the alley, talked to the guard in the back for a moment, put Beau in a stall, and ran to the back door.

"Damn," he muttered, when it opened beneath his hand.

"Who's there?" Madeleine called.

Suddenly, the sound of her voice made his throat close.

"Who goes?" she demanded.

Next she would shoot him.

"Rafe," he said.

He heard the quick intake of her breath.

"Rafe."

The way she said his name, he knew everything was going to be all right.

Madeleine ran down the little hallway to meet him in the kitchen. Her blood thundering in her veins, her heart turning somersaults, she stopped when she saw him.

"How come that door's unlocked?" he asked.

"How come you're here?"

"I have a feeling, Maddie. It'll be tonight."

He knew. She could tell by the way he spoke.

Strangely enough, she felt peace instead of panic or fear.

"What should we do?"

"Douse this light."

"I thought if they knew someone was here . . ."

The thunder of hoofbeats came up out of the night like a quick-moving storm. Then the sound of another horse pounding around the corner, and the next instant a shout, the sparkling sound of crashing glass, and then the quick flash of light that showed all the way down the hall.

Rafe grabbed the kitchen water bucket and ran to the office with Maddie on his heels. All was fine inside.

"Thank God. I thought it was the window again," she cried.

"It would've been, if Tol's man hadn't scared him and spoiled his aim."

She ran ahead of him to open the front door.

The wooden sidewalk was already ablaze,

flames glinting off the broken glass of the
kerosene bottle in a trail along the dusty boards.
Rafe threw water on the flames and ran back for
more, pulling Maddie along by the hand.

"I'm surprised you let the guard do the hon-
ors," she said, running to the cupboard for her
biggest pot while he worked the pump and re-
filled the bucket. "As I recall, you were always
one to perform the heroics yourself."

He cocked his head and flashed her his most
charming sideways grin.

"I didn't miss my train to chase some ugly
outlaw down the street. I'm here to keep my eye
on *you*, Miss Maddie."

Madeleine felt the heat rise to her cheeks and
she couldn't seem to look away from him. Why,
really, had he come back?

He moved the bucket, and she put the pot under the pump.

"Another minute and half the town'll be out
fighting the fire," she said.

"Then let's get it out right now," he said, as
they ran back to the fire with the water. "I don't
want company. I missed that train to talk to you."

Her incorrigible heart leapt with hope. What
could be so important to talk about that he had
missed the train? And the all-important game?

As they separated to attack both ends of the
fire, the second guard ran from the stable with
two buckets of water, and with that, the fire
gave up.

"I'll go for the broom and take care of this glass," Madeleine said. "I've had some practice at that."

When she came back out onto the sidewalk, horses and men had gathered in the street.

"He threw a bottle full of kerosene and a lucifer after it, Sheriff," said the guard who was holding the culprit he'd caught. "I seen 'im do it."

"Good job, Benny. I'll take him now."

Rafe talked to the sheriff while he handcuffed the outlaw, then he came back to Madeleine.

"Let me," he said, and took the broom from her. "You're shaking like a cottonwood leaf in a high wind."

But it wasn't because of the fire. The danger of the fire had hardly penetrated her consciousness, since that was nothing compared to the danger her heart had just leapt into.

"Come on," Rafe said, when the dustpan was full. "Show me where you put that trash can."

After they had finished, he took Maddie's hand and walked her out into the back yard, into the moonlight, over to the live oak where he'd kissed her that day at sunrise. He took her shoulders and gently placed them against the trunk of the tree in a stream of moonlight.

"Stay right there where I can keep my eye on you," he said. "And listen close to me."

She waited, wide-eyed.

"I love you, Madeleine Cottrell. I have loved

you since the moment I first saw you. Will you marry me?"

Joy, surprise, excitement, hope, panic that it wasn't true, that her ears were playing tricks on her—all of those flamed through her in a heartbeat.

"Rafe, do you know what you're saying? I thought you weren't the marrying kind."

Humor glinted in his eyes and his smile flashed in the moonlight.

"Now I have to be," he drawled. "I've gone and destroyed my gambler's reputation, so I might as well give up my renegade ways."

She stood very still, judging his tone and his smile.

"How can you sound so easy and so sure, Rafe Aigner?"

"Because I have other choices for occupation, ma'am," he said with exaggerated politeness. "I have a ranch and a newspaper, among other properties."

"Well, you'd better choose the ranch," she said saucily. "Because in three years the newspaper will belong to me."

"That so?" He held her gaze so long, so seductively, that her whole body grew warm.

"That's so."

"Well, I was thinking of the ranch first," he said. "I'm considering the racehorse breeding business, because that's risk enough to thrill any gambler's blood."

She couldn't take her eyes from his.

"Will you have me, Maddie?" he said, very low. "Will you have me as breeder, groom, stall picker, and . . . husband?"

"Yes," she said, beaming as she went into his arms.

"You know what's going to be the most fun of all?" he murmured, holding her very tight and dropping a kiss onto her hair.

"Juanito will be happy to have me as his Lena forever, I know that," she said.

"Not what I was thinking, but true," Rafe said. "But you know what he'll be even happier about?"

They answered the question at the same time.

"More horses, faster horses."

Laughing together, their lips met, and they sealed the bargain with a kiss.

Avon Romances—
the best in exceptional authors and unforgettable novels!

THE
POISONED
SERPENT

by

JOAN WOLF

0-06-109746-2/$5.99 US/$7.99 Can

Bestselling author Joan Wolf is back with her
eagerly anticipated second novel of
murder and mystery in medieval times.

Against the backdrop of civil war in 12th-century England,
a young lord must use his considerable powers
of deduction to solve the murder of a nobleman,
save an innocent life, and outwit a devious foe.

"Joan Wolf never fails to deliver the best."
Nora Roberts